ADVENTURES *To go*

Your Home for Multi-Genre Reading Entertainment.

ADVENTURES

PEOPLE AND STORIES THAT SHOULD NOT BE FORGOTTEN

Summer 2023

ISBN: (PAPERBACK) 978-1-950464-46-3
ISBN: (EBOOK) 978-1-950464-47-0

WWW.OFFBEATREADS.COM

ADVENTURES

PEOPLE AND STORIES THAT SHOULD NOT BE FORGOTTEN

SUMMER, 2023 **ISSUE #8**

WHAT

THE LOCKET - KATE CHOPIN.. 1

THE TOWER TREASURE - FRANKLIN W. DIXON.............. 11

OUR AMERICAN COUSIN - TOM TAYLOR........................ 149

DARK CORNERS - ELMEDINA HOTA.................................. 248

TAPPING AT THE DOOR - DAVID PAYNE......................... 249

TREASURES - SUZANNE ELSON...................................... 255

THANOS - MICHAEL FOWLER... 263

SOUTHWEST SCENARIOS - DARRYLE PURCELL............ 274

A SERVICE OF LOVE - O. HENRY....................................... 277

WHERE

Editor's Note

AHEAD FOR YOUR READING ENTERTAINMENT WE AGAIN HAVE A VARIETY OF STORIES. We packed seven complete stories in this issue (#8) like sardines. You have three original stories, and four stories from yesteryear that should not be forgotten. Notice the very first Hardy Boys mystery, *The Tower Treasure*, is one of these. Sure, The Hardy Boys may be considered young adult for the most part. But it's really good, and what multi-genre rag could count itself true without at least one Hardy Boys mystery from author Franklin W. Dixon? (We are aware that Franklin W. Dixon is a pseudonym for several authors who wrote Hardy Boys Mysteries.)

How much you value a story is indeed subjective. Shakespeare said, "Beauty is bought by judgement of the eye…", and that is so true, even when it pertains to the written word. Of course, not every book is everyone's cup of tea, and there is no way to avoid judging a written work, especially when one has finished reading it. But to dismiss the work of someone's mind completely is to devalue their life. A story should not disappear with the vapors of time. Dismissing a written work is forever closing one's brain to enlightenment, and saying the product of a mind is meaningless. Part of our philosophy at OffBeatReads is that no written work should be forgotten, because every individual is unique. When a society hides or destroys someone's writing, (whether we agree with it or not; whether we like it or not), they forever close the ideas and the thoughts recorded therein.

Bibliophiles and historians will likely recall the significance of the three act play, *Our American Cousin*. On April 14, 1865, a true story occurred that should never be forgotten. On the evening of that day, President Lincoln sat with his wife Mary Todd in the Presidential Box at Ford's Theatre. During scene 2 of the final act, a bullet from a .44 caliber Derringer ended the life of our 16th President.

The downhill-spiraling culture today finds a small but loud and aggressive group demonizing many things about the United States, including the Founding Fathers, early Presidents and other historical figures. We choose to publish this play and recognize President Lincoln because, even as a flawed human being, he chose a moral path that had never before been attempted—and men and women became free because of it.

Robert Kimbrell

P.S.
Look for our Two Year
Anniversary Issue coming
out this Fall!

Letters to the editor:

**Comments/Questions are
accepted. Put *Letter to Editor*
in Subject and send to:
OffBeatReads@pm.me
*Email content could
be published in future
Adventures To Go*.**

THE LOCKET
BY KATE CHOPIN

I

One night in autumn a few men were gathered about a fire on the slope of a hill. They belonged to a small detachment of Confederate forces and were awaiting orders to march. Their gray uniforms were worn beyond the point of shabbiness. One of the men was heating something in a tin cup over the embers. Two were lying at full length a little distance away, while a fourth was trying to decipher a letter and had drawn close to the light. He had unfastened his collar and a good bit of his flannel shirt front.

"What's that you got around your neck, Ned?" asked one of the men lying in the obscurity.

Ned—or Edmond—mechanically fastened another button of his shirt and did not reply. He went on reading his letter.

"Is it your sweet heart's picture?"

"'Taint no gal's picture," offered the man at the fire. He had removed his tin cup and was engaged in stirring its grimy contents with a small stick. "That's a charm; some kind of hoodoo business that one o' them priests gave him to keep him out o' trouble. I know them Cath'lics. That's how come Frenchy got permoted an never got a scratch sence he's been in the ranks. Hey, French! aint I right?" Edmond looked up absently from his letter.

"What is it?" he asked.

"Aint that a charm you got round your neck?"

"It must be, Nick," returned Edmond with a smile. "I don't know how I could have gone through this year and a half without it."

The letter had made Edmond heart sick and home sick. He stretched himself on his back and looked straight up at the blinking stars. But he was not thinking of them nor of anything but a certain spring day when the bees were humming in the clematis; when a girl was saying good bye to him. He could see her as she unclasped from her neck the locket which she fastened about his own. It was an old fashioned golden locket bearing miniatures of her father and mother with their names and the date of their marriage. It was her most precious earthly possession. Edmond could feel again the folds of the girl's soft white gown, and see the droop of the angel-sleeves as she circled her fair arms about his neck. Her sweet face, appealing, pathetic, tormented by the pain of parting, appeared before him as vividly as life. He turned over, burying his face in his arm and there he lay, still and motionless.

The profound and treacherous night with its silence and semblance of peace settled upon the camp. He dreamed that the fair Octavie brought him a letter. He had no chair to offer her and was pained and embarrassed at the condition of his garments. He was ashamed of the poor food which comprised the dinner at which he begged her to join them.

He dreamt of a serpent coiling around his throat, and when he strove to grasp it the slimy thing glided away from his clutch. Then his dream was clamor.

"Git your duds! you! Frenchy!" Nick was bellowing in his face. There was what appeared to be a scramble and a rush rather than any regulated movement. The hill side was alive with clatter and motion; with sudden up-springing lights among the pines. In the east the dawn was unfolding out of the darkness. Its glimmer was yet dim in the plain below.

"What's it all about?" wondered a big black bird perched in the top of the tallest tree. He was an old solitary and a wise one, yet he was not wise enough to guess what it was all about. So all day long he kept blinking and wondering.

The noise reached far out over the plain and across the hills and awoke the little babes that were sleeping in their cradles. The smoke curled up toward the sun and shadowed the plain so that the stupid birds thought it was going to rain; but the wise one knew better.

"They are children playing a game," thought he. "I shall know more about it if I watch long enough."

At the approach of night they had all vanished away with their din and smoke. Then the old bird plumed his feathers. At last he had understood! With a flap of his great, black wings he shot downward, circling toward the plain.

A man was picking his way across the plain. He was dressed in the garb of a clergyman. His mission was to administer the consolations of religion to any of the prostrate figures in whom there might yet linger a spark of life. A negro accompanied him, bearing a bucket of water and a flask of wine.

There were no wounded here; they had been borne away. But the retreat had been hurried and the vultures and the good Samaritans would have to look to the dead.

There was a soldier—a mere boy—lying with his face to the sky. His hands were clutching the sward on either side and his finger nails were stuffed with earth and bits of grass that he had gathered in his despairing grasp upon life. His musket was gone; he was hatless and his face and clothing were begrimed. Around his neck hung a gold chain and locket. The priest, bending over him, unclasped the chain and removed it from the dead soldier's neck. He had grown used to the terrors of war and could face them unflinchingly; but its pathos, someway, always brought the tears to his old, dim eyes.

The angelus was ringing half a mile away. The priest and the negro knelt and murmured together the evening benediction and a prayer for the dead.

II

The peace and beauty of a spring day had descended upon the earth like a benediction. Along the leafy road which skirted a narrow, tortuous stream in central Louisiana, rumbled an old fashioned cabriolet, much the worse for hard and rough usage over country roads and lanes. The fat, black horses went in a slow, measured trot, notwithstanding constant urging on the part of the fat, black coachman. Within the vehicle were seated the fair Octavie and her old friend and neighbor, Judge Pillier, who had come to take her for a morning drive.

Octavie wore a plain black dress, severe in its simplicity. A narrow belt held it at the waist and the sleeves were gathered into close fitting wristbands. She had discarded her hoopskirt and appeared not unlike a nun. Beneath the folds of her bodice nestled the old locket. She never displayed it now. It had returned to her sanctified in her eyes; made precious as material things sometimes are by being forever identified with a significant moment of one's existence.

A hundred times she had read over the letter with which the locket had come back to her. No later than that morning she had again pored over it. As she sat beside the window, smoothing the letter out upon her knee, heavy and spiced odors stole in to her with the songs of birds and the humming of insects in the air.

She was so young and the world was so beautiful that there came over her a sense of unreality as she read again and again the priest's letter. He told of that autumn day drawing to its close, with the gold and the red fading out of the west, and the night gathering its shadows to cover the faces of the dead. Oh! She could not believe that one of those dead was her own! with visage uplifted to the gray sky in an agony of supplication. A spasm of resistance and rebellion seized and swept over her. Why was the spring here with its flowers and its seductive breath if he was dead! Why was she here! What further had she to do with life and the living!

Octavie had experienced many such moments of despair, but a blessed resignation had never failed to follow, and it fell then upon her like a mantle and enveloped her.

"I shall grow old and quiet and sad like poor Aunt Tavie," she murmured to herself as she folded the letter and replaced it in the secretary. Already she gave herself a little demure air like her Aunt Tavie. She walked with a slow glide in unconscious imitation of Mademoiselle Tavie whom some youthful affliction had robbed of earthly compensation while leaving her in possession of youth's illusions.

As she sat in the old cabriolet beside the father of her dead lover, again there came to Octavie the terrible sense of loss which had assailed her so often before. The soul of her youth clamored for its rights; for a share in the world's glory and exultation. She leaned back and drew her veil a little closer about her face. It was an old black veil of her Aunt Tavie's. A whiff of dust from the road had blown in and she wiped her cheeks and her eyes with her soft, white handkerchief, a homemade handkerchief, fabricated from one of her old fine muslin petticoats.

"Will you do me the favor, Octavie," requested the judge in the courteous tone which he never abandoned, "to remove that veil which you wear. It seems out of harmony, someway, with the beauty and promise of the day."

The young girl obediently yielded to her old companion's wish and unpinning the cumbersome, sombre drapery from her bonnet, folded it neatly and laid it upon the seat in front of her.

"Ah! that is better; far better!" he said in a tone expressing unbounded relief. "Never put it on again, dear." Octavie felt a little hurt; as if he wished to debar her from share and parcel in the burden of affliction which had been placed upon all of them. Again she drew forth the old muslin handkerchief.

They had left the big road and turned into a level plain which had formerly been an old meadow. There were clumps of thorn trees here and there, gorgeous in their spring radiance. Some cattle were grazing off in the distance in spots where the grass was tall and luscious. At the far end of the meadow was the towering lilac hedge, skirting the lane that led to Judge Pillier's house, and the scent of its heavy blossoms met them like a soft and tender embrace of welcome.

As they neared the house the old gentleman placed an arm around the girl's shoulders and turning her face up to him he said: "Do you not think that on a day like this, miracles might happen? When the whole earth is vibrant with life, does it not seem to you, Octavie, that heaven might for once relent and give us back our dead?" He spoke very low, advisedly, and impressively. In his voice was an old quaver which was not habitual and there was agitation in every line of his visage.

She gazed at him with eyes that were full of supplication and a certain terror of joy.

They had been driving through the lane with the towering hedge on one side and the open meadow on the other. The horses had somewhat quickened their lazy pace. As they turned into the avenue leading to the house, a whole choir of feathered songsters fluted a sudden torrent of melodious greeting from their leafy hiding places.

Octavie felt as if she had passed into a stage of existence which was like a dream, more poignant and real than life. There was the old gray house with its sloping eaves. Amid the blur of green, and dimly, she saw familiar faces and heard voices as if they came from far across the fields, and Edmond was holding her. Her dead Edmond; her living Edmond, and she felt the beating of his heart against her and the agonizing rapture of his kisses striving to awake her. It was as if the spirit of life and the awakening spring had given back the soul to her youth and bade her rejoice.

It was many hours later that Octavie drew the locket from her bosom and looked at Edmond with a questioning appeal in her glance.

"It was the night before an engagement," he said. "In the hurry of the encounter, and the retreat next day, I never missed it till the fight was over. I thought of course I had lost it in the heat of the struggle, but it was stolen."

"Stolen," she shuddered, and thought of the dead soldier with his face uplifted to the sky in an agony of supplication.

Edmond said nothing; but he thought of his messmate; the one who had lain far back in the shadow; the one who had said nothing.

THE HARDY BOYS IN
THE TOWER TREASURE

BY FRANKLIN W. DIXON

CHAPTER I
THE SPEED DEMON

"**A**fter the help we gave dad on that forgery case I guess he'll begin to think we *could* be detectives when we grow up."

"Why shouldn't we? Isn't he one of the most famous detectives in the country? And aren't we his sons? If the profession was good enough for him to follow it should be good enough for us."

Two bright-eyed boys on motorcycles were speeding along a shore road in the sunshine of a morning in spring. It was Saturday and they were enjoying a holiday from the Bayport high school. The day was ideal for a motorcycle trip and the lads were combining business with pleasure by going on an errand to a near-by village for their father.

The older of the two boys was a tall, dark youth, about sixteen years of age. His name was Frank Hardy. The other boy, his companion on the motorcycle trip, was his brother Joe, a year younger.

While there was a certain resemblance between the two lads, chiefly in the firm yet good-humored expression of their mouths, in some respects they differed greatly in appearance. While Frank was dark, with straight, black hair and brown eyes, his brother was pink-cheeked, with fair, curly hair and blue eyes.

These were the Hardy boys, sons of Fenton Hardy, an internationally famous detective who had made a name for himself in the years he had spent on the New York police force and who was now, at the age of forty, handling his own practice. The Hardy family lived in Bayport, a city of about fifty thousand inhabitants, located on Barmet Bay, three miles in from the Atlantic, and here the Hardy boys attended high school and dreamed of the days when they, too, should be detectives like their father.

As they sped along the narrow shore road, with the waves breaking on the rocks far below, they discussed their chances of winning over their parents to agreement with their ambition to follow in the footsteps of their father. Like most boys, they speculated frequently on the occupation they should follow when they grew up, and it had always seemed to them that nothing offered so many possibilities of adventure and excitement as the career of a detective.

"But whenever we mention it to dad he just laughs at us," said Joe Hardy. "Tells us to wait until we're through school and then we can think about being detectives."

"Well, at least he's more encouraging than mother," remarked Frank. "She comes out plump and plain and says she wants one of us to be a doctor and the other a lawyer."

"What a fine lawyer either of us would make!" sniffed Joe. "Or a doctor, either! We were both cut out to be detectives and dad knows it."

"As I was saying, the help we gave him in that forgery case proves it. He didn't say much, but I'll bet he's been thinking a lot."

"Of course we didn't actually *do* very much in that case," Joe pointed out.

"But we suggested something that led to a clue, didn't we? That's as much a part of detective work as anything else. Dad himself admitted he would never have thought of examining the city tax receipts for that forged signature. It was just a lucky idea on our part, but it proved to him that we can use our heads for something more than to hang our hats on."

"Oh, I guess he's convinced all right. Once we get out of school he'll probably give his permission. Why, this is a good sign right now, isn't it? He asked us to deliver these papers for him in Willowville. He's letting us help him."

"I'd rather get in on a real, good mystery," said Frank. "It's all right to help dad, but if there's no more excitement in it than delivering papers I'd rather start in studying to be a lawyer and be done with it."

"Never mind, Frank," comforted his brother. "We may get a mystery all of our own to solve some day."

"If we do we'll show that Fenton Hardy's sons are worthy of his name. Oh boy, but what wouldn't I give to be as famous as dad! Why, some of the biggest cases in the country are turned over to him. That forgery case, for instance. Fifty thousand dollars had been stolen right from under the noses of the city officials and all the auditors and city detectives and private detectives they called in had to admit that it was too deep for them."

"Then they called in dad and he cleared it up in three days. Once he got suspicious of that slick bookkeeper whom nobody had been suspecting at all, it was all over but the shouting. Got a confession out of him and everything."

"It was smooth work. I'm glad our suggestion helped him. The case certainly got a lot of attention in the papers."

"And here *we* are," said Joe, "plugging along the shore road on a measly little errand to deliver some legal papers at Willowville. I'd rather be on the track of some diamond thieves or smugglers—or something."

"Well, we have to be satisfied, I suppose," replied Frank, leaning farther over the handlebars. "Perhaps dad may give us a chance on a real case some time."

"Some time! I want to be on a real case *now*!"

The motorcycles roared along the narrow road that skirted the bay. An embankment of tumbled rocks and boulders sloped steeply to the water below, and on the other side of the road was a steep cliff. The roadway itself was narrow, although it was wide enough to permit two cars to meet and pass, and it wound about in frequent curves and turnings. It was a road that was not often traveled, for Willowville was only a small village and this shore road was an offshoot of the main highways to the north and the west.

The Hardy boys dropped their discussion of the probability that some day they would become detectives, and for a while they rode on in silence, occupied with the difficulties of keeping to the road. For the road at this point was dangerous, very rough and rutty, and it sloped sharply upward so that the embankment leading to the ocean far below became steeper and steeper.

"I shouldn't want to go over the edge around here," remarked Frank, as he glanced down the rugged slope.

"It's a hundred-foot drop. You'd be smashed to pieces before you ever hit the shore."

"I'll say! It's best to stay in close to the cliff. These curves are bad medicine."

The motorcycles took the next curve neatly, and then the boys confronted a long, steep slope. The rocky cliffs frowned on one side, and the embankment jutted far down to the tumbling waves below, so that the road was a mere ribbon before them.

"Once we get to the top of the hill we'll be all right. It's all smooth sailing from there to Willowville," remarked Frank, as the motorcycles commenced the climb.

Just then, above the sharp put-put of their own motors, they heard the high humming roar of an automobile approaching at great speed. The car was not yet in sight, but there was no mistaking the fact that it was coursing along with the cut-out open and with no regard for the speed laws.

"What idiot is driving like that on this kind of road!" exclaimed Frank. They looked back.

Even as he spoke the automobile flashed into sight.

It came around the curve behind and so swiftly did the driver take the dangerous turn that two wheels were off the ground as the car shot into view. A cloud of dust and stones arose, the car veered violently from left to right, and then it roared at headlong speed down the slope.

The boys glimpsed a tense figure at the wheel. How he kept the car on the road was a miracle, for the racing automobile swung from side to side. At one moment it would be in imminent danger of crashing over the embankment, down on the rocks below; the next instant the car would be over on the other side of the road, grazing the cliff.

"He'll run us down!" shouted Joe, in alarm. "The idiot!"

Indeed, the position of the two lads was perilous.

The roadway was narrow enough at any time, and this speeding car was taking up every inch of space. In a great cloud of dust it bore directly down on the two motorcyclists. It seemed to leap through the air. The front wheels left a rut, the rear of the car skidded violently about. By a twist of the wheel the driver pulled the car back into the roadway again just as it seemed about to plunge over the embankment. It shot over toward the cliff, swerved back again into the middle of the roadway, and then shot ahead at terrific speed.

Frank and Joe edged their motorcycles as far to the right of the road as they dared. To their horror they saw that the car was skidding again.

The driver made no attempt to slacken speed.

The automobile came hurtling toward them!

CHAPTER II
THE STOLEN ROADSTER

The auto brakes squealed.

The driver of the oncoming car swung the wheel viciously about. For a moment it appeared that the wheels would not respond. Then they gripped the gravel and the automobile swerved, then shot past.

Bits of sand and gravel were flung about the two boys as they crouched by their motorcycles at the edge of the embankment. The car had missed them only by inches!

Frank caught a glimpse of the driver, who turned about at that moment and, in spite of the speed at which the automobile was traveling and in spite of the perils of the road, shouted something they could not catch at them and shook his fist.

The car was traveling at too great a speed to enable the lad to distinguish the driver's features, but he saw that the man was hatless and that he had a shock of red hair blowing in the wind.

Then the automobile disappeared from sight around the curve ahead, roaring away in a cloud of dust.

"The road hog!" gasped Joe, as soon as he had recovered from his surprise.

"He must be crazy!" Frank exclaimed angrily. "Why, he might have pushed us both right over the embankment!"

"At the rate he was going I don't think he cared whether he ran any one down or not."

Both boys were justifiably angry. On such a narrow, treacherous road there was danger enough when an automobile passed them traveling at even a reasonable speed, but the reckless and insane driving of the red-headed motorist was nothing short of criminal.

"If we ever catch up to him I'm going to give him a piece of my mind!" declared Frank. "Not content with almost running us down he had to shake his fist at us."

"Road hog!" muttered Joe again. "Jail is too good for the likes of him. If it was only his own life he endangered it wouldn't be so bad. Good thing we only had motorcycles. If we had been in another car there would have been a smash-up, sure."

The boys resumed their journey and by the time they had reached the curve ahead that enabled them to see the village of Willowville lying in a little valley along the bay beneath them, there was no trace of the reckless motorist.

Frank delivered the legal papers his father had given to him, and then the boys had the rest of the day to themselves.

"It's too early to go back to Bayport just now," he said to Joe. "What say we go out and visit Chet Morton?"

"Good idea," agreed Joe. "He has often asked us to come out and see him."

Chet Morton was a school chum of the Hardy boys. His father was a real estate dealer with an office in Bayport, but the family lived in the country, about a mile from the city. Although Willowville was some distance away, the boys knew of a road that would take them across country to the Morton home, and from there they could return to Bayport. It would make their journey longer, but they would have the pleasure of visiting their chum. Chet was a great favorite with all the boys, not the least of the reasons for his popularity being the fact that he had a roadster of his own, in which he drove to school every day and with which he was very generous in giving rides to his friends after school hours.

The Hardy boys drove along the country roads in the spring sunlight, enjoying the freedom of their holiday as only boys can. When they had reached a culvert not far from the Morton place Frank suddenly brought his motorcycle to a stop and peered down into a clump of bushes in the deep ditch.

"Somebody's had a spill," he remarked.

Down in the bushes lay an upturned automobile. The car was a total wreck, and lay bottom upward, a mass of tangled junk.

"Must have been hitting an awful clip to crumple up like that," Joe commented. "Perhaps there's some one underneath. Let's go and see."

The boys left their motorcycles by the road and went down to the wrecked car. But there was no sign of either driver or passengers.

"If any one was hurt they've been taken away by now. Probably this wreck is a day or so old," said Frank. "Let's go. We can't do any good here."

They left the wreckage and returned to the road again, resuming their journey.

"I thought at first it might be our red-headed speed fiend," said Frank. "If it was, he was sure lucky to get out of it alive."

The boys gave little further thought to the incident and before long they were in sight of the Mortons' house, a big, homelike, rambling old farmhouse with an apple orchard at the rear. When the boys drove down the lane they saw a figure awaiting them at the barnyard gate.

"That's Chet," said Frank. "I'm glad we found him at home. I thought he might have gone out in the car."

"It is strange," Joe agreed. "On a holiday like this he doesn't usually stay around the farm."

As they approached, they saw Chet leave the gate and come down the lane to meet them. Chet was one of the most popular boys at the Bayport high school, one reason for his popularity being his unfailing good nature and his ability to see fun in almost everything. He was full of jokes and good humor and was rarely seen without a smile on his plump, freckled face.

But to-day the Hardy boys saw that there was something wrong. Chet's face had an anxious expression, and as they brought their motorcycles to a stop they saw that their chum's usually cheery face was clouded.

"What's the matter?" asked Frank, as their friend hastened up to them.

"You're just in time," replied Chet hurriedly. "You didn't meet a fellow driving my roadster, did you?"

The brothers looked at each other blankly.

"*Your* roadster? We'd recognize it anywhere. No, we didn't see it," said Joe. "What's happened?"

"It's been stolen."

"Stolen?"

"An auto thief stole it from the garage not half an hour ago. He just went in as cool as you please and made away with the car. The hired man saw the roadster disappearing down the lane, but he supposed I was in it so he didn't think anything of it. Then he saw me out in the yard a little while later, so he got suspicious—and the roadster was gone."

"Wasn't it locked?"

"That's the strange part of it. The car was locked, although the garage door was open. I can't see how he got away with it."

"A professional job," commented Frank. "These auto thieves always carry scores of keys with them. But we're losing time here. The only thing is to set out in pursuit and to notify the police. The hired man didn't see which way the fellow went, did he?"

"No."

"There is only the one road, and we didn't meet him, so he must have taken the turning to the right at the end of the lane."

"We'll chase him," said Joe. "Climb onto my bike, Chet. We'll get the thief yet."

"Wait a minute," cried Frank suddenly. "I have an idea! Joe, do you remember that car we saw wrecked in the bushes?"

"Sure."

"Perhaps the driver stole the first automobile he could lay his hands on after the wreck."

"What wreck was that?" asked Chet.

The Hardy boys told him of the wrecked car they had found by the roadside. It had occurred to Frank that perhaps the smash-up might have occurred just a short while before and that the driver of the wrecked car had resumed his interrupted journey in a stolen automobile.

"It sounds reasonable," said Chet. "Let's go and take a look at this wreck. We can get the license number and that may help us find the name of the owner."

The motorcycles roared as the three chums set out back along the road toward the place where the upturned automobile had been seen among the bushes. The boys lost no time in reaching the place, for they realized that every second was precious and that the longer they delayed the greater was the advantage to the car thief.

The car had not been disturbed and apparently no one had been near it since the boys had discovered the wreck. They parked their motorcycles by the roadside and again went down into the bushes to examine the wrecked car.

To their disappointment the car bore no license plates.

"That looks suspicious," said Frank.

"It's more than suspicious," said Joe, who had withdrawn a little to one side and was examining the automobile from the rear. "Don't you remember seeing this car before, Frank? It didn't occur to me until you mentioned the matter of license plates."

"I have been wondering if this isn't the same car that passed us on the shore road at the curve," replied Frank slowly.

"It is the same car. There's no doubt of it in my mind. It didn't have a license plate, I noticed at the time, for I wanted to get the fellow's number. And it was a touring car of the same make as this."

"You're right, Joe. There's no mistake. The red-headed driver came to grief in the ditch, just as we said he would, and then he went on to the nearest farmhouse, which happened to be Chet's place, and stole the first car he saw."

"The busted car was the one the fellow was running who nearly sent us over the cliff," Joe declared. "And it's ten chances to one that he's the fellow who stole Chet's roadster. And he's red-headed. We have those clues, anyway."

"And he went on past our farmhouse instead of turning back the way he came," cried Chet. "Come on, fellows—let's get after him! There was only a little bit of gas in the roadster anyway. Perhaps he's stalled by this time."

Thrilling with the excitement of a chase, the boys clambered back onto the motorcycles and within a few moments a cloud of dust rose from the road as the Hardy boys and Chet Morton set out in swift pursuit of the red-headed automobile thief.

CHAPTER III
TRACES OF THE THIEF

Chet Morton's roadster was a brilliant yellow, not easily mistaken, and the Hardy boys were confident that it would not be difficult to pick up the trail of the auto thief.

"The car is pretty well known around Bayport," said Chet. "It was certainly a gay-looking speed-wagon. Any one who saw it would remember it."

"Seems strange that a thief would take a car like that," remarked Frank. "Auto thieves usually take cars of a standard make and standard color. They're easier to get rid of. He would know that a car like yours could be easily traced."

"I don't think he stole the car to sell it," Joe pointed out. "Take it from me, that chap was getting away from some place in a hurry and when his own car was smashed he just took the first one that came to hand. If we keep after him before he has a chance to get rid of it we'll run him to earth."

A number of men in a hay-field near by attracted Frank's attention, and he brought his motorcycle to a stop.

"I'm going to ask these chaps if they saw him pass."

Frank scrambled over the fence and went over to talk to the farmhands, who watched his approach with curiosity.

"Didn't see a yellow roadster pass here within the last hour, did you?"

One of them, a lanky old farmer with a sun-burned nose, carefully laid down his scythe, put his hand to his ear and shouted:

"Eh?"

"Did you see a fellow pass along here in a roadster?" Frank repeated, in a louder tone.

The farmer turned to his companions, removed a plug of tobacco from the pocket of his overalls and took a hearty chew.

"Lad here want to know if we saw a roadster come by here!" he said slowly.

There were three other farmhands and all gathered around. They put down their scythes very deliberately, and the plug of tobacco was duly passed around the group.

Frank waited.

"A roadster, eh?" asked one.

"A yellow roadster," Frank told him.

One of the men removed his hat and mopped his brow.

"Seems to me," he observed, "I *did* see a car come by here a while ago."

"A yellow car?"

"No—twan't a yeller car. It was a delivery truck, if I remember rightly."

Frank strove to conceal his impatience.

"It was a roadster I was asking about. A yellow roadster."

"Not one of them there coops, hey?" asked the oldest man in the group doubtfully.

"No, not a coupé. A roadster."

"Roadster, eh?" remarked the old farmer. "That's one of them there autymobiles with just two seats and a little cupboard in the back, eh?"

"My cousin has one," observed another member of the group. "He got it secondhand in Bayport. I never *could* see why he bought the doggone thing, for you can't take the folks out for a ride in it without havin' 'em all crowded somethin' fearful. Give me the old tourin' car every time."

"Cain't say as I agree with you," returned the old farmer. "What good's a tourin' car if you want to haul a load of grain into town. Once of them leetle trucks is the best, I've always thought. Then, if you want to go on a picnic or anythin' the family can all climb in the back. You get the *use* out of a car like that."

"Nope. Nothin' like a tourin' car."

"Rank extravagance, buyin' tourin' cars," put in another. "Horse and wagon is good enough for me."

"That's what I say," agreed the fourth.

"What with taxes the way they are—"

"And last year's crops wasn't any too good—"

"I tell ye a tourin' car is the only thing nowadays—"

Somewhat astonished by the sudden turn the argument had taken, Frank vainly tried to make himself heard above the uproar.

"But about this roadster?" he asked. "Did any of you see it?"

But the four men in the field were not listening. Instead they were deep in a highly complicated argument regarding the faults and merits of various makes of cars and they paid no further attention to the youth.

"Can't afford to waste any more time here," he said to himself, and turned away. At the fence, he looked back. One of the farmhands was shaking his fist beneath the nose of a companion, while the other two were engrossed in a heated discussion. Their voices floated across the hay-field in the drowsy summer morning.

"It looks as if you started something," laughed Joe, as his brother returned to the motorcycle.

"I certainly did. Just asked them if they had seen a yellow roadster and they started to fight about what was the best car for a farmer to buy."

"And didn't they see the roadster?" asked Chet.

"I don't think so. If they had they would have told me. I guess they were glad of an excuse to quit work."

"Well, we'd better be getting on our way then. We've lost enough time already."

So, while the four farmhands wrangled loudly in the field, in an argument that bade fair to last until dinner-time at least, the three boys set out again in pursuit of the red-headed auto thief.

They were approaching Bayport when they saw a girl walking along the road ahead of them. There was something familiar about her appearance, and as they drew nearer Frank's face lighted up, for he recognized the girl as Callie Shaw, who was in his own class at Bayport high school. Of all the girls at the school, Callie was the one most greatly admired by Frank. She was a pretty girl, with brown hair and brown eyes, always neatly dressed, and quick and vivacious in her manner.

As the boys brought their motorcycles to a stop, Frank saw that Callie was not in her usual bright and cheery humor. Under one arm she was carrying a parcel that had evidently become untied and the paper of which was badly torn. Her face was distressed and it appeared that she had been crying.

Callie looked up and, recognizing the boys, ran over toward them.

"That awful man!" she wailed, even before they had time to ask her what the matter was. "He ran right over my parcel and smashed nearly all the cakes and jelly I was bringing to Mrs. Wills!"

And with that she held out the torn parcel. Frank knew that Callie, who was a generous and good-hearted girl, had been in the habit of taking little delicacies to a widow, Mrs. Wills, who lived just on the outskirts of Bayport.

Now he saw that the parcel had been smashed so that only one glass of jelly and a few of the cakes had been left intact.

"What man, Callie?" he asked. "What happened?"

"He ran right over my parcel!" Just then Callie spied Chet Morton, and she pouted at him. "He was a friend of yours, too, Chet Morton, for he was driving your car!"

"My car!" gasped Chet.

"Your yellow roadster. He came driving along this road at such a terrible speed that I was frightened and I dropped my parcel. Then he ran right over it."

"Why, Callie, that's just the fellow we've been looking for!" said Frank quickly. "Chet's car has been stolen!"

"Well, whoever stole it, came by here not ten minutes ago," said the girl. "And he's a madman—by the way he was driving."

"Why, we're right on his trail then!" declared Frank. "He must have gone into Bayport."

"He was heading that way," Callie told them. "But at the rate he was going, you'll have a hard time catching him. Oh, Chet, I'm so sorry your car was stolen."

"Don't worry. We'll get it back," replied Chet grimly.

"Are you going back home, Callie?" asked Frank.

"No, I'm going on up to Mrs. Wills' place. You needn't bother to drive me up. It's only a few yards farther on. I know you're anxious to chase that awful man."

"We'll chase him, all right!" declared Frank, as the motorcycles roared.

They bade good-bye to the girl and sped on their way into Bayport, leaving Callie to continue her journey to the home of Mrs. Wills, with the remains of the cakes and jelly over which she had spent so much time and care.

They sped down the main street of Bayport and headed directly to the police station, where they intended to report the theft of Chet's car and a description of the thief, assuming him to be the red-headed man who had so nearly run down Frank and Joe on the shore road.

But when they reached the police station a further surprise was in wait for them.

CHAPTER IV
THE HOLD-UP

Chief Ezra Collig, of the Bayport police force, was a burly, red-faced individual, much given to telling long-winded stories.

Usually, Collig was to be found reclining in a swivel chair in his office, with his feet on the desk, reading the comic papers or polishing up his numerous badges, but this day something had happened to shake him out of his customary calm.

When the boys went into his office they found the chief painfully writing in a huge notebook and confronted by three excited figures. One of these was Ike Harrity, the old ticket seller at the city steamboat office. The others were Detective Smuff, of the police force, and Policeman Con Riley, both trying their best to look important and composed.

Ike Harrity was frankly frightened. It was plain that something very much out of the ordinary had happened. Harrity was a timid and inoffensive old chap who had perched on a high stool behind the wicket at the steamboat office day in and day out for as many years as any one in Bayport could remember.

"I was just countin' up the mornin's receipts," he was saying, in a frightened and high-pitched voice, "when in comes this fellow and he sticks a revolver in front of my nose—"

"Just a minute," interrupted the chief grandly, as the boys entered. He dipped his pen in the inkwell and poised it in the air, as he peered at the lads over his spectacles.

"What are you boys doing here? Can't you see we're busy?"

"I came to report a theft," said Chet Morton. "My roadster has been stolen."

"Why, it was a roadster this fellow drove up to my office in!" cried Ike Harrity. "A yellow roadster."

"Ha!" said Detective Smuff. "A clue!" He immediately fished a notebook out of his pocket and began rummaging around for a pencil.

"Never mind, Detective Smuff," observed the chief heavily. "I'll take any notes that are needed."

Detective Smuff, duly squelched, put back his notebook in confusion.

"What fellow?" Frank asked. "Who drove up to your office in a yellow roadster?"

"The hold-up man," declared Harrity. "I was held up this morning. A fellow tried to steal the steamboat money on me."

"Now just a minute. Just a minute!" demanded the chief. "Let *me* say a word here. The situation is this. A man drove up to the steamboat office a little while ago and tried to hold up Mr. Harrity. But a passenger happened to come into the office just then and the fellow got frightened and ran away. Is that right?"

"That's right," said Harrity.

"I'll make a note of it," said the chief, suiting the action to the word. When he had scribbled industriously for some time he raised the pen again and pointed it at Chet.

"Now *you*," he observed, "say that somebody stole a yellow roadster on you this morning."

"Yes, sir! From our farm. He was seen driving into Bayport just a little while ago."

The chief made a note of it.

"And *you*," he said, pointing the pen at Ike Harrity, "say the hold-up man drove up to the office in a yellow roadster?"

"That's right, chief. That's right. A yellow roadster, it was. And now that I come to think of it, I've seen Chet Morton's car before and it was the spittin' image of it."

"Then," declared the chief, putting down his pen with the air of one making a momentous discovery, "it looks to me very much as if the hold-up man and the fellow that stole the car is one and the same man."

Detective Smuff wagged his head solemnly in admiration of this feat of deduction. "I believe you're right, chief," he declared.

"Of course he's right," said Frank. "It couldn't be any one else. The point is this—where did the hold-up man go? Did he leave in the car? Did any one follow him?"

"He left in the car all right," said Harrity. "But nobody followed him. I telephoned for the police."

"Did you notice the color of this man's hair?" asked Frank suddenly.

"What's that got to do with it?" asked Detective Smuff.

"Never mind. It may have a great deal to do with it. Did you notice the color of his hair?" repeated Frank, turning to Harrity.

"It was short," said Harrity firmly. "Short and dark."

Frank and Joe looked blankly at one another.

"Are you sure?" asked Joe.

"I'm positive," declared Harrity. "I was face to face with him. He was a dark-haired man, and his hair was cut awful short. I noticed that."

"You're sure he wasn't red-headed?"

"I'm sure of it."

"What's all this about?" asked Chief Collig suspiciously. "What has the color of his hair to do with it?"

"Well," admitted Frank, "we were pretty sure that the man who stole Chet's car had long, red hair."

"Hum!" muttered the chief doubtfully. "Then if *that* was the case, the man who stole the car and the man who tried to hold up the office *isn't* one and the same fellow after all."

"I don't know what to make of it," confessed Frank.

Just then a short, nervous little man was ushered into the office. He introduced himself as the passenger who had gone into the steamboat office at the time of the attempted hold-up, and he presented himself in answer to a call from the chief.

In reply to questions, the newcomer, who gave the prosaic name of Henry J. Brown and said he was from New York, told of entering the office and seeing a man run away from the wicket with a revolver in his hand.

"What color was his hair? Did you notice?" asked Frank eagerly.

"I can't say I did," answered the little man. "It all happened so quickly I didn't realize that it was a hold-up until the man was out the door. Then I saw him jump into the roadster and drive away. But—wait a minute. I did notice the color of his hair. Just as the car was disappearing down the street. You couldn't help notice. He was red-headed. He had long red hair."

Detective Smuff looked blankly at the chief and the chief looked blankly at everybody else, particularly at Henry J. Brown of New York.

"I knew it!" declared Joe exultantly. "It's the same man!"

"It can't be the same man!" said the chief wearily. "You boys don't know what you're talking about. Mr. Harrity says he had short, dark hair. Now how could he have short, dark hair and long, red hair at the same time? I ask you that! How could he?"

Chief Collig propounded this query with the expression of one who has triumphantly settled all difficulties.

"He had short, dark hair!" said Harrity doggedly.

"And I'm sure he had long, red hair!" shouted Henry J. Brown, very indignantly. "Do you think I'm blind? Do you think I'd tell a lie about it?"

"He had dark hair."

"It was red."

"It was dark."

"It wasn't."

"It was!"

"Stop it!" commanded Chief Collig. "I don't think either of you know what kind of hair he had. Probably he was bald-headed. But I'll send word out to keep a watch for the yellow roadster. I'll notify the police in other towns too. I guess that's all that can be done now."

And with that, the Hardy boys and Chet Morton had to be content.

When they left the office it was with little hope that the thief or the car would be found. Their misgivings were justified. When they returned to see Chief Collig that night they learned that no word had been received concerning the yellow roadster from any of the outlying towns or villages and that despite a diligent search conducted by Detective Smuff and other members of the Bayport force, the roadster had not been located in the city.

CHAPTER V
CHET'S AUTO HORN

Fenton Hardy, the internationally famous detective, was reading in the library of his home that evening when his sons tapped on the door.

Although he was a busy man, Mr. Hardy was not the type of father who maintains an air of aloofness from his family, the result being that he was on as good terms with his boys as though he were an elder brother.

"Come in," he shouted cheerfully, putting aside his book, and when Frank and Joe entered the room he motioned to a deep leather sofa near the window. "Sit down. What have you been doing all day? Burning up all the roads in the country, I suppose?" He grinned amiably at them and puffed vigorously at his pipe.

"Well, we didn't travel very far to-day, dad," Frank replied. "We were—well, we—we were—"

"Investigating," prompted Joe.

"Aha!" exclaimed Mr. Hardy, in mock surprise. "So my sons were investigating, eh? What was it? A murder? A plot to blow up the White House? A train wreck? Something big, I hope."

"No—not quite that bad," admitted Frank. "It was a car theft."

Mr. Hardy shook his head.

"I'm disappointed in you," he said solemnly. "I really am. To think that sons of mine should investigate a car theft. I thought you wouldn't bother about anything less than a murder!" His eyes twinkled, and the Hardy boys, who were accustomed to their father's good-natured banter, smiled back at him.

"We weren't just practicing detective work, dad," explained Frank. "You see, Chet Morton's roadster was stolen this morning."

"Is that so!" exclaimed Mr. Hardy, genuinely concerned. "Why, that's too bad. Chet was mighty proud of that car, wasn't he?"

"Yes, he was. And it hasn't been found yet."

"No trace of the thief?"

"He tried to hold up the steamboat ticket office after he stole the car." Mr. Hardy whistled.

"Why you *have* been on a case worth while. Tell me all about it."

He settled back in his chair while his sons told him the story of the day's doings. When they told of the difference of opinion as to the color of the man's hair he did not laugh with them, as they had expected, over the argument between Harrity and Mr. Brown. On the contrary, he knitted his brows and his face wore a serious expression.

"It wasn't any ordinary auto thief you were dealing with," he said slowly. "I've no doubt the man who tried to rob the ticket office and the man who almost ran you down on the shore road were one and the same. And the same man stole Chet Morton's car."

"But how about the color of his hair? There must have been two men," said Joe.

"Think so? I have my own theories. But then—the average witness is very unreliable. For instance, I'll give you a test. You have each seen Superintendent Norton of Bayport high school—well, how often?"

"About two or three thousand times, I guess," answered Frank.

"Over a period of three years. Well, what color is his hair?"

Frank looked blankly at Joe.

"Why, it's—it's—"

Joe scratched his head.

"Brown, isn't it?"

"I think it's black."

"You see?" said Mr. Hardy, smiling. "Your powers of observation have not been trained. A good detective has to school himself to remember all sorts of little facts like that, until it gets to be a habit with him. Both of you have been looking at Mr. Norton for about three years and you don't know the color of his hair. And if I asked you whether he was in the habit of wearing laced shoes or buttoned shoes you would be stumped altogether. As a matter of fact, Mr. Norton is bald and he wears a chestnut wig. You never noticed that? He always wears buttoned shoes, he belongs to the Elks, and his favorite author is Dickens."

The boys looked at their father in amazement.

"But, dad, you've never met him."

"I've never been introduced to him, but I've passed him on the street a number of times. When your powers of observation have been trained as mine have been it's no trick at all to take away a mental photograph of a man after seeing him once. If you are specially observant it isn't hard to notice such details as that regarding the wig. A wig never has the same appearance as natural hair."

"But how do you know he belongs to the Elks?" asked Joe.

"He wears the lodge emblem as a watch charm."

"And how do you know his favorite author is Dickens?"

"On three separate occasions that I met Mr. Norton I noticed that he was carrying a book. Once it was 'Oliver Twist.' Another time it was 'A Tale of Two Cities.' The third time it was 'David Copperfield.' So I judge that his favorite author must be Dickens. Am I right?"

"He always talks Dickens to us at school," said Frank.

"It's simple enough, once you get the habit," remarked Mr. Hardy. "You must train yourselves to be observant, so that in time you will automatically remember little details about people you meet and places you've visited. Now, if Harrity and Mr. Brown had been at all observant, in spite of the fact that they were surprised and frightened, they would have been able to give the police a very thorough description of the man who tried to hold up the steamboat office. And if the man happened to be a professional thief the description would have helped the officers ascertain who he was, because once a man has served a prison term his description is kept on file. As it is, all we know about him is that he is probably red-headed. That isn't very much to go on."

"I'm afraid Chet hasn't much chance of recovering his roadster," said Joe.

"You never can tell," remarked his father. "It may turn up some time. Perhaps the thief will get himself into trouble yet. Keep your ears and eyes open. And now, if you don't mind, I have some reports to write—"

Frank and Joe took the hint and left their father to his work. But although they talked long into the night on possible ways and means of recovering Chet's car, they were able to devise no plan for tracing the thief.

And through the week that followed there were no further clues. Chet had given up all hope of seeing the roadster again.

"I sure miss the old bus," he told the Hardy boys after school on Friday afternoon. "I have to take my chances on catching rides in and out of town now. Why, last night I walked half way home before a car came along and gave me a lift."

"Saturday will be a pretty dull day for you now."

"You just bet your sweet life it will be dull! Nothing to do but sit around the farm."

"Better come with us to-morrow," suggested Joe. "A bunch of us are going fishing up near the dam. You can meet us at the crossroads near Willow River."

"Good idea!" said Chet. "What time?"

"Ten o'clock."

"Fine! I'll be there. Gosh, I see where I get a ride home. There goes a hay wagon, and it's heading right for the next farm."

A long wagon rumbled slowly toward the boys. A lean and solemn farmer perched on the front seat, half asleep. The horses dawdled along.

"That's Lem Billers—the laziest man in nine counties," said Chet. "Watch me have some fun with him."

Chet took from his pocket an automobile horn. He had originally bought it for the roadster but had not had time to install it before the car was stolen. The horn was of a new type, very small, yet it had a particularly raucous shriek.

The Hardy boys grinned as they saw Chet step out into the road and swing himself lightly up on the back of the wagon. Mr. Billers was bringing some supplies back to the farm and Chet was hidden from view by a bag of flour.

As the wagon rumbled past, Chet sounded the automobile horn.

It shrieked sharply and insistently.

Mr. Billers, being a lazy man, did not even look behind. He simply tugged lightly at the reins and the horses edged over to the side of the road.

Having heard the horn, Mr. Billers expected an automobile would pass. But when no car flashed by he turned indolently in his seat and looked behind. The roadway was clear. There was not an automobile in sight. He did not see Chet, doubling up with laughter, on the back of the wagon. He gazed doubtfully at the Hardy boys, who were standing at the curb, trying to conceal their smiles.

"Could 'a' swore I heard a horn," grunted Mr. Billers. Then he tugged at the lines and brought the horses into the middle of the road again.

Instantly the horn shrieked again. This time it was even louder and more insistent than before. It seemed that an automobile was right behind the wagon, clamoring to pass.

Almost automatically, Mr. Billers yanked at the reins and the horses again went to the side of the road.

But again no car went by.

Again Mr. Billers looked behind. Again, to his astonishment, he saw that the roadway was clear.

"Hanged if I didn't think I heard a horn!" exclaimed Mr. Billers, greatly puzzled, as he drove on again. "My ears must be goin' back on me."

But in a few minutes the horn shrieked again. Frank and Joe, who were walking along the sidewalk, keeping abreast of the wagon so as not to miss the fun, chuckled as they saw Mr. Billers once more pull on the reins to guide the horses to the roadside. Then the farmer recollected how he had been fooled on the previous occasions and he looked quickly around. But there was no car in sight.

Mr. Billers gazed down the roadway for a long time. Then he sighed, with the air of one whose patience has been long tried.

"Must be somethin' the matter with my ears," he muttered, and drove on.

At this moment a luxurious sedan swept around a corner and drew up close behind the wagon. There was a chauffeur at the wheel and he sounded his horn impatiently, for the road was narrow and he was unable to get past.

Lem Billers smiled darkly to himself and paid no attention.

"There it goes again," he grumbled. "I *must* be hearin' things. Hang me if I'll turn out any more when there ain't no car there to turn out for."

The wagon continued in the center of the road. The chauffeur of the car glared at Lem Billers' back and sounded the horn again. Still the farmer paid no attention.

Chet, limp with laughter, almost rolled off the wagon. Frank and Joe could control their mirth no longer, and leaned against a telephone post with shouts of glee.

The chauffeur, believing that the boys were laughing at him because he could not get past, became purple with anger. He sounded the horn again and again, and finally, when Lem Billers obstinately refused to pay any attention, he looked wildly about for a policeman.

As luck would have it, Constable Con Riley was ambling along Main Street at that moment, wondering if it would soon be supper time and hoping his wife would serve corned beef and cabbage that evening. He was aroused from his trance by the chauffeur, who brought the sedan to a stop and ran over to him.

"Officer—arrest that man!" roared the chauffeur, pointing to Lem Billers.

"What for?" demanded Con, taking off his helmet and scratching his head.

"Obstructing the traffic. He won't let me pass. I've been sounding my horn for the last five minutes, and he won't let me go past."

"Oh, ho!" said Constable Riley. "He can't get away with that. Not while Con Riley's on the beat." And with that he ran out into the road, shouting to Lem Billers to stop.

At the constable's command, the farmer halted his team and gazed in amazement at the chauffeur and the officer as they came running up to him.

"Why won't you let him pass?" demanded the constable.

"Don't say you didn't hear me?" roared the chauffeur. "I sounded my horn fifty times."

"Sure, I heard a horn," admitted Billers. "But," he added triumphantly, "I didn't see no car."

"Are you blind?" asked Riley. "There's the car."

Lem Billers looked behind. At sight of the sedan, his jaw dropped.

"Well, I'll be hanged!" he declared sadly. "It must be my eyes is goin' back on me. Not my ears. I looked behind three times and I couldn't see no car."

"Don't believe him, officer," said the chauffeur. "He didn't even turn around."

"I did so!" contended Mr. Billers.

"Then why didn't you let me pass?"

"You didn't have no car. I heard a horn but I didn't see no car."

Thereupon the argument grew fast and furious. Constable Riley was vastly puzzled. He didn't know what to make of it. Both the chauffeur and Lem Billers appeared to be telling the truth, yet there was something wrong somewhere. He took it all down in a notebook, while Mr. Billers and the chauffeur grew angrier and angrier at each other until finally they were on the point of settling the matter with their fists.

In the meantime there was a steadily lengthening line of cars and wagons blocking the street, unable to get past because of the hay wagon and the sedan. A constant chorus of automobile horns sounded. Angry drivers roared at the officer to clear the road.

Constable Riley threw up his hands in disgust.

"Get on your way, both of you," he commanded. "I can't stand here arguin' all afternoon."

And while Lem Billers, wondering whether his eyes or his ears had deceived him, drew his horses to the side of the road and muttered strong threats of vengeance against the chauffeur, the traffic tangle gradually abated. When he finally resumed his journey, the Hardy boys could see Chet Morton lying limply in the back of the wagon with tears of laughter running down his face. As for Frank and Joe, they laughed all the way home and during supper that evening their spasmodic outbursts of chuckles puzzled their parents extremely.

CHAPTER VI
TIRE TRACKS

Next day was Saturday, and immediately after breakfast the Hardy boys asked their mother to make up a lunch for them, as they intended to spend the day in the woods with a number of their school chums.

Mrs. Hardy quickly made up a generous package of sandwiches, not forgetting to slip in several big slices of the boys' favorite cake, and the lads started out in the bright morning sunshine, with the whole holiday before them.

They met the other boys, half a dozen in all, on the road at the outskirts of the town and so, whistling and chattering and telling jokes, the group trudged along the dusty highway. Once in a while they would explore along the fences for berry bushes, and occasionally a friendly scuffle would start, to end with both laughing contestants covered with dust.

When they reached the crossroads Chet had not yet appeared, so they rested in the shade of the trees until at length the chubby youth came panting along the road, his lunch under his arm.

"If I only had my roadster I wouldn't be late," he said, as he came up to them. "I've been so used to it that I've forgotten how long it takes to walk this far."

"Well, are we all set?" asked Frank.

"Everybody's here. Where are we going?"

"What do you say to Willow Grove?"

"All those in favor say 'Aye'," demanded Chet, and there was a chorus of "Aye" from the crowd.

"It's unanimous," Chet decided. "Willow Grove it shall be. Let's go."

Willow Grove was about a mile farther on. It was some distance in from the road, and was on the banks of Willow River, from which it got its name. It was an ideal place for a picnic, and as it was somewhat early in the season it was hardly likely that other parties from the city would be in the grove that day.

Frank told the other boys about Chet's adventure with the auto horn and the story was greeted with shouts of laughter, which were redoubled when Chet told how he had later jumped down from the wagon and run along behind, shouting to Lem Billers to give him a ride.

"It was a shame!" he confessed. "The poor old chap reined in his horses and made me come up and sit on the seat beside him. He asked me if I had walked very far and then he told me all about his argument with the policeman and the chauffeur. I could hardly keep my face straight."

When the boys reached the lane that led in toward Willow Grove from the main road they broke into a run and raced into the woods, shouting and yelling like wild Indians. Once in the friendly shade of the trees they capered about in the joy of their Saturday freedom. Chet took charge of the lunches and stored them in a convenient clearing, and then began the rush for the river.

The day passed in the usual fashion of such days. They swam, they ate, they loafed about under the trees, they played games at imminent risk of life and limb, they explored the woods, and otherwise enjoyed themselves with all the happy energy of healthy lads. Joe Hardy, who was an amateur naturalist in his way, went roaming off by himself during the afternoon while the other boys were enjoying their third swim of the day, and penetrated deeper into the woods.

He poked about in the undergrowth, examining various flowers and plants that came to his attention, but discovered no specimens that he had not seen before. He was just on the point of going back to the other lads when he saw before him a small clearing. It was a part of the grove in which he had never been, so he ploughed on through the bushes until he found himself in a clearing that appeared to be part of an abandoned roadway.

It was in a low-lying part of the grove and the ground was wet. At one point it was muddy, and in this mud Joe saw something that aroused his curiosity.

"Tire tracks, eh! There's been an automobile in here," he muttered to himself. "I wonder how on earth a car could get this far into the woods!"

Then he remembered his father's remarks on the value of developing his powers of observation, so he went over closer and examined the marks in the mud.

"That's a strange tread," he thought. "I've never seen a tire mark quite like that before."

He gazed at it until he was sure that if he ever saw a similar auto tread again he would recognize it.

"That just goes to prove that dad was right," said Joe. "Probably I've seen auto tires like that often, but I've never noticed the markings, and now that I do notice one in particular it seems strange to me. But I wonder what an automobile was doing in here and how it came to get here in the first place!"

However, he gave the matter little further thought and retraced his steps through the woods until he returned to the other boys, who were getting dressed after their swim.

"I thought automobiles weren't allowed in Willow Grove," he said casually to Chet Morton.

"Neither they are. You have to park just inside the fence."

"Well, somebody brought a car right down into the grove."

"They couldn't. There's no road."

"Well, there's a sort of clearing over there," said Joe, motioning in the direction from which he had just returned. "It looks as if it had been a road at one time."

"That's probably the old creek road. It hasn't been used for years."

"Well, it was used just this week. I saw the marks of an automobile tire over there not ten minutes ago. And it was a mighty peculiar tread, too. Like this—," and Joe commenced to draw a replica of the design in the sand, using a thin stick of wood as a pencil.

Chet Morton stared.

"Why," he exclaimed, "there's only one car in the city has tires like that!"

"Whose car?"

"Mine!" exclaimed Chet, springing to his feet. "Where *is* this road you found?"

Joe Hardy quickly led the way and all the other boys came trooping along behind, the whole band thrown into a state of great excitement by this unexpected discovery. They all knew that Chet's car was of an unusual make and that the tires were distinctive. When they reached the clearing and Chet had examined the imprint in the mud he exclaimed:

"There's no mistake about it! My car has been here! No other car in the city has a tread like that!"

"Perhaps the car is still around here," suggested Frank quickly. "For all we can tell, the thief may have abandoned it and picked this road as a good place to hide it."

"It would be an ideal place," agreed Chet. "This road leads off the main highway, and it isn't often used. Let's take a look around, anyway."

The boys quickly scattered, some taking one side of the road, the rest taking the other.

For a while the search continued without success, but at last Frank and Chet, who were following the abandoned road farther down, gave a simultaneous cry.

"Here's a bypath!"

Before them was a narrow roadway, over-grown with weeds and low bushes that almost hid it from view. It led from the abandoned road into the very depths of the wood. Without hesitation the two boys plunged into it.

The narrow roadway widened out farther on, then wound about a heavy clump of trees, until it came to an end in a wide clearing.

And in the clearing stood Chet Morton's lost roadster!

"My car!" yelled Chet, in delight.

His shout was heard by all the other boys, and the sound of snapping twigs and crackling branches soon told Frank and Chet that the others were losing no time in reaching the scene.

Chet's delight was boundless. He examined the car with minute care, in every particular, while the other boys crowded about. At last he straightened up with a smile of satisfaction.

"She hasn't been damaged a bit. All ready to run. The thief just hid the old bus in here and made a getaway. Come on, fellows, we don't walk back home to-day. We ride."

He clamored into the car and in a few seconds the engine roared. There was sufficient room in the clearing to permit him to turn the roadster about, and when he swung the car around and headed up the bypath the boys gave a cheer and hastened to clamber on board.

Lurching and swaying, the roadster reached the abandoned road and from there it was an easy run to the main highway. In spite of the fact that it had been left in the bush for probably a week, the roadster was in perfect condition and the engine ran smoothly. Joe was given the seat of honor beside the driver, because he had discovered the tire marks that had led to the recovery of the car, and the other boys distributed themselves as best they could. They clung to the running boards, hung precariously to the back, and one lad even straddled the hood. In this manner the triumphal procession returned to Bayport.

But as the cheering lads came down the main street they noticed that there was an unwonted air of excitement in the town. People were standing on the street corners in little groups, talking earnestly, and when the boys spied Detective Smuff, of the police force, striding along with a portentous frown, they called out to him.

"What's on your mind to-day, detective? Chet got his car back!"

"I've got something more important than stolen cars to worry about," declared Detective Smuff. "The Tower Mansion has been robbed."

CHAPTER VII
THE MANSION ROBBERY

Tower Mansion was one of the show places of Bayport. Few people in the city had ever been permitted to enter the place and the admiration the palatial building excited was solely by reason of its exterior appearance, but the first thing a newcomer to Bayport usually asked was, "Who owns that magnificent house on the hill?"

It was an immense, rambling stone structure situated on the top of the hill overlooking the bay, and it could be seen for miles, silhouetted against the skyline, like some ancient feudal castle. This resemblance to a castle was heightened by the fact that at each end of the mansion rose a high tower.

One of these towers had been built when the mansion was first erected by Major Applegate, an eccentric old army man who had made millions by lucky real estate deals and had laid the foundation for the Applegate fortune. The mansion had been the admiration of its day, and in its time had seen much gaiety.

But as the years passed the Applegate family became scattered until at last there remained but Hurd Applegate and his sister Adelia, who continued living in the vast and lonely old mansion.

Hurd Applegate was a man of about sixty years of age. He was a tall, stooped man, eccentric in his ways, and his life seemed to be devoted to the collection of rare stamps. He was an authority on the subject, and nothing else in life appeared to hold a great deal of interest for him. The only visitors at Tower Mansion were philatelists from New York or experts desirous of appraising some new stamp that Hurd Applegate had managed to secure from some remote part of the world. It had often been said in Bayport that Hurd Applegate had accomplished only two things in life— he had collected stamps and he had built a new tower on the mansion. The new tower, a duplicate of the original tower at the opposite end of the great building, had been built but a few years—even well within the memory of the two Hardy boys.

Adelia Applegate, who lived in the Tower Mansion with her brother, was a maiden lady of uncertain years. The records in Bayport's city hall gave her age as fifty-five, but Miss Applegate admitted it to no one. She was as eccentric as her brother, and lived very much to herself, being seldom seen in the city. She was at one time a blonde, but she had endeavored to retain her youth by dyeing her hair, with the result that it was now a sort of dusty black. Chet Morton was fond of saying that "Miss Applegate used to be a blonde but she dyed."

She dressed in all colors of the rainbow, and her infrequent excursions into Bayport stores, when she would order the clerks about like so many soldiers, shouting at them in her high, cracked voice, had become historic on account of the wild and colorful garments she would carry off with her.

These eccentric people were reputed to be enormously wealthy, although they lived simply and kept only a few servants. So when Hurd Applegate came into the Bayport police station that afternoon and reported that the safe in his library had been broken open and that it had been robbed of all the securities and jewels it contained, the rumors that soon spread about the city magnified the actual loss until it became common talk that the loss amounted anywhere from one hundred thousand to a million dollars.

When Frank and Joe Hardy arrived home that evening they met Hurd Applegate just leaving the house. The man tapped the steps with his cane as he came out and when he met the boys he gave them an abrupt and piercing glance.

"Good day!" he growled, in a grudging manner, and went on his way.

"He must have been asking dad to take up the case," said Frank to his brother, as soon as Hurd Applegate was out of earshot.

They hurried into the house, eager to find out more about the robbery, and in the hallway they met Fenton Hardy, who had just seen Mr. Applegate to the door.

"I hear the Tower Mansion was robbed," said Joe.

Mr. Hardy nodded.

"Yes—Mr. Applegate was just here. He wants me to handle the case."

"How much was taken?"

"Quite curious, aren't you?" remarked Mr. Hardy, with a smile. "Well, I don't suppose it will do any harm to tell you. The safe in the Applegate library was opened. The loss will be about forty thousand dollars, I believe."

"We heard it was over a hundred thousand!" exclaimed Joe.

"Rumors always exaggerate. Forty thousand dollars is the figure Mr. Applegate puts it at. And it's quite enough, too. All in securities and jewels."

"Whew!" exclaimed Frank. "Quite a haul! When did it happen?"

"Either last night or this morning. He did not get up until after ten o'clock this morning and he did not go into the library until nearly noon. Then he discovered the theft."

"How was the safe opened?"

"It was either opened by some one who knew the combination or else by a very clever crook. It wasn't dynamited at all. I'm going up to the house in a few minutes. Mr. Applegate is to call for me."

"Can't we go along?" asked Joe eagerly.

Mr. Hardy looked at his sons with a smile.

"Well, if you are so anxious to be detectives, I suppose it is about as good a chance as any to watch a crime investigation from the inside. If Mr. Applegate doesn't object, I suppose you may come along."

In a few minutes an automobile drew up before the Hardy home. Mr. Applegate was sitting in the rear seat, resting his chin on his cane. When Mr. Hardy mentioned the boys' request he merely grunted assent, so Joe and Frank clambered into the car with their father. They were tremendously excited at the prospect of being "on the inside" in the mysterious case.

While the car bowled along over the city roads toward the Tower Mansion that was gloomily silhouetted against the sky, Mr. Hardy and Mr. Applegate discussed the robbery.

"I don't really need a detective in this case," snapped Hurd Applegate. "Don't need one at all. It's as clear as the nose on your face. I *know* who took the stuff. But I can't prove it."

"Whom do you suspect?" asked Fenton Hardy.

"Only one man in the world could have taken it. Robinson!"

"Robinson?"

"Yes. Henry Robinson—the caretaker. He's the man."

The Hardy boys looked at one another in consternation.

Henry Robinson, the caretaker of the Tower Mansion, was the father of one of their closest chums. Perry Robinson, nick-named "Slim", was to have accompanied them on their jaunt to the woods that day but had failed to appear. The reason was now evident.

But that Henry Robinson should be accused of the robbery seemed absurd. The boys had met Slim's father and he had appeared to them as a good-natured, easy-going man, the soul of truth and honesty.

"I don't believe it," whispered Frank.

"Neither do I," returned his brother.

"What makes you suspect Robinson?" asked Mr. Hardy of Hurd Applegate.

"He's the only person besides my sister and me who ever saw that safe opened and closed. He could have learned the combination if he kept his eyes and ears open. I believe he did."

"But is that your only reason for suspecting him?"

"More than that. This morning he paid off a note at the bank. It was a note for nine hundred dollars, and I know for a fact that he didn't have more than one hundred dollars to his name a few days ago. The Robinsons have been hard up, for they had sickness in the family last winter and Henry Robinson has had a hard time meeting his debts since then. Now where did he raise nine hundred dollars so suddenly?"

"Perhaps he has a good explanation," said Mr. Hardy mildly. "It doesn't do to jump at conclusions."

"Oh, he'll have an explanation all right!" sniffed Mr. Applegate. "But it will have to be a mighty good one to satisfy me."

"Luckily, he'll not have to satisfy Mr. Applegate, but will have to convince a jury—if it gets that far," whispered Joe in his brother's ear.

The automobile was speeding up the wide driveway that led to Tower Mansion, and within a few minutes it drew up at the front entrance. Mr. Applegate dismissed the driver, and Mr. Hardy and the two boys accompanied the eccentric man into the house.

Nothing had been disturbed in the library since the discovery of the theft. Mr. Hardy examined the open safe, then drew a magnifying glass from his pocket and with minute care inspected the dial of the combination lock. Then he examined the windows, the door-knobs, all places where there might be finger-prints. At last he shook his head.

"A smooth job," he observed. "The fellow must have worn gloves. Not a finger-print in the room."

"No need of looking for finger-prints," said Applegate. "It was Robinson—that's who it was."

"Better send for him," advised Mr. Hardy. "I'd like to ask him a few questions."

Mr. Applegate rang for one of the servants and instructed him to tell Mr. Robinson he was wanted in the library at once. Mr. Hardy glanced at the boys.

"You had better wait in the hallway," he suggested. "I want to ask some questions, and it might embarrass Mr. Robinson if you were here."

The lads readily withdrew, and in the hallway they met Henry Robinson, the caretaker, and his son Perry. Mr. Robinson was calm but pale, and at the doorway he patted his son on the shoulder.

"Don't worry, son," he said. "It'll be all right." With that he entered the library.

Slim Robinson turned to his two chums.

"My dad is innocent!" he cried.

CHAPTER VIII
THE ARREST

There was something in Perry Robinson's tone that made Frank and Joe extremely sorry for their chum, for it seemed that the boy realized that the case looked black against his father.

Although the Hardy lads realized that it was only natural that Perry should stand up for his father, they shared some of his conviction that Mr. Robinson was not guilty.

"Of course he's innocent," agreed Frank. "He'll be able to clear himself all right, Perry."

"But everything looks pretty black against him," said Perry, who was pale and shaken. "Unless your father can catch the real thief I'm afraid dad will be blamed for it."

"Everybody knows your father is honest," said Joe consolingly. "He has a good record—even Applegate will have to admit that."

"A good record won't help him very much if he is blamed for this and can't clear himself. And dad admits that he did know the combination of the safe."

"He knew it?"

"Accidentally. He was cleaning the library fireplace one day when he found a slip of paper with numbers marked on it. The combination was so simple that any one could remember it if he read it once. Dad didn't realize what it was until he had studied it a while, and then he put it back on Mr. Applegate's desk. The window was open and the breeze had blown the paper to the floor."

"Does Applegate know that?"

"Not yet. But dad is going to tell him now. He says he knows it will look bad for him, but he's going to tell the truth about it. He knew the combination, although of course he would never think of using it."

From the library came the dull hum of voices. The harsh tones of Hurd Applegate occasionally rose above the murmur of conversation and once the boys heard Mr. Robinson's voice rise sharply.

"I *didn't* do it. I tell you I *didn't* take that money."

"Then where did you get the nine hundred you paid on that note?" demanded Mr. Applegate.

There was silence for a while.

"Where did you get it?"

"I'm not at liberty to tell you."

"You won't tell?"

"I can't."

"Why not?"

"I got the money honestly—that's all I can say about it."

"Oh, ho!" exclaimed Applegate. "You got the money honestly, yet you can't tell me where it came from! That's very likely, isn't it? If you got it honestly you shouldn't be ashamed to tell where you got it."

"I'm not ashamed. But I'm not at liberty to tell."

"Mighty funny thing that you should get nine hundred dollars so quickly. You were pretty hard up last week, weren't you? Had to ask for an advance on your month's wages."

"I admit it."

"And then the day of this robbery you suddenly have nine hundred dollars that you can't explain."

Mr. Hardy's calm voice broke in.

"Of course, I don't like to pry into your private affairs, Mr. Robinson," he said; "but it would be best if you could clear up this matter of the money. You must admit yourself that it doesn't look promising."

"I know it looks bad," replied the caretaker doggedly. "But I can't tell you where that money came from."

"And you admit knowing the combination of the safe, too!" broke in Applegate. "I didn't know that before. Why didn't you tell me?"

"I didn't consider it important enough. I had found the combination by accident and I had no intention of using it. As a matter of fact, I don't think I could remember it accurately right now. I just put the paper back and decided to say nothing about it, to save trouble."

"And yet you come and tell me about it now!"

"I have nothing to conceal. If I had taken the money I wouldn't very likely be telling you now that I knew the combination."

"Yes," agreed Mr. Hardy, "that's a point in your favor."

"Is it?" asked Applegate. "You're just clever enough to think up a trick like that, Robinson. You think that if you come to me now and admit you knew the combination I'll believe that you are so honest that you couldn't have committed this robbery. Very clever. But not clever enough. There's enough evidence right here and now to convict you, and I'm not going to delay another minute."

There was the sound of a telephone receiver being lifted, and then Applegate's voice continued—

"Police station." After a short wait, he went on. "Hello—police station?—This is Applegate speaking—Applegate—Hurd Applegate.—Well, I think we've found our man.—In that robbery.—Yes, Robinson.—You thought so, eh?—So did I, but I wasn't sure.—He has practically convicted himself by his own story.—Yes, I want him arrested.—You'll be up right away?—Fine.—Good-bye."

The telephone tinkled.

"You're not going to have me arrested, Mr. Applegate?"

"Why not? You took the money!"

"But I'm innocent! I swear it! Haven't I always been honest, ever since I came to work for you? Have you ever had any fault to find with me?"

"Not until now," returned Applegate grimly.

"It might have been better to wait a while," suggested Mr. Hardy mildly. "Of course, it is entirely in your hands, Mr. Applegate, and I admit the case looks rather bad against Mr. Robinson. But perhaps some more evidence may turn up."

"What more evidence do we want? The man's guilty. It's as plain as the nose on your face. If he wants to return the rest of the jewels and securities I'll see what can be done toward having the charge reduced—but that's all."

"But I can't return them! I didn't take them!"

"I suppose you have them hidden safely away by now, hoping to get them when you get out of penitentiary, eh? It'll be a long time, Robinson—a long time."

In the hallway, the boys listened in growing excitement. The case had taken an abrupt and tragic turn. Both the Hardy boys were sorry for their chum Slim, who looked as though he might collapse under the strain.

"He's innocent," muttered the boy, over and over again. "I *know* he's innocent. They can't arrest him. My dad never stole a dollar in his life!"

Frank patted him on the shoulder.

"Brace up, old chap," he advised. "It looks pretty bad just now, but your father will be able to clear himself, never fear."

"I—I'll have to tell mother—," stammered Slim. "This will break her heart. And my sisters—"

Frank and Joe led him down through the hallway and along a corridor that led to a wing of the mansion, where the Robinson family had rooms. There, in a neat, but sparsely furnished apartment, they found Mrs. Robinson, a gentle, kindly-faced woman, somewhat lame, who was sitting anxiously in a chair by the window. Her two daughters, Paula and Tessie, twins, were by her side, and all looked up in expectation as the lads came in.

"What news, son?" asked Mrs. Robinson bravely, after she had greeted the Hardy boys.

"Bad, mother."

"They're not—they're not—arresting him?" cried Paula, springing forward.

Perry nodded, dumbly.

"But they can't!" cried Tessie protestingly. "He's innocent! He *couldn't* do anything like that! It's wrong—"

Mrs. Robinson began to cry, quite silently. Perry went over to his mother and awkwardly patted her shoulder, his face white and stern. The twins gazed at one another with desperate eyes.

Frank and Joe, their hearts too full for utterance, withdrew softly from the room.

CHAPTER IX

RED HAIR

The arrest of Henry Robinson caused a sensation in Bayport, for the caretaker of Tower Mansion was one of the last men in the city whom one would have suspected of dishonesty. There was a great deal of public sympathy for the family, but little for the accused, as most people seemed to take it for granted that he would not have been arrested if he had not had something to do with the crime.

But the Hardy boys were not satisfied.

"I'm positive Henry Robinson is innocent," said Frank to his brother the next morning. "There's a great deal about this case that hasn't come to the surface yet. I have a sort of sneaking idea that the man who stole Chet Morton's car had something to do with this."

"He was a criminal—that much is certain," agreed Joe. "He stole an automobile and he tried to hold up the ticket office."

"I'd like to go back to the place where we saw the wrecked car. You never know what evidence we might find. There might be something there that would identify the chap."

"I'm with you. Let's go this morning."

So within the hour the boys were on their motorcycles, speeding along the shore road toward the place where the speed fiend's car had been wrecked in the bushes.

"I'd certainly like to do something to help clear Mr. Robinson," said Frank. "It's pretty tough on Slim and his mother and sisters."

"We probably won't be able to do very much. If dad can't clear him, I don't think we can help a great deal. But it's worth while trying."

"It sure is. And I've had a hunch all along that we didn't investigate the wreck of that car closely enough."

"Well, we'll make a thorough job of it this time."

When the boys reached the scene of the wreck they found the smashed car just where they had seen it last. The tires had been taken and some of the accessories that had escaped destruction had been stripped from the automobile, but the car had been so badly smashed that there were few evidences of disturbance.

Leaving their motorcycles by the side of the road, the lads plunged down into the bushes and busied themselves examining the wreckage. Joe hunted through the side pockets in the hope that there might be papers or some other means of identification, but in this he was disappointed. There were no license plates, but Frank managed to secure the engine number, and this he jotted down in a notebook he carried.

"Perhaps this will give us a clue. Although I have an idea that the fellow got this car in the same way he got Chet's. It's probably a stolen automobile."

For a time they rummaged around among the wreckage without success. Then, at last, Frank gave a low cry.

"Here's something!" he exclaimed. "Look!"

Joe came over to where he was standing, and Frank plucked something from the front seat of the wrecked car.

"Red hair!"

In his hand Frank held a small tuft of vivid red hair. It was very coarse in texture, and the surprising part of it was that the hairs were not separate but were attached to a sort of tough linen.

"Why, it's part of a wig!" said Frank, examining the hair more closely.

"You're right," agreed his brother. "No human hair ever grew like that."

"Part of the fellow's wig was torn when the car was smashed up!"

"And that explains why Harrity and his witness couldn't agree on the color of the fellow's hair!" exclaimed Joe, in excitement.

"I see it now! The man didn't wear the wig when he held up the steamboat office, and the minute he reached the car he put it on again. That explains why Brown saw a red-haired man driving away in Chet's roadster and why Harrity was positive that man wasn't red-headed."

"That's a *real* clue!" exclaimed Joe. "We ought to tell dad about this."

"And we will, too," said Frank, beginning to scramble through the bushes back toward the road.

He put the fragment of the red wig carefully in an inner pocket, and then the Hardy boys started back toward Bayport. The clue was slight, of course, but, still, it served to clear up the disagreement as to the color of the hold-up man's hair. It also served to prove conclusively that the man who had passed Frank and Joe on the shore road at such break-neck speed, and who had later wrecked his car, was the same man who had stolen Chet's roadster and had attempted to hold up the steamboat ticket office.

"I guess dad will think we aren't such poor detectives after all," Joe exulted, as they brought their motorcycles to a stop in the yard of the Hardy home.

Their father was in the library, but in their excitement the lads forgot to rap at the door and rushed into the room without ceremony.

"Dad, we've found a clue!" cried Joe, when he saw his father sitting at the huge oak desk. Then he fell back, embarrassed, when he saw that there was some one else in the room.

"Beg pardon!" said Frank, and the boys would have retreated, but Mr. Hardy's visitor turned around and they saw that it was Perry Robinson.

"It's only me," said Slim. "Don't go."

"Perry has been trying to shed a little more light on the Tower robbery," explained Mr. Hardy. "But what is this clue you are talking of?"

"It isn't about the robbery," replied Frank. "Although it *might* have something to do with it, for all we know. It's about the red-headed man who stole Chet's car and who tried to hold up the steamboat ticket office."

"What about him?"

"This!" said Frank, taking the fragment of red hair from his pocket and showing it to his father. "The fellow wore a wig."

Mr. Hardy examined the little tuft of hair closely.

"Where did you find it?" he asked.

"In the wreckage of that smashed car."

Mr. Hardy nodded.

"That seems to link up a pretty good chain of evidence. The man who passed you on the shore road wrecked his car, then stole Chet's roadster and afterward tried to hold up the ticket office. When he failed in that he abandoned the roadster. He wore a red wig that he took off occasionally to confuse pursuers. If we could only find the wig we might be able to get further information."

"Do you think it might help us solve the Tower robbery?" asked Perry.

"Possibly."

"The man was evidently a professional thief," explained Frank. "If he was smart enough to wear a wig he was evidently an old-timer at the game. And if he failed in the ticket office hold-up, who knows but what he might have been hanging around the city waiting for another chance."

"Gosh, you may be right, at that!" exclaimed Perry. "I was just telling your father that I saw a strange man lurking about the grounds of Tower Mansion two days before the robbery. I didn't think anything of it at the time, and in the shock of dad's arrest I forgot about it."

"Did you get a good look at him? Could you describe him?" asked the detective.

"I'm afraid I couldn't. It was in the evening, and I was sitting by the window, studying. I happened to look up and I saw this fellow moving about under the trees near the wall. Later on I heard one of the dogs barking in another part of the grounds, and shortly afterward I saw some one running across the lawn. But I thought it was probably just a tramp."

"Did he wear a hat or a cap?"

"As near as I can remember, it was a cap. His clothes were dark."

"And you couldn't see his face?"

"No."

"Well, it's not much to go on, but it might be linked up with Frank's idea that the man who stole the roadster might have still been hanging around." Mr. Hardy thought deeply for a few moments. "I am going to bring all these facts to Mr. Applegate's attention and I am also going to have a talk with the police authorities. I don't think they have enough evidence to warrant holding your father, Perry."

"Do you think you can have him released?" asked the boy eagerly.

"I'm sure of it. In fact, I think Mr. Applegate is beginning to realize now that he made a mistake and I don't think the police are any too anxious to go ahead with the case on the meager evidence in their possession."

"It will be wonderful if we can have dad back with us again," said Perry. "Although it won't be quite the same. He'll be under a cloud as long as this mystery isn't cleared up. And of course Mr. Applegate won't employ him any more."

"All the more reason why we should get busy and clear up the affair," returned Mr. Hardy. "You boys can help."

"How?"

"By keeping your eyes and ears open and by using your wits. That's all there is to detective work."

"Well, you can just bet that if it will clear Slim's dad we'll be listening and looking for every clue there is," Joe assured his father.

CHAPTER X

AN IMPORTANT DISCOVERY

When the Hardy boys returned from school next afternoon they saw that a crowd had collected about the bulletin board in the post office.

"Wonder what's up now?" said Joe, pushing his way forward. Boylike, he was able to make his way through the crowd with the agility of an eel, and Frank was not slow in following.

On the board was a large poster, the ink on which was scarcely dry. At the top, in enormous black letters, they read:

$1000 REWARD

Underneath, in slightly smaller type, came the following:

The above reward will be paid for information leading to the arrest of the person or persons who broke into Tower Mansion and stole from a safe in the library jewels and securities, as follows—

Then came a list of the jewels and negotiable bonds that had been taken from Tower Mansion, the jewels being fully described and the numbers of the bonds being given. It was announced that the reward was offered by Hurd Applegate.

"Why, that must mean that the charge against Mr. Robinson has been dropped!" exclaimed Joe.

"It looks like it. Let's go and see if we can't find Slim."

All about them people were commenting on the size of the reward, and there were many expressions of envy for the person who should be fortunate enough to solve the mystery.

"A thousand dollars!" said Frank, as they made their way out of the post office. "That's a lot of money, Joe."

"I'll say it is."

"And there's no reason why we haven't as good a chance of getting it as any one else."

"Golly—if we only could!"

"Why not? Let's get at this case in real earnest. Of course, we would do what we could anyway, but—"

"A thousand dollars!"

"It's worth trying for."

"Dad and the police are barred from the reward, for it's their duty to find the thief if they can. But if we find him we get the money."

"And we'll have the satisfaction of clearing Mr. Robinson too. Joe, let's get at this case in earnest. We have some clues right now, and we can follow them up."

"I'm with you. But there's Slim now."

Perry Robinson was coming down the street toward them. He looked much happier than he had been the previous evening, and when he saw the Hardy boys his face lighted up.

"Dad is free," he told them. "Thanks to your father. The charge has been dropped."

"Gee, but I'm glad to hear that!" exclaimed Joe. "I see they're offering a reward."

"Your father convinced Mr. Applegate that it must have been an outside job. That is, that it was the work of a professional crook. And the police admitted there wasn't much evidence against dad, so they let him go. I tell you, it was a great thing for my mother and sisters. They were almost crazy with worry."

"No wonder," commented Frank. "What is your father going to do now?"

"I don't know," Slim admitted heavily. "Of course, we've had to move out of Tower Mansion. Mr. Applegate said that while the charge had been dropped, he wasn't altogether convinced in his own mind that dad hadn't had something to do with it. So he dismissed him."

"That's tough luck. But he'll be able to get another job somewhere."

"I'm not so sure about that. People aren't likely to employ a man that's been suspected of stealing. Dad tried two or three places this afternoon, but he was turned down."

The Hardy boys were silent. They were sorry for the Robinsons, for they knew only too well that the family were badly off financially and that in view of the robbery it would indeed be difficult for Mr. Robinson to get another position.

"We've rented a small house just outside the city," went on Slim. "It is cheap, and we'll have to get along." There was no false pride about Perry Robinson. He faced the facts as they came, and made the best of them. "But if dad doesn't get a job it will mean that I'll have to go to work."

"But, Slim—you'd have to quit school!"

"I can't help that. I wouldn't want to, for you know I was trying for the class medal this year. But—oh, well—"

The Hardy boys realized how much it would mean to their chum to leave school at this stage. Perry Robinson was an ambitious boy and one of the cleverest in his class. He had always wanted to continue his studies, go to a university, and his teachers had predicted a brilliant career for him. Now it seemed that all his ambitions would have to be thrown overboard because of this misfortune.

"Don't worry, Slim," comforted Frank. "Joe and I are going to plug away at this affair until we get at the bottom of it."

"It's mighty good of you, fellows," said Slim gratefully. "I won't forget it in a hurry. You've been pretty white to me all through this—"

"Aw, shucks!" muttered Frank, embarrassed. "It's the reward we're after. Applegate is offering a thousand dollars."

"Oh, I know it isn't altogether the reward. You would do it to help us anyway, and you know it. Look what you've already done!"

"Well, we're going to get busy," Joe said hastily. "See you later, Slim. Don't worry too much. I think everything will be all right."

Slim tried to smile, but it was evident that he was deeply worried, and when he walked away it was not with the light, springy, carefree step his chums had previously known.

"What's the first move, Frank?"

"We had better get a full description of those jewels. Perhaps the thief tried to pawn them. We can call at all the pawnshops and see what we can find out. Then we may be able to get a line on the thief. You know, he might pawn something here—if he had to have money with which to get out of town."

"Good idea! Do you think Applegate will give us a list?"

"We won't have to ask him. Dad should have all that information."

"Let's go and ask him right now."

But when the lads returned home and asked their father for a description of the jewels, they met with a disappointment.

"I'm quite willing to give you all that information," said Fenton Hardy; "but I don't think it will be much use. Furthermore, I'll bet I can tell just what you are going to do."

"What?"

"You're going to make the rounds of the pawnshops and see if any of the jewels have been turned in."

The Hardy boys looked at one another in consternation.

"How did you ever guess that?" asked Frank.

Their father smiled.

"Because it is just what I have already done. Not an hour after I was called in on the case I had a full description of all those jewels in every pawnshop in the city. More than that, the description has been sent to jewelry firms and pawnshops in other cities near here, and also to the New York police. Here's a duplicate list if you want it, but you'll just be wasting time by going around to the shops. They are all on the lookout for the stuff."

Mechanically, Frank took the list.

"And I thought it was such a bright idea!"

"It *is* a bright idea. But it has been used before. Most jewel robberies are solved in just this manner—by tracing the thief when he tries to get rid of the gems."

"Well," said Joe gloomily, "I guess *that* plan is all shot to pieces. Come on, Frank. We'll think of something else."

"Out after the reward, eh?" said Mr. Hardy shrewdly.

"Yes; and we'll get it, too!"

"I hope you do. But you can't ask me to help you any more than I've done. It's my case too, remember. So from now on, you are part of my opposition."

"It's a go!"

"More power to you, then," and Mr. Hardy returned to his desk. He had a sheaf of reports from shops and agencies in various parts of the State, through which he had been trying to trace the stolen jewels and securities, but in every case the report was the same. There had been no trace of the gems or bonds taken from Tower Mansion.

When the boys left their father's study they went outside and sat on the back steps, silently regarding their motorcycles.

"What shall we do now?" asked Joe.

"I don't know. Dad sure took the wind out of our sails that time, didn't he?"

"I'll say he did. But it was just as well. Saved us a lot of trouble."

"We might have been going around to all the pawnshops in the city and not getting anywhere."

"Looks as if dad has the inside track on the case, anyway. If any of the jewels are turned in he will be the first to hear of it. What chance have we?"

"I'm hanged if I'll give up!" declared Frank, with determination. "We know that there was a strange man hanging around Tower Mansion and we know that there was a red-headed crook in town. Perhaps those two facts aren't connected, but I think they are. And we know he stole Chet's roadster."

"And left it in the woods."

"Yes—and say, Joe! We didn't take much time to look around when that roadster was found, did we?"

"What was the use? The roadster was there and Chet got it back."

"No, but the man who stole the car had been there too. Perhaps he left some clue."

Joe slapped his knee with an open hand.

"I never thought of that, Frank. Let's go right back there now."

"Come on."

Eagerly, the Hardy boys dashed over to their motorcycles. In a few minutes they were speeding through the streets of Bayport, out toward the woods where Chet Morton's roadster had been abandoned.

They were fired with enthusiasm again, in spite of the momentary setback they had received when their father squelched Frank's plan of going around to the pawnshops. They felt now that they were on a new trail.

They came to the abandoned road that led into the woods and they brought their motorcycles as far as possible, finally leaving them by the roadside and going ahead on foot. Frank located the place where the roadster had been driven off into the woods, for the trees were still bent and broken, and the two boys plunged into the depths of the thickets.

At last the Hardy boys emerged into the little cleared space where the roadster had been found. Everything was just as they had left it. They examined the ground carefully.

"He might have dropped letters from his pocket, or something," said Joe hopefully, as they explored the clearing.

But the auto thief had not been so careless. There was not even a footprint, for the boys had trampled the ground thoroughly after the roadster had been discovered.

"If I had only thought to look for footprints at the time!" groaned Joe, in disappointment.

"Or finger-prints. He must have left finger-prints somewhere about the car. If he was a professional crook we could have traced him easily."

"Too late now. Chet has had the car washed since then—we didn't think of it in time."

Their search was without success, and the Hardy boys were about to give up in disappointment when Frank left the clearing and began to hunt about in the bushes.

"I guess we might as well go home," said Joe. "We've come hunting for clues too late. If we had any sense we would have looked for finger-prints and—"

He was interrupted by a shout from his brother.

"Joe! Come here, quick! I've found something!"

There was no mistaking the excitement in Frank's voice. Joe lost no time in scrambling through the bushes until he reached his brother's side.

Frank was standing in the midst of a thicket, holding up something red and bushy.

It was a wig!

"The red wig!" exclaimed Joe, his eyes widening.

"Not only the wig," replied Frank. "But this—" and he bent over to pick up a battered hat from the ground. "And this!" Whereupon he picked up a worn coat.

"They belong to the crook!"

"It couldn't have been any one else. He must have disguised himself here and left the wig and things in the bush when he abandoned the car."

CHAPTER XI

MR. HARDY INVESTIGATES

The Hardy boys looked at one another in growing excitement.

"What ought we do about it?" asked Joe.

"I'm going to tell dad what we've found."

"But didn't he say he would be working the case on his own and that we would be opposition?"

"This is different. We have a real clue here, but we don't know how to use it. You can bet dad will know what to do. He'll act fairly with us. If it leads to anything, he'll see that we get credit for what we've done."

"I guess you're right, Frank. This is a little too big for us to handle ourselves. But imagine finding that wig! What luck!"

"There's nothing else around, is there? Let's look."

Although the Hardy boys scoured the woods in that vicinity thoroughly, they found nothing more. But the wig, the hat and the coat gave promise of interesting developments. Frank hunted through all the pockets of the coat in the faint hope of finding something that would identify the previous wearer, but in this he was disappointed.

So they went back to the abandoned road and remounted their motorcycles, returning to Bayport with the articles they had found in the woods.

Their disappointment had turned to jubilation, for now they felt that they were definitely on the trail of the mysterious man in the red wig, and while ostensibly there was no connection between this fellow and the thief who had robbed Tower Mansion, Frank had, as he said, "a hunch" that the auto thief and the robber of the mansion were one and the same man.

"If we ever lay our hands on the man who stole Chet's roadster I'm sure we'll have gone a long way toward solving the Tower affair," said Frank to his brother. "I may be wrong, but I have an idea that the fellow was a professional crook who first set out to rob the steamboat office. Then, when he was frightened off, he hung around the city and waited his chance to rob Tower Mansion."

Mr. Hardy was still in the library when the boys returned home. The great detective was frankly surprised when his sons again entered the room, and he looked up with the suspicion of a twinkle in his eyes.

"What! More clues!" he exclaimed. "Surely not so soon."

"You bet we have more clues!" exclaimed Frank eagerly. "And real clues this time. We're going to turn them over to you."

"But I thought the two of you were working on this case in your own way. Remember, I'm the opposition."

"Well, to tell the truth, we don't know just what to do with what we've found," admitted Frank. "And, anyway, we know you'll be fair with us, so it doesn't matter. Look!"

And with that he tossed the red wig on the table. He kept the coat and hat behind his back.

Fenton Hardy leaned forward quickly and picked up the wig with an inquiring glance at his sons.

"So!" he murmured. "You found the wig?"

He examined it intently. Then he opened a drawer of his desk and produced the fragment of wig that the boys had found in the smashed car by the road. This he applied to a torn part of the wig itself. It fitted perfectly.

"It's the wig all right," he declared, looking up. "Where did you find it? By the smashed car?"

"No. Hidden in the bushes near the place where Chet's roadster was found."

Mr. Hardy whistled solemnly.

"Good work." He turned the wig over and over in his hands, carefully examined it under a microscope, and then tossed it back on the desk.

"There aren't so many wigs sold that one can't trace them," he observed. "This happens to be made by a small company that doesn't turn out a great many wigs in a year. It's a sort of side line with them."

"How can you tell?"

"There's a little mark on the inside that distinguishes the manufacturer. Just a trademark—hardly noticeable."

"And we found these as well," said Frank, handing over the coat and hat.

Mr. Hardy's eyes opened wide.

"Well, well!" he exclaimed. "You *have* been busy, haven't you?"

"They were all hidden in the same place."

"And well hidden, too, I'll warrant."

"We were sure there must be clues of some kind around that car, so we searched every inch of the woods roundabout."

"Good!" said Mr. Hardy approvingly. "You didn't miss any chances. I'm not saying these clues will lead to the capture of the fellow, but they will go a long way toward finding him."

"What should we do with them?"

Mr. Hardy looked up at his sons and smiled.

"Well, you've shared your clues with me, so I suppose I may as well share some of my experience with you. What do you say if I go to the city and try to trace up some of these labels? This hat, for instance—" and he picked it up from the table, examining the band intently. "There is a label here. Of course, the hat may have been sold a long time ago, and it isn't likely that the man who sold it would remember who bought it. But there is always the chance that the store may not be far from where the fellow lives. You get my idea? And the coat, too. If we can find any trace of who bought the wig we may be able to connect up the other things as well."

"Gosh, I never thought of that!" admitted Frank.

"It's a slim chance, but, as I said before, we can't afford to overlook any chances. I'll take them to the city and see what I can do. It may mean everything and it may mean nothing. Don't be disappointed if I come back empty-handed. And don't be surprised if I come back with some valuable information."

Mr. Hardy tossed the wig, the coat and the hat into a club bag that was standing open near his desk. The great detective was accustomed to being called away suddenly on strange errands, and he was always prepared to leave at a moment's notice.

"Not much use starting now," he said, glancing at his watch. "But I'll go to the city the first thing in the morning. In the meantime, don't rest on your oars, as the saying is. Keep your eyes and your ears open for more clues. The case isn't over yet by any means."

Mr. Hardy picked up some papers on his desk, as a hint that the interview was over, and the boys left the library. They were in a state of high excitement, for they were confident now that they had made valuable progress in the case and they were sure that if the wig and the garments could be of any use at all toward locating the crook, Mr. Hardy would be the man to use them.

When they went to bed that night they could hardly sleep, so elated were they over their discovery near the abandoned roadway.

"He must have been a pretty smart crook," murmured Joe, after they had talked long into the night. "That idea about the wig was clever. I'll bet he was an experienced guy!"

"The smarter they are, the harder they fall," replied Frank. "It's the experienced crook that the police always look for. If this fellow has any kind of a record at all it won't take long for dad to run him down. I've heard dad say that there is no such thing as a clever crook. If he was really clever he wouldn't be a crook at all."

"Yes, I guess there's something in that, too. But it shows that we're not up against any ordinary amateur. This fellow must be a slippery customer."

"He'll have to be mighty slippery from now on. Once dad has a few clues to work on he never lets up till he gets his man."

"Well, let's hope he gets this one. He'll think a lot more of us as detectives if he does." And with that, the boys fell asleep.

When they went down to breakfast the following morning they found that Fenton Hardy had left for New York on an early morning train.

The Hardy boys went to school, but all through that morning they could scarcely keep their minds on their work. Their thoughts were far afield. They were wondering how Fenton Hardy was faring on his quest in New York and it was not until after Frank had drawn a reprimand from one of his teachers because he absent-mindedly answered, "Red wig," when asked to name the capital of Kansas that they settled down to work and tried to put the affair of the wig and the abandoned clothes from their minds.

Slim Robinson was at school that day, but after four o'clock he confided to the Hardy boys that he was leaving.

"It's no use," he said. "Father can't keep me in school any longer and it's up to me to pitch in and help the family. I'm to start work to-morrow for a grocery company."

"And you wanted to go to college!" exclaimed Frank. "It's a shame, that's what it is!"

"Can't be helped," replied Perry, with a grimace. "I can consider myself lucky I got this far. I guess I'll have to give up all those ideas now and settle down to learn the grocery business. There's one good thing about it—I'll have a chance to learn it from the ground up. I'm starting in the delivery department. Perhaps in about fifty years I'll be head of the firm."

"You'll make good at whatever you tackle," Joe assured him. "But I'm sorry you won't be able to go through college as you wished. Don't give up hope yet, Slim. You never know what may happen. Perhaps they'll find the fellow who *did* rob Tower Mansion."

Both boys wanted to tell their chum about the clues they had discovered the previous day, but the same thought was in their minds—that it would be unwise to raise false hopes. It would go much harder with Perry, they knew, if he began to think the capture of the thief was imminent, only to have the hope dashed to earth again. So they said good-bye to him and wished him good luck. Perry tried hard to be cheerful, but his smile was very faint as he turned away from them and walked off down the street.

"Gosh, but I'm sorry for him," said Frank as they went home. "He was such a hard worker in school and he counted so much on going to college."

"We've just *got* to clear up the Tower robbery, that's all there is to it!" declared his brother.

"Perhaps dad is back by now. There's a train from New York at three o'clock. Let's hurry home and see."

But when the Hardy boys arrived home they found that their father had not yet returned from the city.

"We'll just have to be patient, I guess," said Frank. "No news is good news."

And with this philosophic reflection the Hardy boys were obliged to comfort themselves against the impatience that possessed them to learn what progress their father was making in the city toward following up the clues they had given him.

CHAPTER XII
DAYS OF WAITING

Fenton Hardy had high hopes of a quick solution of the mystery when he went to New York. Possession of the wig, the hat and the coat gave him three clues, any one of which might lead to tracing the previous owner quickly, and the detective was confident that it would not be long before he would unravel the tangled threads. He had not stated his optimism to the boys, being careful not to arouse their hopes, but in his heart he thought it would be but a matter of hours before he ran the owner of the red wig to earth.

But obstacles presented themselves before him in bewildering succession.

The wig appeared to be his chief clue, and when he arrived in the city he went directly to the head office of the company that had manufactured it. When he sent his card in to the manager he was readily admitted, for Fenton Hardy's name was known from the Atlantic to the Pacific.

"Some of our customers in trouble, Mr. Hardy?" asked the manager, when the great detective tossed the red wig on his desk.

"Not yet. But one of your customers *will* be in trouble if I can ever trace the purchaser of this wig."

The manager picked it up. He inspected it carefully and frowned.

"We are not, as you know, a wig-making firm," he said. "That is, the wig department is a very small side line with us."

"The very reason I thought it would be easier to trace this," replied Mr. Hardy. "If you turned out thousands of them every year it might be more difficult. You sell to an exclusive theatrical trade, I believe."

"Exactly. If an actor wants a wig of some special nature, we do our best to please him. We only make the wigs to order."

"Then you will probably have a record of this one."

The manager turned the wig over in his hands, glanced carefully at the inside, felt of the weight and texture, then pressed a button at the side of his desk. A boy came and departed with a message.

"It may be difficult. This wig is not new. In fact, I would say it was turned out about two years ago."

"A long time. But still—"

"I'll do the best I can."

A bespectacled old man shuffled into the office at that moment, in response to the manager's summons, and stood waiting in front of the desk.

"Kauffman, here," said the manager, "is our expert. What he doesn't know about wigs isn't worth knowing." Then, turning to the old man, he handed him the red wig. "Remember it, Kauffman?"

The old man looked at it doubtfully. Then he gazed at the ceiling.

"Red wig ... red wig ..." he muttered.

"About two years old, isn't it?" prompted the manager.

"Not quite. Year'n a half, I'd say. Looks like a comedy character type. Wait'll I think. There ain't been so many of our customers playin' that kind of a part inside a year and a half. Let's see. Let's see." The old man paced up and down the office, muttering names under his breath. Suddenly, he stopped, snapping his fingers.

"I have it," he said. "It must have been Morley who bought that wig. That's who it was! Harold Morley. He is playing in Shakespearian repertoire with Hamlin's company. Very fussy about his wigs. Has to have 'em just so. I remember he bought this one because he came in here about a month ago and ordered another just like it."

"Why would he do that?" asked Mr. Hardy.

Kauffman shrugged his shoulders.

"Ain't none of my business. Lots of actors keep a double set of wigs. Morley's playin' down at the Crescent Theater right now. Call him up."

"I'll go and see him," said Mr. Hardy, rising. "You're sure he is the man who ordered that wig?"

"Positive!" replied Kauffman, looking hurt. "I know every wig that goes out of my shop. I give 'em all my pers'nal attention. Morley got the wig—and he got another like it a month ago. I remember."

"Kauffman is right," put in the manager. "Morley has a very good account with us. If Kauffman says he remembers the wig, it must be so."

"Well, thank you for your trouble," answered Fenton Hardy. "I may be able to see Mr. Morley in his dressing room if I hurry. It lacks about half an hour of theater time."

"You'll just about make it. Glad to have been of service, Mr. Hardy. Any time we can do anything for you, just ask."

"Thank you," and Fenton Hardy shook hands with Kauffman and the manager, then left the office, bound for the Crescent Theater.

But the detective's hopes were not as high as they had been. He knew that Morley, the actor, was certainly not the man who had worn the wig on the day the roadster was stolen, for the Shakespearian company of which Morley was a member had been playing a three months' run in New York. It would be impossible for the actor to get away from the theater long enough for such an escapade, just as it was improbable that he would even try to do so.

He presented his card to a suspicious doorman at the Crescent and was finally admitted backstage and shown down a brilliantly lighted corridor to the dressing room of Harold Morley. It was a snug little place, the dressing room, for Morley had fitted it up to suit his own tastes once it was assured that the company would remain at the Crescent for an extended run. There were pictures on the walls, a potted plant in the window overlooking the alleyway, and a rug on the floor.

Seated before a mirror with electric lights at either side, was a stout little man, almost totally bald. He was diligently rubbing cold cream on his face, and when Fenton Hardy entered he did not turn around but, eyeing his visitor in the mirror, casually told him to sit down.

"Often heard of you, Mr. Hardy," he said, in a surprisingly deep voice that had a comical effect in contrast to his diminutive appearance. "Often heard of you. Glad to meet you. What kind of call is this? Social—or professional?"

"Professional."

Morley continued rubbing cold cream on his jowls.

"Spill it," he said briefly. "What's it all about?"

"Ever see this wig before?" asked Mr. Hardy, tossing the red wig on the table.

Morley turned from the mirror, and an expression of delight crossed his plump countenance.

"Well, I'll say I've seen it before!" he declared. "Old Kauffman—the best wig-maker in the country—made that for me about a year and a half ago. That's the kind of wig I wear for *Launcelot Gobbo* in 'The Merchant of Venice.' Where did you get it? I sure didn't think I'd ever see *that* wig again."

"Why?"

"Stolen from me. Some low-down egg cleaned out my dressing room one night. During the performance. Nerviest thing I ever heard of. Came right in here while I was doing my stuff out front, grabbed my watch and money and a diamond ring I had lying by the mirror, took this wig and a couple of others that were lying around, and beat it. Nobody saw him come or go. Must have got in by that window."

Morley talked in short, rapid sentences, and there was no mistaking his sincerity.

"How many wigs did he take?"

"About half a dozen. Funny thing about that, too. They were all red. Took nothin' but red wigs. I told the cops to be on the lookout for a red-headed thief. I didn't worry so much about the other wigs, for they were for old plays, but this one was being used right along. Kauffman made it specially for me. I had to get him to make another. But say—where did you find it?"

"Oh, just a little case I'm investigating. The crook left this behind him. I was trying to trace it."

"Well, you've traced it all right. But that's all the help I can give you. The cops never *did* find out who cleaned out my dressing room."

Mr. Hardy was disappointed. The clue of the red wig had led only to a blind alley. But he concealed his chagrin and tossed the wig over to Morley.

"Gee, and I'm sure glad to get it back again," declared the actor. "Things haven't gone right with me at all since I lost that wig. Losing it brought me a whole flock of bad luck. Sorry I can't help you find the guy that took it. What's he been up to now?"

Fenton Hardy evaded the question.

"Oh, I'll probably get him some other way. Give me a list and description of the stuff he took from you. Probably I can trace him through that."

"Hop to it," said Morley breezily. "Hop right to it, old man. Here's a list of the stuff right here." He reached in a drawer and drew out a sheet of paper which he handed over to the detective. "That's the same list I gave to the cops when I reported the robbery. Number of the watch, and everything."

Mr. Hardy folded the list and put it in his pocket. Morley glanced at his watch, lying beside the mirror, face up, and gave an exclamation.

"Suffering Sebastopol! Curtain in five minutes and I'm not half made up yet. Excuse me, Mr. Hardy, but I've got to get busy. In this business 'I'll be ready in a minute' doesn't go."

He seized a stick of grease paint and feverishly resumed the task of altering his appearance to that of the character he was portraying at the matinee that day. Mr. Hardy, smiling at the actor's casual informality, withdrew from the dressing room and made his way out to the street.

"A blind alley!" he muttered. "I was sure I could trace the fellow by means of the wig. Oh, well!" He shrugged his shoulders. "I still have the hat and coat. And if the worst comes to the worst I can try to trace the chap through the stuff he stole from Morley—for it was probably the same man. But it looks like a big job."

It was a big job.

Efforts to trace the purchaser of the hat and coat were fruitless. The search ended at a secondhand store where the owner vainly tried to sell Mr. Hardy a complete outfit of clothing at a bargain, but could not or would not remember who had bought the coat from him. He sold so many coats, and at such bargains, that he could not remember the customers who came into his store. Mr. Hardy was forced to retire, defeated.

The predominating quality of the detective's character was patience. When he found that he could not trace the thief through the wig, the hat or the coat, he doggedly set to work trying to trace the man who had broken into the dressing room of the actor, Morley, and this, in spite of the fact that the police had already given up that case as hopeless.

Then, in his spare time, Mr. Hardy spent hours at police headquarters, poring over records, searching for particulars of hundreds of red-headed criminals.

It was over a week before he found what he wanted and it came from a chance note at the bottom of a police description of a thief who was at that time out on parole. But when Fenton Hardy saw the note he knew he had stumbled on the clue he needed. And he smiled grimly.

"It won't be long now," he remarked, in the popular phrase of the day, as he went back to his hotel.

CHAPTER XIII

IN POOR QUARTERS

In the meantime, the Hardy boys were finding the suspense almost unbearable. They had expected that their father would be away but a day at the most, but when two days dragged by, then three, and finally an entire week, without word from Mr. Hardy further than a brief note from New York stating that he was well and that the case was not as easy of solution as he had hoped, they became depressed.

"If dad can't get the thief, no one can," declared Joe, with conviction, "and I'm beginning to think that even dad is falling down in this affair."

"Better wait till he admits it himself," suggested Frank. "Although I don't mind telling you I'm not very hopeful myself."

Frank's preoccupied air had not gone unobserved. Callie Shaw had noticed his abstraction. More than once, when she had smiled pleasantly at him as they met one another in the hallways or in the classroom at the high school, he had merely nodded moodily. Callie was too sensible to be hurt by this, but she wondered what was worrying Frank. So one afternoon, when they happened to leave school together, she taxed him with it.

"What's on your mind, Frank?" she asked gaily. "You've been going around looking like a human thundercloud for the last week."

"Who, me? I didn't notice," returned Frank heavily.

"Yes, you!" she replied, mimicking his lifeless tone. "You used to be full of fun. What's the matter? Can't I help?" She glanced up at him eagerly.

Frank shook his head.

"No, you can't help, Callie. It's about Slim."

"Slim Robinson! Oh, yes! Wasn't that too bad?" said Callie, with quick sympathy. "He had to leave school. They tell me he's working."

"In a grocery."

"And he was so anxious to be a lawyer!"

"I was talking to him this morning. He pretends he likes the work he's at, but I could tell he wishes he could get back to school again. I'm real sorry for him. And all on account of that confounded Tower robbery!"

"But nobody really believes Mr. Robinson did it!"

"Of course not. Nobody but Hurd Applegate. But until they find who *did* take the stuff, Mr. Robinson is out of a job and nobody will hire him."

"Isn't that too bad? I'm going over to see Paula and Tessie and Mrs. Robinson to-night. Where are they living?"

Frank gave Callie the address. Her eyes widened.

"Why that's in one of the poorest sections of the city! Frank, I had no idea it was that bad!"

"It is—and it'll be a lot worse unless Mr. Robinson gets work pretty soon. Slim's earnings aren't nearly enough to keep the family yet."

"Isn't there any chance that Mr. Robinson will be cleared?"

"That's what's worrying me. Dad is working on the case."

"Then why should you worry?" said Callie triumphantly. "Why, that means it'll be all cleared up. Your father can do anything!"

"I used to think so, too. But he seems to be stuck, this time."

"What's the matter?"

"He went to New York almost a week ago with some clues that Joe and I were certain would clear up the affair, and so far we haven't heard from him, only to know that the case was harder than he expected."

"But he hasn't given up, has he?"

"Well—no—"

"Then what are you worrying about, silly? If your father had given up the case there would be something to worry about. If he is still working on it there's always hope."

They walked on in silence for a while.

"Let's go out to see the Robinsons," Callie said suddenly.

"I've been intending to go, but—I sort of—well—you know—"

"You thought it might embarrass them. Well, it won't. I know Paula and Tessie well, and they're not that kind. They'd appreciate a friendly visit."

Frank hesitated. He had the natural shyness of his age and he felt awkward about visiting the Robinsons in their new home, for he knew they were now in reduced circumstances and might not wish their former friends to see them in their present plight. But Callie's words reassured him.

"All right. I'll go. We can't stay long, though."

"We can't. I must be back in time for supper. We'll just drop in on them so they'll know we haven't forgotten all about them."

"I thought you were going over to see them to-night?"

"I was, but I've changed my mind. I want you to come with me now."

Frank hailed a passing street car bound for the section of the city in which the Robinsons lived and they got on board. It was a long ride and the streets became poorer and meaner as they neared the outskirts of Bayport.

"It's an outrage, that's what it is!" declared Callie abruptly. "Mrs. Robinson and the girls were always accustomed to having everything so nice! And now they have to live away out here! Oh, I hope your father catches the man that committed that robbery!"

Her eyes flashed and for a moment she looked so fierce that Frank laughed.

"I suppose you'd like to be the judge and jury at his trial, eh?" he chuckled.

"I'd give him a hundred years in jail!"

When at length they came to the street to which the Robinsons had moved they found that it was an even poorer thoroughfare than they had expected. There were squalid shacks and tumbledown houses on either side of the narrow street, and ragged children were playing in the roadway. At the far end of the street they came to a small, unpainted cottage that somehow contrived to look neat in spite of the surroundings. The picket fence had been repaired and the yard had been cleaned up.

"This is where they live," said Frank. "It's the neatest place on the whole street."

Paula answered their knock. Her face lighted up with pleasure when she saw who the callers were.

"Frank and Callie!" exclaimed the girl. "You've come to see us! Come in. We're dying of loneliness. There hasn't been a soul out this way since we moved."

Callie flashed Frank a look of triumph, and whispered:

"There, now! Didn't I tell you they'd be glad?" as they went into the house.

They were greeted with kindly dignity by Mrs. Robinson and with girlish good humor by Tessie. Mrs. Robinson received them with the same self-possession she would have shown had they been back at Tower Mansion, and Frank wondered at himself for thinking that these good people might be ashamed to meet their old friends in this new and humbler home.

"We can't stay long," explained Callie. "But Frank and I just thought we'd run out to see how you all are."

"We're all well—that's one mercy to be thankful for," answered Mrs. Robinson. "Perry is working. I suppose you knew that."

"And Mr. Robinson?" inquired Frank.

She shook her head.

"Not yet." Mrs. Robinson's lips quivered. "It's so hard for him," she said. "Without a recommendation, you know. It looks as though he might have to go to another city to get work."

"And leave you here?"

"I suppose so. We don't know what to do."

"It's so unjust!" flared Paula. "Papa didn't have a thing to do with that miserable robbery, and yet he has to suffer for it just the same!"

"Has your father—discovered anything—yet, Frank?" asked Mrs. Robinson hesitantly.

"I'm sorry," admitted Frank. "We haven't heard from him. He's been away in New York following up some clues. But so far there's been nothing. Of course, it isn't often he falls down on a case."

"We hardly dare hope that he'll be able to clear Mr. Robinson. The whole case is so mysterious."

"I've given up thinking of it," Tessie declared. "If it is cleared up, all well and good. If it isn't—we won't starve, at any rate, and papa knows we all believe in him."

"Yes, I suppose it doesn't do much good to keep talking about it," agreed Mrs. Robinson. "We've gone over it all so thoroughly that there is nothing more to say."

So, by tacit consent, the subject was changed, and for the rest of their stay Frank and Callie chatted of doings at school. Mrs. Robinson and the girls invited them to remain for supper, but Callie insisted that she must go. When they left they promised faithfully to pay another visit in the near future. Only once again was the subject that was nearest their hearts brought up, and that was when Mrs. Robinson drew Frank to one side as he was leaving.

"Promise me one thing," she said. "Let me know as soon as your father returns—if he has any news."

"I'll do that, Mrs. Robinson," agreed the boy. "I know what this suspense must be like for you."

"It's terrible. But as long as Fenton Hardy is working on the case I'm sure that it will be cleared up if it is humanly possible."

And with that, the matter rested. Callie was unusually silent all the way home. It was evident that she had been profoundly affected by the change that the Tower Mansion mystery had caused in the lives of the Robinsons. Naturally sympathetic and tender-hearted, she felt keenly the injustice of it all, and she realized even more than Frank what it had meant to Mrs. Robinson and the girls to move from their comfortable home in the Mansion to the squalid and distant part of the city in which they now lived.

Callie lived but a few blocks away from the Hardy home, and Frank accompanied her to the gate.

"Mercy!" she exclaimed, glancing at her watch, "it's after six. I'm away late for supper."

"So am I. See you to-morrow."

"Surely. But, Frank—"

"Yes?"

Callie hesitated, then looked directly into his eyes. "Frank," she said, "if your father, somehow, doesn't clear up this affair, you and Joe simply *must* do it! You *must*! For the Robinsons. It means so much to them."

"Dad won't fall down on it. Don't worry. And Joe and I are giving all the help we can."

His confidence was contagious. Callie brightened up immediately.

"In that case," she said, gaily, "the mystery is as good as solved. The three best detectives in the world are working on it. Good-bye, Frank."

With that she ran lightly into the house.

CHAPTER XIV

RED JACKLEY

It was another week before Fenton Hardy returned to Bayport.

Contrary to the expectations of the boys, he did not arrive from New York. Instead, he came home early one morning, having reached the city by a train from the west. He had sent no advance notice of his arrival, and the first his sons knew of it was when a servant told them that their father had reached the house in the early hours of the morning, plainly careworn and travel-stained. He had gone immediately to bed, leaving orders that he was on no account to be disturbed.

This was at breakfast, and although the boys were wild with impatience to learn the outcome of their father's trip, they were obliged to curb their curiosity. Mr. Hardy was still sleeping when they left for school that morning and, to their surprise, he was asleep when they came back home for lunch.

"He must be mighty tired!" remarked Joe. "I wonder where on earth he came from?"

"Probably been up all night. When dad gets hard at work on a case he forgets all about sleep. I'll bet he found something."

"Hope so. But I wish he'd wake up and tell us. I hate to go back to school without knowing."

But Mr. Hardy had not awakened by the time the boys set out for school again, although they lingered until they were in danger of being late.

All afternoon they were tormented by curiosity. Where had their father been? What had he discovered? As soon as school was out they fled down the steps, broke away from a group of boys anxious to get up a baseball game, and shattered all records in their race for home.

Fenton Hardy was in the library, and as they rushed panting into the room he grinned broadly at his sons, for he was quite well aware that they were impatient to hear an account of his trip.

He looked refreshed after his long sleep and it was evident that his trip had not been entirely without success, for his manner was cheerful. The Hardy boys knew their father well, and they knew that when a case was difficult of solution the great detective became moody and worried.

"What luck, dad?" asked Frank, perching on the arm of an easy chair.

Mr. Hardy raised his eyebrows, pretending not to understand.

"About what?" he inquired.

"About the case. The Tower Mansion case. The red wig. Did you find out who owned it? Did you catch the thief?"

"Whoa! Whoa! Not all at once. A question at a time please. Now, do I understand that you want to know if I found out anything about the Tower Mansion affair?"

"Don't keep us waiting, dad," pleaded Joe. "You know that's what we're asking you about."

"Well," answered Mr. Hardy, "yes—and no!"

"That's not much of an answer," objected Frank, in disappointment.

"It's the best answer I can give, unfortunately. I *did* find out something about the red wig. But as for connecting its wearer with the Tower robbery—that is still to come."

"You traced the fellow who wore the wig?"

"I did. And he turned out to be a well-known criminal—well known to the police, that is."

"What's his name?" asked Joe.

"Jackley. John Jackley—commonly known as 'Red'."

"Because he has red hair?"

"No. Because he *hasn't* red hair. That reverses the usual order of nicknames, I imagine. This fellow Jackley has a fondness for wearing red wigs."

"And was he the man who stole Chet's roadster?"

"It seems almost certain. I traced the wig, which had been originally stolen from an actor in New York. I traced it to Jackley because his habit of wearing red wigs is well known to the police, and by locating him and keeping a close watch on him and paying a call at his room one night when he was out, I managed to find some of the loot that he had taken when he robbed the actor. That seemed to connect everything up very well."

"Where did you find him?" asked Frank.

"In New York. He wasn't in hiding, for he hadn't been sought for any particular crime at the time. The police seemed to overlook him in their investigation of the dressing-room theft."

"Did you accuse him?"

"No. I wanted to learn more. When I found the articles that had been stolen from the actor and knew that the wig found by the roadster had been taken at the same time, I knew Red Jackley was the auto thief. But I wanted to get some information on the Tower Mansion affair if possible. So I took a room in the house in which Jackley was living, and kept a close watch on him."

"Did you learn anything?"

Mr. Hardy shook his head.

"Jackley himself spoiled everything. He got mixed up in a jewel robbery and cleared out of the city. Luckily, I heard him packing up, and I trailed him. The police were watching for him and he couldn't get out by railway—that is, not in the ordinary manner. Instead, he tried to make his escape by jumping a freight."

"And you still followed?"

"I lost him two or three times, but luck was with me, and somehow I managed to pick up his trail again. He got out of the city, out into New Jersey, and then his luck failed him. A railway detective recognized him and then the chase was on. Up to that time I had been content with just keeping behind him, I had hoped to pose as a fellow fugitive and win his confidence. But when the chase started in real earnest I had to join with the other officers."

"And they caught Jackley?"

"Not without a chase. Jackley, by the way, was once a railroad man. Strangely enough, he once worked not many miles from here. He managed to steal a railway gasoline speeder and got away from us. But he didn't last long, for the speeder jumped the tracks on a curve and Jackley was badly smashed up."

"Was he killed?"

"I don't think he'll live. He's in a hospital right now and the doctors say he hasn't much of a chance."

"But he's under arrest."

"Oh, yes. He is being held for the jewel robbery and also for the robbery from the actor's dressing room. But I don't think he'll live to answer either charge."

"Didn't you find out anything that would connect him with the Tower robbery?"

"Not a thing."

The Hardy boys were disappointed, and their expressions showed it. If Red Jackley died, the secret of the Tower robbery would die with him, for by now Frank and Joe were convinced that the notorious criminal had indeed been the thief for whose misdeeds Mr. Robinson was now suffering. And if the secret died with him, Mr. Robinson would be doomed to spend the rest of his life under a cloud, suspected of being a thief.

"Have you seen Jackley yet?" asked Frank.

"After the smash-up. But I didn't have a chance to talk to him."

"You might have been able to get a confession from him."

Fenton Hardy nodded.

"I may be able to get one yet. If he is sure he is going to die he may admit everything. I intend to make an effort to see him in the hospital and ask him about the Tower robbery, anyway."

"Is he far away?"

Mr. Hardy named a small city not far distant from Bayport.

"I explained my mission to the doctor in charge and he promised to telephone me as soon as it was possible for Jackley to see any one. I'm convinced that the fellow had something to do with the Tower affair. It's a certainty that he stole the automobile—the wig proves that. By the same token it's certain that he was the man who tried to hold up the ticket office. Having failed in that attempt, it seems more than likely that an old-time criminal like Jackley would look around for something else to do before he left Bayport."

"You say he used to work near here?" asked Joe.

"He was once employed by the railroad, and he knows all the country around here well. Then he got mixed up in some thefts from freight cars and after he got out of jail he became a professional criminal. It was when I was looking over the records that I found out about his fondness for wearing a red wig. That was what eventually proved his undoing. If he had not robbed the actor's dressing room to get the wig that he used when he was in Bayport, I would never have traced him."

At that moment it was announced that Chief Collig of the Bayport police force wished to see Fenton Hardy. The detective winked at the boys, and told the servant to show the chief in.

Chief Collig entered the room, mopping his brow with a handkerchief, for it was a hot day and he was a stout man. Behind him came Detective Smuff, fanning himself with a straw hat.

"Good afternoon, gentlemen," said Mr. Hardy genially, "Won't you sit down?"

Chief Collig eased himself into an arm chair. Detective Smuff leaned against the table. Both glanced inquiringly at the two boys.

"Unless your business is *very* private, I'd just as soon have the boys stay," suggested Mr. Hardy pleasantly. He did not trust Chief Collig and Detective Smuff, who came to him only in emergencies and who usually took all the credit for themselves whenever he helped them out of their difficulties. He preferred to have the boys present as witnesses.

"How about it, chief?" asked Smuff heavily. "Can they stay?"

"I guess so," grunted Chief Collig, undoing the collar of his uniform. "Can't do no good and they can't do no harm."

"Well, gentlemen, to what do I owe the honor of this visit?" asked Mr. Hardy.

"We've been hearin' things about this Tower Mansion case," observed Chief Collig gravely. "You've been workin' on it, eh?"

"Perhaps."

"You've been out of town for quite a few days. You *must* have been workin' on it."

"That's what we dedooce, anyway," put in Detective Smuff.

"Perhaps it's my own business."

"Police business is everybody's business," declared Collig judicially. "What we want to know is—did you find any clues?"

Detective Smuff fished out the inevitable notebook and pencil.

"I'll note 'em down, chief," he remarked.

"You may as well put back the notebook, Smuff," snapped Fenton Hardy, with annoyance. "If I went away, it is my own business, and if I am still working on the Tower robbery, that's my business too. I'll thank you to keep to your own affairs."

Chief Collig opened his mouth, then closed it again. He took out his handkerchief and mopped his brow, all the while staring at Fenton Hardy. Then he turned and gazed at Smuff.

"Detective Smuff," he said, in a solemn voice, "did you hear that?"

"I did."

"What do you think of it, Detective Smuff?"

"I think—I think—" Detective Smuff groped for an expression that would encompass the magnitude of the offence, "I think Mr. Hardy is guilty of obstructin' the cause of justice," he said grandly.

"Obstructing fiddlesticks!" said Mr. Hardy. "I'm minding my own business. Which is more than some police officers seem capable of doing."

Chief Collig sighed.

"The trouble with you, Mr. Hardy," he said, "is that you won't co-operate. If you co-operated a little more, we would all be farther ahead. There ain't any co-operation at all. Here is me and Smuff, doin' our best to drive crime out of Bayport, and you won't co-operate."

"Perhaps the fact that there is a thousand dollars reward in the case isn't making you anxious for some co-operation?" suggested Fenton Hardy dryly.

"It ain't got nothin' to do with it," replied Chief Collig virtuously. "We're just anxious to see this affair cleared up, that's all. Now, Mr. Hardy, we hear you were with the officers that chased this here notorious criminal Red Jackley."

Mr. Hardy gave a perceptible start. He had no idea that news of the capture of Jackley had reached Bayport, much less that news of his own participation in the chase had reached the city.

"What of it?"

"Did Jackley have anything to do with this here Tower case?"

"How should I know?"

"Wasn't that what you were working on?"

"That's my affair."

Detective Smuff and Chief Collig looked at one another.

"You ain't co-operatin'," complained Chief Collig. "You're goin' to put us to a whole lot of worry and expense just because you won't give us a little co-operation."

"Just what do you mean?"

"Detective Smuff and me was thinkin' of goin' over to the hospital where this man Jackley is and givin' him the third degree about the Tower case."

Fenton Hardy's lips narrowed into a straight line.

"You can't do that. The doctor won't let you see him."

"We're going to try, anyway. There's a train at seven o'clock, and we aim to have a talk with this fellow Jackley to-night."

Mr. Hardy shrugged his shoulders.

"Go ahead. It means nothing to me. But if you take my advice you'll stay away. You'll just spoil everything. Jackley will talk when the time comes."

"Oh, ho!" said Detective Smuff triumphantly. "Then there *is* something to it, hey?"

"I knew there was," said Chief Collig. "Come on, Smuff. We'll make this man Jackley talk yet. We're officers of the law, we are, and I'd like to see any doctor keep us from doin' our duty."

He mopped his brow again, put on his hat, nodded to Fenton Hardy, and clumped out of the room. Detective Smuff, putting his notebook into his pocket, followed. The door closed behind them.

Mr. Hardy sat back with a gesture of despair.

"They'll spoil everything," he said. "They're just so clumsy that Red Jackley will close up like a clam if they try to make him talk."

"Perhaps," remarked Frank significantly, "they'll miss their train."

At that moment the telephone rang. Mr. Hardy answered it.

"Hello—yes, this is Fenton Hardy—yes—oh, yes, doctor—he is—well, well—is that so?—won't live until morning—I can see him?—fine—thank you—good-bye."

He put back the receiver.

"There," he said wearily, "just my luck! Red Jackley is dying, and the doctor says I can see him to-night. But Collig and Smuff will have first right to talk to him, for they are officials and I'm only a private detective. If Jackley confesses, they'll have the credit for it."

"They'll just have to miss their train," said Frank. "Come on, Joe. Let's see what we can do."

CHAPTER XV
THE CHIEF GETS A BOMB

"What's up now?" asked Joe, when the Hardy boys had left the house.

"Chief Collig and Detective Smuff must miss that train."

"But how?"

"I don't know just yet, but they've got to miss it. If they reach the hospital to-night they'll interview Jackley first. One of two things will happen. They'll either get a confession and take all the credit for clearing up the case, or they'll go about it so clumsily that Jackley will say nothing and spoil everything for dad."

The Hardy boys walked along the street in silence. They realized that the situation was urgent, but although they racked their brains trying to think of some way in which to prevent Chief Collig and Detective Smuff from catching the train, it seemed hopeless.

"Let's round up the gang," suggested Joe. "Perhaps they can think of something."

"The gang" consisted of the boys who had been with Frank and Joe the day they held the picnic in the woods. There was, of course, Chet Morton. Besides him were Allen Hooper, otherwise known as "Biff", because of his passion for boxing, Jerry Gilroy, Phil Cohen and Tony Prito, all students at the Bayport high school. They were usually to be found on the school campus after hours, playing ball, and there the Hardy boys soon located them. The game was just breaking up.

"Pikers," grinned Chet Morton when he saw the Hardy boys approaching. "You wouldn't play ball when we asked you to, and now you come around when the game's all over."

"We had something more important on our minds," replied Frank. "We need your help."

"What's the mattah?" asked Tony Prito. Tony was the son of a prosperous Italian building contractor, but he had not yet been in America long enough to talk the language without an accent, and his attempts were frequently the cause of much amusement to his companions. He was quick and good-natured, however, and laughed as much at his own errors as any one else did.

"Chief Collig and Detective Smuff are butting into one of dad's cases," said Frank. "We can't tell you much more about it than that. But the whole thing is that they mustn't catch the seven o'clock train."

"What do you want us to do?" asked Biff Hooper. "Blow up the bridge?"

"We might lock Collig and Smuff in one of their own cells," suggested Phil Cohen.

"And get locked in ourselves," added Jerry Gilroy. "Be sensible. Are you serious about this, Frank?"

"Absolutely. If those two catch that train dad's case will be ruined. And I don't mind telling you it has something to do with Perry Robinson."

Chet Morton whistled.

"Ah, ha! I see now. The Tower affair. In that case, we'll see to it that the seven o'clock train leaves here without our worthy chief and his equally worthy—although dumb—detective." He hated Smuff, for the sleuth had once or twice tried to arrest the boys for bathing in a forbidden section of the bay.

"There is only one question left," said Phil solemnly.

"And what is that?"

"How to keep them from getting on the train."

"Get your brains to work, fellows—if you have any," ordered Jerry Gilroy. "Let's figure out a plan."

A dozen plans were suggested, each wilder than the one before. Biff Hooper was in favor of kidnapping the chief and his detective, binding them hand and foot and setting them adrift in the bay in an open boat.

Phil Cohen suggested putting the chief's watch an hour ahead. That plan, as Frank observed, would have been a good one but for the little difficulty of laying hands on the watch.

Chet Morton thought it would be a good idea to start a fight in front of the police station just as Collig and Smuff were about to leave for the train. The possibility that they might all land in jail as a result made this suggestion unpopular.

"If we were in Italy we could get the Black Hand to help," said Tony Prito.

"The Black Hand!" declared Chet. "That's a good idea!"

"We got no Black Hand society in Bayport," objected Tony.

"Let's get one up. Send the chief a Black Hand letter warning him not to take that train."

"And if he ever found who wrote it, we'd all be up to our necks in trouble," pointed out Joe. "I'd like to put a bomb under his old police station."

"Fine idea!" applauded Tony. "Where we get the bomb?"

"Leave it to me," announced Chet Morton mysteriously. "I'll get a bomb. I'll guarantee to keep the chief in town."

"Not a real bomb?" asked Frank.

"Why not?" said Chet. "Listen to me."

Chet proceeded to lay forth his plan in a stealthy whisper. It was received with chuckles and murmurs of admiration. His companions clapped him on the back, and when he had finished the boys hastened down the street toward the Hardy home.

In the rear of the house were a garage and an old barn. In the barn was a gymnasium that the Hardy boys had fitted out for themselves, and here was the usual collection of old toys, footballs, broken baseball bats and such paraphernalia, to be found wherever boys store their cherished possessions. Frank groped about among the rubbish in one corner until at last he rose with an exclamation of triumph, holding aloft a shining object.

"It's here!" he said. "Let's get busy. There's no time to lose."

An old box was quickly produced, and in it the shining object was placed. The box was then carefully wrapped up, and in a few minutes the boys left the barn, Tony carrying the package under one arm.

Not far from the Bayport police station was a fruit stand over which presided an Italian by the name of Rocco. He was a simple, genial soul, who believed almost everything he heard and, like most of his countrymen, he was of an excitable nature. Toward Rocco's fruit stand the boys made their way. Rocco was sorting over his oranges when they approached. Tony, with the box under his arm, hung in the background, while Chet stepped boldly forward.

"How much are your oranges, Rocco?" he asked.

Rocco, with much explanatory waving of arms, recited the prices of the various grades of oranges.

"Too much. There's a fellow at another fruit stand on the next street sells them a nickel a dozen cheaper."

"He no can do!" shrieked Rocco. "My price is da low." Then, angered by this reflection on the prices of his wares, he burst into a lengthy explanation of the struggles confronting a poor Italian trying to get along in a new country. He grabbed Chet by the coat collar, dragged him to a corner of the fruit stall, bade him inspect the fruit, gabbled off prices, and generally worked himself into a state of high indignation. In the meantime, Tony Prito made good use of his time to shove the mysterious package under the front of the stall. Then he joined the other boys who had screened his movements by gathering about Rocco.

"You'll have the Black Hand after you if you keep on charging such high prices—that's all I can say!" declared Chet, as the boys moved away.

"Poof! W'at do I care for da Blacka Hand. No frighten me!" said Rocco bravely, but he gulped when he said it and there was no doubt that the shot had gone home.

It was now after six o'clock, and the boys decided that in the interests of their plan they would have to brook the parental wrath by being late for supper. Frank had assumed that Chief Collig and Detective Smuff would be leaving to catch the train at about ten minutes to seven, so shortly after six-thirty, Phil Cohen, who had remained in the background during the interview with Rocco, walked smartly up to the fruit stand again. The others were viewing the scene from around the corner of a near-by building.

"Banana," said Phil briefly, tossing a nickel on the counter. When he had received the fruit he began to eat it, at the same time chatting with Rocco.

"W'at you t'ink?" snickered the Italian, "some boys come here a while ago and say da Blacka Hand t'ink I charga too much for da fruit."

"Well, you *do* charge too much, Rocco. Everybody says so."

"I sella da good fruit at da good price."

Phil turned aside and at the same time accidentally knocked an apple to the ground. He bent to pick it up, Rocco eyeing him narrowly in case he tried to slip it into his pocket. But Phil did not get up at once. Instead, he said:

"Oi! What's this?"

"W'at you find?"

"What's this, Rocco?" Phil rose from in front of the stand, with the package in his hands. "I found this under the counter."

Rocco stared. His mouth opened in dismay. For, sounding clearly from the inside of the package, came a steady "tick-tock, tick-tock."

"A bomb!" he shrieked. "Put heem down!"

Thereupon he scrambled wildly over the array of fruit at the back of the stand, knocked over a tray of oranges, and went sprawling over the opposite counter, roaring, "Police!" at the top of his lungs.

Phil, with a fine imitation of fright, put the package on top of the counter and fled.

Rocco, in his white apron, was dancing about in the middle of the street, yelling, "Bombs! Police! Da Blacka Hand!" Then, suddenly fearing that the supposed bomb might explode at any moment, he whirled rapidly about and raced down the street away from the stand, in the general direction of the police station.

He reached the doorway just as Chief Collig and Detective Smuff were leaving for the train. Panting with fear and excitement, Rocco implored them to save him from the Black Handers who had put a bomb under his fruit stand.

"Da bomb, she go 'teek-tock',", he wailed. "She blowa da stand into da little piece!"

"A bomb!" exclaimed Chief Collig. "Surely not in Bayport!"

"I always thought there was Black Handers around here," said Smuff.

"She blowa up da fruit stand! Come queeck!"

Chief Collig and Detective Smuff followed Rocco to the corner. Then they peeped around until they could see the deserted fruit stand, with the package on the counter.

"You say it goes 'tick-tock'?"

"Just lika da clock."

"Must be a bomb, all right," said Smuff. "They run by clockwork."

"Might go off any minute," observed the chief. "I hate to go near it. Smuff, you go and pour a pail of water over it."

"Me?"

"Yes, you. You're not afraid, are you?"

"No—I'm not afraid," muttered Smuff, mopping his brow. "But I got to think of my wife and family."

"Coward!" said the chief. "I'd do it myself, only it wouldn't be right, seein' I'm your superior officer. Bad for discipline."

The worthy officers stared at the package on the fruit stand counter, while Rocco danced with impatience. Neither Collig nor Smuff dared approach closer, but they realized something must be done.

"Where's Riley?" asked the chief at last.

"Out on his beat, around the corner."

"Get him."

Smuff departed hastily, glad of the chance to get away from the vicinity of the bomb. He was some time in locating Con Riley, and when at last that minion of the law was escorted back to the chief, seven o'clock had come and gone. So had the train.

CHAPTER XVI

A CONFESSION

"Riley!" ordered the chief, "see that package on the counter of the fruit stand. Go and get it and pour a pail of water over it."

"Huh?" exclaimed Riley, gaping.

"Pour a pail of water over it."

Riley took off his helmet and scratched his head. He began to wonder if his chief's brain had been affected by the heat.

"Don't stand there staring at me!" snapped Collig. "Hurry up and obey orders."

"This is the meanest job I ever got," observed Con Riley. But he ambled across the street, wondering why a crowd of people had collected—for word had quickly spread that a bomb had been found under Rocco's fruit stand—and when he reached the package he inspected it wonderingly.

"Mebbe she blowa him all to da bits!" suggested Rocco fearfully.

"He has insurance," consoled the chief.

"We'll give him a good funeral," observed Smuff.

Con Riley hunted around the fruit stand until he found a pail, and then he went up the street until he located a tap. Finally, with the pail full of water, he went back to the fruit stand, dumped the water over the package, and stood awaiting further orders.

"Soak it again!" roared the chief, who was taking no chances.

Con Riley sighed, but did as he was told. For five minutes he was kept busy dumping innumerable pails of water over the package, and only then did Chief Collig and Detective Smuff venture forth. Then, with fear and trembling, Chief Collig handed the package to Smuff and bade him open it.

Smuff's hands were shaking so that he could scarcely tear apart the coverings from the water-soaked parcel. The chief withdrew to a safe distance. Con Riley, who had just been told by a friend that he had been pouring water over a live bomb, was trying to achieve a sickly smile as the crowd congratulated him on his bravery.

Detective Smuff opened the package. The coverings fell away. The cardboard box, dripping with water, tumbled apart.

A bright object fell to the pavement with a clatter.

Everybody jumped.

But there was no cause for fear. The bright object was nothing more harmful than an old alarm clock.

The Hardy boys and their chums, mingling with the crowd, roared with laughter, and when the crowd saw how Chief Collig and his assistants had been duped they joined in the merriment.

"An alarm clock!" roared some one. "They thought an alarm clock was a bomb. Pouring water over an alarm clock!"

Chief Collig and Smuff returned to the police station with all the dignity they could muster under the circumstances. The crowd howled and whooped with laughter.

The Hardy boys went home smiling. The seven o'clock train had left half an hour before. Their father was making the trip to the city without the interference of the chief and his assistant, Smuff.

Fenton Hardy returned home late that night, and at the breakfast table next morning he was in high spirits.

"Solved another mystery?" asked Mrs. Hardy gaily, as she poured the coffee. She seldom asked questions about her husband's work, being of a gentle nature that instinctively shrank from any discussion of crime. It frequently distressed her that Mr. Hardy's occupation should be one that meant terms of imprisonment for those whom his cunning and cleverness had brought to justice. But her husband's attitude this morning was so unmistakably jubilant that she was glad for his sake if he had scored another success.

"Practically solved, my dear. If you'd care to hear all about it—"

"Not me. You know I don't care to hear about these terrible things."

"Well, the boys shall hear of it then. They are interested. If they'll come into my den after breakfast I'll tell them all about it."

"That means you succeeded," Frank said.

"Eat your bacon and eggs and don't be impatient."

After breakfast the boys went with their father into the den off the library, eagerly awaiting news of his mission of the previous evening. They had not told him how Chief Collig and Detective Smuff had missed the train, but they were shrewdly certain that their efforts in this respect had been of considerable assistance to Mr. Hardy.

"First of all," said the detective, "Jackley is dead."

"Did he confess?"

"You're not very sympathetic for the poor fellow. Yes, he confessed. Fortunately, Chief Collig and Detective Smuff didn't show up—"

Fenton Hardy saw that Joe and Frank glanced at one another, and he smiled quietly.

"I have an idea that you two scamps know more about that than you would care to tell. However, they failed to show up, and I had a clear field ahead of me. I saw Jackley just before he died. And I questioned him about the Tower robbery."

"He admitted it?"

"He admitted everything. He said he came to Bayport with the intention of robbing the ticket office. When he failed in that attempt he decided to hang around for a few days, and then he hit upon Tower Mansion as his next effort. He entered the place and opened the safe. Then he took the jewels and the bonds."

"What did he do with the loot?"

"That's what I'm coming to. I had quite a time making Jackley confess to the Tower affair and it was not until he was on the point of death that he admitted it. Then he said, 'Yes, I took the stuff—but I couldn't get away with it. You can get it back easily. I hid it in the old tower—'

"That was all he said. He became unconscious then and died in a few minutes. Just why he couldn't get away with the loot and why he hid it in the tower, I don't know. He didn't have time to tell me. But he said it was hidden in the old tower."

"Why, we'll find it in no time!" exclaimed Frank. "Tower Mansion has two towers—the old and the new. We'll search the old tower."

"The story seems likely enough," said Mr. Hardy. "Jackley would gain nothing by lying about it when he was on his deathbed. He probably became frightened after he committed the robbery and hid in the old tower until he saw the coast was clear and he was able to get away. Then no doubt he decided to hide the stuff there and take a chance on coming back for it some time after the affair had blown over."

"That was why he couldn't be traced through the jewels and the bonds," Joe said. "They were never disposed of at all. They've been lying in the old tower all this time."

"I tried to get him to tell me in just what part of the tower the loot was hidden," continued Fenton Hardy, "but he died before he could say any more. 'I hid it in the old tower.' He just managed to gasp that out before he became unconscious."

"It shouldn't be hard to find the stuff, now that we have a general idea of where it is," Frank pointed out. "Probably he didn't hide it very carefully. The old tower has been unoccupied for a long time and it is rarely entered. The stuff would be as safe there as if he had hidden it miles away."

Joe got up from his chair.

"I think we ought to get busy and go search the old tower right away. Oh, boy! If we can only hand old Applegate his jewels and bonds this morning and clear Mr. Robinson. Let's start."

"I'll leave it to you boys to make the search," said Mr. Hardy, with a smile. "I've no doubt the stuff will be easily recovered, and you can have the satisfaction of turning it over to Mr. Applegate. I guess you can get along without me in this case from now on."

"We wouldn't have got very far if it hadn't been for you."

"And I wouldn't have got very far if it hadn't been for you, so we're even," smiled Mr. Hardy. "Be on your way, then, and good luck to you."

"We'll find it, never fear," promised Frank, putting on his cap. "I hope the Applegates don't throw us out when we ask to be allowed to look around in the old tower."

"Just tell them you have a pretty good clue to where the bonds and jewels are hidden and they'll let you search to your heart's content," Mr. Hardy advised.

"Come on then, Joe. We'll have that thousand dollar reward before the morning is over."

Their father glanced at them shrewdly.

"Don't count your chickens before they are hatched," he said. And then, as the boys hastened out of the den, he called after them: "Also, you might remember the old proverb that there is many a slip between the cup and the lip."

But the Hardy boys scarcely heard him, so eager were they to begin searching the old tower and so confident were they that the mystery was about to be cleared up.

CHAPTER XVII
THE SEARCH OF THE TOWER

When the Hardy boys reached Tower Mansion that morning the door was answered by Hurd Applegate himself. The tall, stooped gentleman peered at them through his thick-lensed glasses. In one hand he held a sheet of stamps, for it was his custom to devote the mornings to his collection.

"Yes?" he said testily, for he was annoyed at being disturbed. "What do you boys want here at this hour of day?"

"You remember us, don't you?" asked Frank politely. "We're Mr. Hardy's sons."

"Fenton Hardy, the detective? Are you his boys?"

"Yes, sir."

"Well, what do you want?"

"We'd like to take a look through the old tower, if you don't mind. We've got a new clue about the robbery you had here a while ago."

"Want to look through the old tower? Of all the impudence! What do you want to look through the tower for? And what has that got to do with the robbery?"

"We have evidence that leads us to believe the jewels and bonds were hidden in the tower by the thief."

"Oh! You have evidence, have you?" The old man peered at them very closely. "It's that rascal Robinson, I'll warrant. He hid the stuff there, and now he's put you up to going and finding it, just to clear himself."

The Hardy boys had not considered the affair in this light, and they gazed at Mr. Applegate in consternation. At last Joe found his tongue.

"Mr. Robinson isn't mixed up in this at all," he said. "The real thief was found. He said the stuff was hidden in the old tower. If you will just let us take a look around, we'll find it for you."

"Who was the real thief, then?"

"We can't tell you just now, sir. Wait till we find the stolen goods and we'll tell you the whole story."

Mr. Applegate took off his glasses and wiped them with his handkerchief. He glared at the boys suspiciously for a few moments. Then he called out:

"Adelia!"

A high cracked voice from the dim regions of the hallway answered.

"What d'you want?"

"Come here a minute."

There was a rustle of skirts, and then Adelia Applegate, maiden sister of the owner of Tower Mansion, appeared. She was a faded blonde woman, of thin features, and she was dressed in a gown of a fashion fifteen years back, in which every color of the spectrum fought for supremacy.

"What's the matter now?" she demanded. "Can't a body sit down to do a bit of sewin' without you hollerin' at them?"

"These boys want to look through the old tower."

"What for? Up to some mischief, I'll be bound."

"They think they can find the bonds and jewels."

"Oh, they do, do they?" sniffed the woman. "And what would the bonds and jewels be doin' in the old tower?"

"We have evidence that they were hidden there after the robbery," replied Frank.

Miss Applegate sniffed again and viewed the boys with frank suspicion.

"As if any thief would be fool enough to hide them right in the house he robbed!"

"These are Mr. Hardy's boys," explained Hurd Applegate. "He is the big detective, you know."

"All detectives," said Miss Applegate, "are nosey. Always pryin' into other people's affairs."

"We're just trying to help you," put in Joe politely.

"Go ahead, then. Go ahead," said Miss Applegate, with a sigh. "Come around at this hour of morning, disturbing honest folks. Go ahead, and tear the old tower to pieces if you like. But I'll be bound you won't find anything. It's all foolishness. You won't find anything."

Consent having been given, Hurd Applegate led the way through the gloomy halls and corridors of the mansion toward the old tower. He was inclined to share his sister's view that the boys' search would be in vain.

"Might as well save yourselves the trouble," he declared. "You won't find anything in the old tower. If anything was hidden there it's been taken away by this time."

"We'll make a try at it, anyway, Mr. Applegate."

"Don't ask me to help you. I've got better things to do. Just got some new stamps in this morning and you interrupted me when I was sortin' them out. I've got to get back to my work."

The man led the way into a corridor that was heavy with dust. It had not been in use for a long time and it was bare and unfurnished. Leading off this corridor was a heavy door. It was unlocked, and when Mr. Applegate opened it the boys saw that a flight of stairs lay beyond.

"There you are. Those stairs lead up into the tower. Search away. You won't find anything."

"I hope we do, Mr. Applegate," said Frank. "And I'm pretty sure we shall."

"Yes—boys are always goin' to do wonders. Go ahead. Live and learn. Waste your time."

And with this parting shot, Hurd Applegate turned and hobbled back along the corridor, the sheet of stamps still in his gnarled hand. He was muttering to himself as he departed. The Hardy boys looked at one another.

"Not very encouraging, is he, Frank?"

"Not a bit of it. But it will be so much the better for us if we get the stuff back for him. He won't think we were wasting our time then."

"Let's get up into the tower. I'm anxious to start."

The tower was about five stories in height, as compared with the rest of the mansion, which had but three stories. The lower floor was empty. The floors and walls were heavy with dust. Frank and Joe first examined the stairs carefully for footprints, but there were none to be seen.

"That seems queer," remarked Frank. "If Jackley had been in here within the past month you'd think his footprints would still show. By the appearance of this dust, there hasn't been any one in the tower for at least a year."

"Perhaps the dust collects more quickly than we think. It may have covered his footprints over even within a couple of weeks."

An inspection of the ground floor revealed the fact that there was no place where the loot could have been hidden, save under the stairs, and there was nothing in that place of concealment. Accordingly, the Hardy boys ascended to the next floor, finding themselves in a room as drab and bare as the one they had just left. Here again the dust lay heavy and the murky windows were thick with cobwebs. There was an atmosphere of age and decay about the entire place. It seemed to have been abandoned for years.

"Nothing here," said Frank, after a quick glance around. "On we go."

They made their way up to the next floor, after again poking about under the stairs, but again without success.

The next room was a duplicate of the first. It was bare and cheerless, deep in dust. There was not the slightest sign of a hiding place. Much less was there any indication that another human being had been in the tower for years.

"Doesn't look very promising, Joe. Still, he may have gone right to the top of the tower."

So the search continued, until at last the Hardy boys had reached the top of the tower. Here they emerged into the open air, coming through a trapdoor that led through the roof from the upper room. They were now standing on a platform, and far below them lay the city of Bayport. To the east was Barmet Bay, the waters sparkling in the sun.

The platform was quite bare. The stone walls gave no opportunity of a hiding place. Their search had been in vain.

"We were fooled, I guess," Frank admitted. "There hasn't been any one in this tower for years. I knew it as soon as I saw there were no footprints."

The boys gazed moodily down over the city, and then down over the grounds of Tower Mansion. The roofs of the mansion itself were far below, and directly across from them rose the heavy bulk of the new tower.

"Do you think he might have meant the *new* tower?" exclaimed Joe suddenly.

"Dad said he specified the old one."

"But he may have been mistaken. In the darkness and everything, perhaps he didn't know the difference."

"That's possible, too. It's certain that he didn't hide anything in this tower, at any rate. Although why he should say 'the old tower'—"

"Let's ask Mr. Applegate if we can search the new tower, too."

"What a fine chance we have! He'll crow over us now in real earnest when we go back and tell him we didn't find anything. He'll say 'I told you so', and if we try to get into the new tower he'll just laugh at us."

"It's worth trying, anyway. We can tell him the whole story about Jackley. That ought to convince him."

Disappointed, the Hardy boys descended through the trapdoor, and then made their way down through the tower until at last they were in the long gloomy hallway again. Their clothes were covered with dust and their hands and faces were grimy. Slowly, they trudged back into the main part of the mansion again, and there they met Adelia Applegate, who popped out of a doorway as they were passing and cackled with delight.

"So these are the fine boys who were going to find the stolen stuff for us, eh!" she exclaimed, in her cracked voice. "So these are the boys who were so sure it was hidden in the old tower! Well, well! And they didn't find anything after all!"

"I'm afraid we didn't, Miss Applegate," Frank answered, with a smile. "But if you and Mr. Applegate will let us tell our story I think we can convince you that we really thought the stuff was hidden there. Even yet I believe it is hidden somewhere in the mansion—probably in the new tower."

"In the new tower!" she sniffed. "Absurd! I suppose you'll want to go poking through there now."

"If it wouldn't be too much trouble."

"It *would* be too much trouble, indeed!" she shrilled. "I shan't have any boys rummaging all through *my* house on a wild-goose chase like this. You'd better leave right away, and forget all this nonsense."

Her voice had attracted the attention of Hurd Applegate, who came hobbling out of his study at that moment.

"Now what's the matter?" he demanded. Then, seeing the boys, his face became creased in a triumphant smile.

"Ah, ha! So you didn't find anything after all! Heh! Heh!" he began to chuckle, immensely pleased with himself. "I told you so."

CHAPTER XVIII
THE NEW TOWER

"They have the audacity to want to go looking through the new tower now," said Miss Applegate, in high indignation.

Hurd Applegate's smile vanished.

"You can't do anything of the sort!" he snapped. "Are you boys trying to make a fool out of me? I knew mighty well you wouldn't find anything in the old tower."

"And we were pretty sure we would," answered Frank. "Listen, Mr. Applegate—we'll be fair with you. We'll tell you exactly why we wanted to make this search."

"Go ahead and tell me. Why didn't you tell me before?"

"Because we wanted to work this out ourselves, as far as possible. But the information we had came from the man who stole the jewels and the bonds."

"What! Has he been caught?"

"He was captured—but he will never come to trial."

"Did he escape again?"

"He escaped—by death. The thief is dead."

"Dead? What happened?" asked Hurd Applegate excitedly.

"His name was Red Jackley, and he was a notorious criminal. He was tracked down by our father, and when he tried to escape on a railroad hand-car he got into a smash-up, and he was fatally injured. But before he died, he admitted robbing Tower Mansion."

"He admitted it? He confessed?"

"He confessed everything."

"I don't believe it," sniffed Adelia Applegate. "Nothing will ever convince me that it wasn't that rascal Robinson."

"Jackley confessed the whole business," Frank persisted. "And on his deathbed he said that he hadn't been able to get away with the loot. That he had hidden it."

"Where?"

"In the old tower."

"And it isn't there?"

"Joe and I have just searched the place high and low. The stuff isn't there. And from the fact that there are no footprints or marks of any kind in the dust, I don't think any one has been in the place for a long time."

"The old tower has been closed for years."

"So we thought," Joe interjected, "that he might have been mistaken and that he had really hidden the stuff in the new tower instead."

Hurd Applegate rubbed his chin meditatively. His manner toward the boys had undergone a change, and it was evident that he was impressed by their story.

"So this fellow confessed to the robbery, eh?"

"He admitted everything. He was a man who once worked around Bayport and he knew this locality pretty well. He had been hanging around the city for some days before the robbery."

"Well," said Applegate slowly, "if he says he hid the stuff in the old tower and it isn't there, he must have meant the new tower, just as you say."

"Will you let us search it?"

"I'll do more than that. I'll help you. I'm just as anxious to get the jewels and bonds back as anybody."

"All nonsense!" declared Adelia Applegate. "It's all a pack of falsehoods. I don't believe a word of it."

"Now, now, Adelia," said her brother soothingly, "these boys may be right after all. It won't hurt to take a look around, at any rate."

"And much you'll find, I'm sure! I declare, Hurd Applegate, you're just as bad as those boys are."

"Maybe, maybe," he answered. "But I'm going to help them search the new tower, anyway."

"Don't ask *me* to brush the dust off your clothes when you come back, then. For that's all you'll get. Dust. Nothing more. The jewels and bonds are no more in the new tower than they are back in the safe right now."

"All right, Adelia. Perhaps you're right. But it won't hurt to make a search, anyway. Come on, boys."

With that, Hurd Applegate led the way down the hall and opened the door leading to a corridor that extended toward the new tower. Frank and Joe, tingling with excitement, followed.

Although the new tower had been built just a few years back and although its rooms had been furnished, it had been seldom occupied, save on the rare occasions when the Applegates had visitors from the city. The new caretaker, employed to replace Robinson, was a lazy and slovenly fellow, who did not bother to extend his duties to the tower, knowing that the Applegates seldom went near that part of the mansion and realizing that any laxity in his duties in that respect would scarcely be discovered. It came as a surprise to Hurd Applegate, then, to find out that the new tower was dusty, that the windows had not been cleaned, that there were cobwebs on the ceilings.

In the first room they found nothing, although they rummaged about in all the corners, looked beneath the table, behind the chairs—looked everywhere, in fact. Not until they were quite satisfied that the loot had not been hidden there, did they ascend the stairs to the next room, and there again their search was fruitless.

Hurd Applegate, being a quick-tempered man, fell back into his old mood. The boys' story had convinced him, and he had been even more certain than they that the stolen bonds and jewels would indeed be found in the new tower. But when two of the tower rooms had been thoroughly searched without success, his disappointment increased.

"Don't believe there was anything in that yarn, after all," he muttered, as they went up the stairs to the third room.

"I don't see why he should lie about it, after he confessed," remarked Frank thoughtfully. "Dad told us that he admitted not being able to get away with the stuff."

"Then where did he hide it?" demanded Applegate. "If he wasn't lying, the stuff must be around here some place."

"Perhaps he hid it a little more carefully than we imagine," put in Joe.

"Haven't we hunted carefully enough?" Hurd Applegate snapped.

In the third room their search was again in vain. They even inspected the window ledges and tapped the floors and ceiling in the faint hope of finding some secret cupboard that was unknown to them.

But the loot was not found.

When at last they emerged through the trapdoor in the roof, out on top of the rear tower, and found it to be bare and empty, Applegate could not disguise his chagrin.

"Wild-goose chase!" he snorted. "Adelia was right. I've been made a fool of."

"You don't think we would make up a story like that, do you, Mr. Applegate?" Frank asked.

"I don't see any reason why you should. But there's something wrong somewhere. I've wasted half a morning poking around through this confounded tower—all for nothing."

"So have we."

"If that fellow did hide the stuff in one of the towers, some one else must have come along and got it. That's the only way I can figure it out. He had some one working with him. Or else Robinson found the stuff—That's more likely! Probably Robinson found the loot right after the robbery and kept it for himself."

"I don't think he would do that. He isn't that kind of man," Joe objected.

"With all that money in front of him? I wouldn't put it past him for a minute. Where did he get that nine hundred dollars, then? Explain that. He can't. He won't tell."

As they descended the stairs and went back into the main part of the mansion, Hurd Applegate elaborated on this theory. The fact that the loot had not been found in the face of Red Jackley's story, seemed to strengthen his conviction that Robinson had something to do with the affair.

"Either Robinson found the stuff and kept it, or else he was in league with Jackley!" said Applegate. "He's mixed up in it some way. I'm sure of that."

The boys could say nothing. They realized that the theory was probable, although in their hearts they found it hard to believe that their chum's father could have had anything to do with the theft. They were deeply puzzled and tremendously disappointed, for they had been practically certain that the loot would be found. Now they saw that the only consequence of the whole affair was to involve Mr. Robinson more deeply than ever in the mystery.

Back in the hallway they endured the taunts of Adelia Applegate, who cackled jubilantly when she saw that the searching party had returned empty-handed.

"There now!" she crowed. "Who's right now? Didn't I tell you it was all nonsense? Hurd Applegate, you've simply been made a fool of by these two boys."

"Now, Adelia, I think they meant well—"

"Meant well! Of course they meant well! And what did it gain you? They have prowled through the place all morning and all the good that's come of it is that perhaps you won't be so ready to believe the next cock-and-bull story some one tells you. Go back to your stamps, Hurd Applegate, and let it be a lesson to you. As for you boys, you should be ashamed of yourselves, disturbing folks like this!"

Whereupon she escorted the Hardy boys to the door, while Hurd Applegate, muttering sadly, went back to his study with a puzzled air.

CHAPTER XIX
THE MYSTERY DEEPENS

Fenton Hardy was dumbfounded when his sons returned to him with the news that the loot had been found in neither the old tower nor the new. So implicitly had he believed in the dying confession of Red Jackley that he had not even bothered to join in the search, preferring to let his sons have the satisfaction of recovering the stolen goods that he was positive were hidden in the old tower.

"And you're sure you searched the place thoroughly?" he asked, for the third time.

"Every inch of it. There was nothing in the old tower. No one had been there in weeks," answered Frank.

"How could you tell?"

"By the dust. It hadn't been disturbed. There wasn't a footprint of any kind."

"But you searched anyway."

"We went through the tower from top to bottom," Frank replied. "It wasn't any use. No one had been there. So then we thought Jackley might have been mistaken and that he had left the stuff in the other tower."

"And Applegate let you search that as well?" and Fenton Hardy's eyes twinkled.

"Not until we had told him our reasons. We told him about Jackley, and then he became enthusiastic and even helped us in the search. But we didn't find anything."

"Strange," muttered the detective. "I know Jackley wasn't lying. He had nothing to gain by deceiving me. Absolutely nothing. He was in real earnest if ever a man was. 'I hid it in the old tower.' Those were his words. He would have told more if he had been able. And what could he mean but the old tower of Tower Mansion? Why should he be so careful to say the *old* tower. Every one knows the mansion has two towers, the old and the new."

"Of course, it may be that we didn't search thoroughly enough," Joe said. "The stuff may be hidden in the flooring or behind the walls."

"That's the only solution I can think of," replied Fenton Hardy. "I'm not satisfied yet that the loot isn't there. I'm going to get in touch with Applegate and ask permission for a real, thorough search of both towers. It's to his interest as well as mine."

"Applegate thinks possibly Jackley hid the stuff all right but that Robinson found it and sold it," said Frank. "He hinted that he was of the opinion that Robinson was in league with the thief."

"It does look rather bad," Mr. Hardy admitted. "One couldn't blame Applegate very much for thinking Robinson found the stuff after it was hidden and made away with it."

"Robinson wouldn't do that!" cried Joe. "He's too honest!"

"I don't think he would do it, either. But sometimes, if a man is in need of money and temptation is placed in his way, he gives in. I'd hate to believe that of Robinson, but if that stuff isn't found in the tower I'll have to admit that it looks very much as if he were mixed up in it."

The interview with their father left the Hardy boys feeling far from cheerful, for they saw that Mr. Robinson was now more deeply involved in the affair than before. On the face of it, circumstances seemed to be against the caretaker.

"Just the same," said Frank, as the boys left the house and went down the street, "I don't believe Jackley ever hid the stuff in the tower. If he had ever so much as opened the tower door he would have left some marks in the dust and we would have seen them. So I don't believe Robinson came along later and got the loot."

"As we saw it, the dust in the tower hadn't been disturbed in weeks. Why, there was even dust on the door-knob, when Mr. Applegate let us in."

"Then, why should Jackley say he hid the stuff there?" exclaimed Frank, puzzled.

"Don't ask me. I'm just as much in the dark as you are."

When the boys reached the business section of the city they found that already Jackley's confession had become common property. People were discussing the deathbed confession on the street corners and newsboys were busy selling copies of papers in which the story of the criminal's last statement was featured on the front page under black headlines.

Policeman Con Riley was ambling along Main Street in the morning sunshine, swinging his club with the air of a man without a care in the world. When he saw the boys he frowned, for there was no love lost between the Hardys and the Bayport police department.

"Well," he grunted, "I hear you got the stuff back."

"I wish we had," said Frank.

"What?" said the constable, brightening up at once. "You didn't get it? I thought it said in the paper this morning that this fellow Jackley told where he had hidden it."

"He did."

"And you can't find it! Ho! Ho!" Con Riley indulged in a hearty laugh. "What a fine detective your father is! Didn't Jackley say the stuff was hidden in the old tower? What more does he want?"

"Our father didn't search for the stuff," retorted Frank. "We did. And it wasn't there. Jackley must have made a mistake."

"It wasn't there?" exclaimed Riley, in high delight. "That's a good one. That's the best I've heard in years." He chuckled exceedingly, and slapped his knee. "Jackley put a good one over on your father that time. Ho! Ho! Ho! The stuff wasn't there!"

Riley wiped the tears from his eyes and went on his way, trying to laugh and at the same time retain his dignity as an officer of the law. The joke, he decided, was too good to keep, so as he proceeded back toward the police station, there to edify Chief Collig and Detective Smuff with the tale, he buttonholed various passers-by and poured the story into their willing ears. It was not long before the yarn had spread throughout the city with that swiftness peculiar to stories spread by word of mouth, and in the telling the story was exaggerated, the net effect being that Fenton Hardy was made to look ridiculous by believing a false confession.

Highly colored accounts of the boys' search of the old tower quickly spread, and throughout the day they were subjected to many caustic and sarcastic inquiries on the part of friends and acquaintances alike. They took all these remarks in good part, although they did not enjoy their sudden prominence.

"Never mind," said Frank, "we'll show them yet."

"I hope they find that stuff when they search the towers again," added Joe. "Then the people will have to eat crow. It'll be our turn to laugh."

"Yes," agreed Frank; "but just now our laughter seems to be in a far-distant future."

When they returned home they found that Fenton Hardy had been busy in the meantime and had convinced Hurd Applegate that a thorough search of the towers would be advisable. True, he had not accomplished this without a great deal of opposition on the part of Adelia and without misgivings on the part of Hurd Applegate himself, who had by that time come to the conclusion that Robinson had indeed been mixed up in the affair all along.

In this conviction he was sustained by Chief Collig, who had paid a call at the Applegate home as soon as Collig had told him of the vain search of the towers.

"The chief says Robinson is behind it, and I'm beginnin' to think he's right," said Applegate.

"But how about the confession?" Mr. Hardy asked.

"The chief says that's all a blind. Jackley did it to protect Robinson. They were both working together."

"I know it looks bad for Robinson, but I don't think it would hurt to give the towers another thorough search. I was the one who heard Jackley make the confession and I don't believe he was lying. I believe he was trying to tell me all he knew."

"Maybe. Maybe. I think he was too smart for you, Mr. Hardy, and everybody else thinks so too. It was all a hoax."

"I'll believe that after I've searched the towers inside and out."

"Well, go ahead. Go as far as you like. But I don't think you'll find that treasure."

With that, Mr. Hardy was content. He made preparations for a search of the towers, although Adelia Applegate flatly declared that the detective was making a laughing-stock of her and her brother and that if the nonsense continued she would leave Tower Mansion forever and carry out her oft-expressed intention of going to one of the South Sea Islands as a missionary.

In spite of the protestations of the worthy lady, however, the search was carried out. The old tower was visited first, and for the greater part of the following morning the place was searched from top to bottom. Even the floors were torn up in places in the quest for some secret hiding place in which Jackley might have left the loot.

But although Fenton Hardy, accompanied by the boys and Hurd Applegate, who soon became infected with the dogged enthusiasm of the others and lent every assistance in his power, hunted throughout the old tower in every conceivable place, the missing jewels and bonds were not recovered.

"Nothing left but to search the new tower," Mr. Hardy commented briefly, when the search was over, and throughout the whole afternoon the new tower was the scene of a search that was as thorough as it was fruitless.

Walls and partitions were tapped, floors were sounded, furniture was minutely examined—not an inch of space escaped the minute scrutiny of the detective and his helpers. But as the search wore on and the loot still evaded discovery, the chagrin of Fenton Hardy deepened and Hurd Applegate finally lost his temper.

"A hoax!" he declared. "A hoax from start to finish."

"The man was in earnest!" the detective insisted.

"Then where is the stuff?"

"Some one else may have found it. That's the only explanation I can think of."

"Who else could have taken it but Robinson?"

To this, Mr. Hardy was silent. In spite of his knowledge of and liking for the man, he was beginning to suspect that the caretaker may have had a hand in the affair after all.

"Either that or Jackley simply told that yarn to shield Robinson," declared Applegate.

"I'm not going to give up this search yet," said Mr. Hardy patiently. "Perhaps the loot was hidden somewhere about the grounds."

So the grounds of Tower Mansion, particularly in the vicinity of the two towers, were thoroughly searched. The shrubbery was inspected but to no avail.

The search continued until sundown, and by that time Adelia Applegate was pale with wrath, for the place, as she expressed it, had been "turned upside down," Hurd Applegate was outspoken in his rage and disappointment, while Fenton Hardy was deeply chagrined. As for the boys, although they had expected that the additional search would be without success, they shared their father's bewilderment.

"I can't understand it," admitted the detective. "I could have sworn that Jackley was in earnest when he made that confession. He knew he was near death and that he had nothing to gain by concealment. I can't understand it at all."

And there the mystery remained, deeper than it had ever been.

CHAPTER XX
THE FLASH IN THE TOWER

For two days after the unsuccessful search of Tower Mansion, there were no further developments in the affair of the robbery. But on the third day, Chief Collig took a hand.

The first intimation the Hardy boys had of it was when they met Callie Shaw and Iola Morton on their way to school. Iola, a plump, dark girl, was a sister of Chet Morton and had achieved the honor of being about the only girl Joe Hardy had ever conceded to be anything but an unmitigated nuisance.

Joe, who was shy in the presence of girls, professed a lofty scorn for all members of the other sex, particularly those of high school age, but had once grudgingly admitted that Iola Morton was "all right, for a girl." This, from him, was high praise.

"Have you heard what's happened?" asked Callie, as they met the boys near the school entrance.

"School called off for to-day?" asked Joe eagerly.

"No, no. Nothing like that. It's about the Robinsons."

"What's happened now?"

"Mr. Robinson has been arrested again."

The Hardy boys stared at her as though thunderstruck.

"What for?" demanded Frank, in astonishment.

"Over that robbery at Tower Mansion. He has been working in the city lately and Chief Collig sent Detective Smuff for him last night. Iola and I were over to see the Robinson girls last night and they told us about it. Smuff should be back by now."

"Well, can you beat that!" exclaimed Frank. "I wonder what's the big idea of arresting him again?"

"It seems the chief has an idea that Mr. Robinson was in league with this man Jackley, the man your father got the confession from. He told Mrs. Robinson last night that he was sure Mr. Robinson had the stuff hidden somewhere and that he was going to find out. He was perfectly mean and nasty about it, and Mrs. Robinson doesn't know what to do."

The Hardy boys looked at one another. The affair had suddenly assumed more serious proportions.

"If Mr. Robinson is brought back, he'll lose his job, and he had a hard time getting it, anyway," said Iola.

"The worst of it is," said Frank slowly, "that the case looks pretty bad against Mr. Robinson."

"You don't think they'll send him to the penitentiary?"

"It looks bad. The thief said he hid the stuff in the old tower. When we looked for it, the stuff wasn't there. About the only person that could have found it and taken it away, was Mr. Robinson himself."

"He wouldn't do it!" declared Iola indignantly.

"We're sure he wouldn't. But a jury mightn't be so easy to convince."

It was time to go into school at that moment and they went to their classrooms, Frank and Joe deeply worried by what they had just heard. At recess that morning they met Jerry, Phil, Tony and Chet Morton, and told them the news. All the boys were highly concerned over this sudden turn in events.

"This will be tough on Perry," said Phil.

"It'll be tough on the whole family," Chet declared. "They've had enough trouble over this dirty affair as it is."

The boys discussed the situation from all angles and racked their brains for some way whereby they could help the Robinsons, but they were reluctantly forced to admit that only by actual discovery of the hidden loot could Mr. Robinson be cleared of suspicion in connection with the robbery.

"Even if he were tried and acquitted, it would be a stain on his reputation for the rest of his life, as long as the treasure isn't recovered," Frank summed up.

"We'll just have to wait and see what happens," Joe said. "We've done all we could, and it hasn't been enough."

"And dad has done the same. I'm sorry, on his account. He was so sure he had cleared the whole thing up when he got the confession from Jackley. But there was something lacking."

"Well, we all helped too," remarked Jerry. "We kept Collig and Smuff from catching that train. Jackley wouldn't have talked at all if they had seen him."

So, reluctantly enough, the boys were forced to admit that they were facing a stone wall. This also was the conclusion of Fenton Hardy, when they talked to him at lunch that day.

"There's nothing to be done," said the detective. "Robinson has been arrested, and while he might be cleared by a skilful lawyer, he hasn't any money to spend on his defence. Whether he is cleared or not, his reputation is ruined."

"Unless the loot is found," put in Joe.

"Yes, unless the loot is found. That is his only hope. But I don't think there's much chance of that."

And there the mystery of Tower Mansion rested for the time being. The arrest of Mr. Robinson furnished a sensation for a day or so and then the case receded into the background, the newspapers finding other things to become excited about. But for the Robinsons it was, naturally enough, a matter of supreme moment. Perry Robinson paid a call at the Hardy home, pleading with the great detective to continue his efforts to clear the accused man.

Mr. Hardy was sympathetic, but, as he said, he was facing a stone wall.

"I've done all I can, my boy," he explained to the grief-stricken lad. "If there was anything more I could do, I would do it. But there are no more clues. If Red Jackley's confession couldn't clear up the affair, then nothing else could. I'm afraid—"

He left the sentence unfinished.

"Do you mean my father will go to jail?"

"I wouldn't say that. But you must be prepared to face the worst."

"He didn't do it," said Perry doggedly.

"I know you have confidence in him. But the law looks only at the facts. Many an innocent man has been convicted on less evidence."

"It will kill my mother."

Mr. Hardy was silent.

"I don't know what to do," said Perry. "I'd do anything to save him. But there's nothing—"

"There is nothing any of us can do now unless by some lucky chance the loot is recovered. That would clear everything up, of course. But in the meantime we just have to wait and hope."

"And you can't do anything more, Mr. Hardy?"

"A detective is not a miracle man, my boy," said Fenton Hardy kindly. "He is only a man who is trained in tracing criminals. He has to go by the facts at his disposal. I have exhausted every line of action in this case. Everything that could be done, has been done."

Perry Robinson got up, twisting his cap nervously in his hands.

"We all thank you very much too, Mr. Hardy," he said huskily. "Don't think I've been ungrateful by coming here and asking you to do more. I guess I didn't realize just how hopeless it is."

"It isn't hopeless, exactly. Don't think that. There's always hope, you know. But—be prepared for the worst."

"I'll have to be."

With that, the boy left. Frank and Joe met him in the hallway and awkwardly tried to express their sympathy. Perry was grateful.

"I know both of you have done a lot for us in this mess," he said. "If it hadn't been for you we wouldn't even have Jackley's story to go on."

"We're only sorry it didn't work out as we hoped, Perry," Frank said. "We thought that would clear the whole thing up. Instead, it seems to have involved your father deeper than ever."

"It wasn't your fault."

"Perhaps something will turn up yet. Joe and I aren't going to lie down on the job now. There isn't much we can do, but we'll have our eyes open for more clues—if there are any."

Perry Robinson shrugged his shoulders disspiritedly. "I guess there isn't much use now," he said. "But I appreciate it of you."

When he went away, the Hardy boys watched him going down the front walk. His carefree stride was gone, and instead he walked mechanically, as though in a daze.

"What a fine pair of detectives we are!" exclaimed Frank, in sudden disgust. "If we had been any good at all we could have got those clues soon enough for dad to have caught Jackley in time."

"No use worrying about that now," replied his brother. "It was just the way things happened."

"Well, there's one thing left. We must find that loot!"

"Haven't we tried?"

"Yes, but we can try some more. We've just *got* to clear Mr. Robinson. And there's only the one way. We must find the loot!"

It was a dull, gloomy day, indicative of rain, and this did not add to the boys' spirits.

To ease their feelings the brothers took a walk, and quite unconsciously their steps took them in the vicinity of Tower Mansion.

"Let's have a squint at the old place from the outside," suggested Joe.

"Don't let Adelia see you, or she'll come after you with a broomstick," chuckled Frank. "Gee, but she's a tartar!"

They walked into the grounds. It was growing darker now and they easily made their way among the trees and bushes to the vicinity of the rambling mansion. They gazed up at the old tower questioningly.

"Some puzzle," was Frank's comment. "Will the case of The Tower Treasure ever be solved?"

"Search me!" was his brother's slangy answer. "Perhaps—oh, Frank, look!" he added suddenly.

He was gazing at the upper windows of the old stone tower. He had seen a strange flash of light. Now this flash was followed by another.

"That's queer," muttered Frank. "What can it mean?"

The light disappeared, then of a sudden it flashed out and downward in the direction of the lads.

"Must be looking for us!" gasped Joe, and started to get behind a bush.

"It's Adelia—and she has a big flashlight," came, a moment later, from Frank. "What do you know about that!"

"She's looking for the treasure herself!" cried Joe. "Huh! And after all she said about our looking being nothing but foolishness!"

They saw the woman gaze out of the window for a few seconds. In one hand she held the flashlight. For a moment she turned the light into her own face, and the boys saw there a look of utter disgust.

"Didn't find it, I'll bet a cookie!" chuckled Joe.

"Come on—let's get away before she spots us," returned his brother, and they were soon on their way.

As they walked home, Joe and Frank talked the matter over. They smiled when they thought of the eccentric woman up in that dusty old tower, but their minds soon went back to Slim and the troubles of the Robinson family.

"We've got to find that loot!" declared Frank emphatically. "No matter where that tower treasure is, we've got to find it!"

"Got to—but can we?"

"We simply have to, I tell you!"

CHAPTER XXI

A NEW IDEA

A week passed, and still the loot was not recovered.

Mr. Robinson had been held for trial at an early court session. The general opinion in Bayport was that he would be sentenced to imprisonment. The fact that he still refused to tell where he had got the nine hundred dollars so near the time of the robbery, weighed heavily against him.

Fenton Hardy was downcast. It was the first case of its kind that he had been unsuccessful in solving completely, and although he was satisfied that he had done good work in tracking down Red Jackley and getting the confession, the result had scarcely been worth the effort.

Chief Collig and Detective Smuff were complacent. They made no effort to conceal their critical opinions of the great detective, who had taken so much time trying to solve the mystery, when the real thief was right under his nose all the time.

"I told you so," was the burden of Chief Collig's song of triumph. "I knew all the time that Robinson was the man. I arrested him right after the robbery, but they all said it couldn't be him. So I let him go. But I knew all the time it couldn't be any one else. Ain't that so, Smuff?"

And the loyal Smuff would dutifully chime in with, "Yes, chief. We have to hand it to you. You had the right man all the time."

"I guess these professional detectives won't think they're so smart after all, eh, Smuff?"

"No, you bet they won't. We can still teach 'em a thing or two."

"I'll say we can, Smuff. I'll say we can."

These stories, naturally enough, reached the ears of Fenton Hardy and the Hardy boys and they felt keenly the arrogant superiority displayed by the Bayport police officials. But they said nothing, suffering their defeat in silence.

On the following Saturday, Frank and Joe decided to take an outing.

"I want to get out of this city for a few hours," said Frank. "We've been so busy worrying about the Tower Mansion case that we've forgotten how to play. Let's take the motorbikes and go out for a run."

"Good idea!" his brother replied. "Mother will make us up some lunch."

Mrs. Hardy, who was in the kitchen with the cook, smiled when they made known their request. Fair-haired and gentle, she had been tolerantly amused by her sons' activities in the Tower affair, but she was glad to see them return to their boyish ways.

"You'll be getting too grown-up altogether," she had said to them a few days previously. And now, when they said they were going on a day's outing with the motorcycles, she hastened to prepare a substantial lunch for them.

"We'll be back in time for supper, mother," Frank promised. "We're just going to follow the highway along the railroad. After that we may cut across country to Chet's place, and then home."

"Take care of yourself," she warned. "No speeding."

"We'll be careful," they promised, as Joe stowed the lunch basket on the carrier of his machine. Then, with a sputtering roar, the motorcycles sped out along the driveway and soon the boys were on the concrete highway leading out of the city.

In a short time they had reached the outskirts of Bayport, and then they turned west on to the State highway that ran parallel to the railway tracks. It was a bright, sunny spring morning, and the highway was not congested with traffic.

Freight trains shunted back and forth on the railway tracks below the embankment, and now and then a passenger train steamed by, trailing a cloud of black smoke. Like most boys, Frank and Joe could not help but feel the fascination of the railway, although they admitted that they preferred the comparative freedom of their own motorcycles, which were not bound to follow the steel rails and did not have to obey the beck and call of despatchers.

Out in the open country they put on a little more speed. The highway was like a city pavement beneath them and the cool breeze stung the color into their cheeks. For more than two hours they rode, passing through villages and small towns, until at last they came to a point where another railway intersected the line they had been following. Here, a road also ran parallel to the tracks, branching off the main highway. Always on the alert for new country to explore, the Hardy boys decided to follow this side road.

"It's off the main stream of traffic," said Frank, "and the country seems to be wooded farther on. We can have lunch in the shade of some trees."

This appeared to be an advantage, for there were no trees along the State road, and the constant stream of vehicles made a roadside lunch something of a public affair. Accordingly, the boys turned their motorcycles down the side road which, although it was not paved, was well graded, and led through a quieter countryside.

"What railroad is this, anyway?" asked Frank, as they sped along.

"The Bayport and Coast line. It's mostly freight."

"The Bayport and Coast! Why, that's the railway that Red Jackley used to work for. Don't you remember dad telling us that? His first crime was stealing freight from the road."

"So he did! I'd forgotten all about it."

The boys looked down at the tracks below the embankment with renewed interest, by virtue of the railway's association with the notorious criminal. Mention of Jackley's name revived recollections of the Tower Mansion case, and when the boys finally decided to stop in the shade of a little grove of trees beside the road for lunch, they reviewed every incident of the mysterious affair.

"It would have been better for every one if Jackley had stayed with the railway," Frank observed, as he bit into a thick roastbeef sandwich.

"He sure caused a lot of trouble before he died."

"And he has caused even more since, by the looks of things. The Robinsons will remember his name for a long time to come."

"I wonder if Mr. Robinson really was in league with him, Frank?"

"I don't think so. And I don't believe Mr. Robinson ever found that treasure after the robbery, either. There is some explanation to this whole affair that none has been able to fathom."

"If I remember rightly, it was in this part of the country that Jackley worked."

"That's what dad told us. He said it was along the right of way near the State road. Jackley was a section hand or signalman, or something."

Both boys gazed down the two lines of railway tracks that gleamed in the sun. Far into the distance, the glittering bands of steel extended, vanishing into a common perspective.

The land along the right of way was thickly wooded. It was an attractive part of the country and here and there the wooded spaces were broken by green fields and meadows. The boys were at the top of a slope, and they had a view of a wide expanse of country below them.

In the far distance, along the tracks, they could see a little red railway station, and back of that the roofs and spires of a village. Nearer still they could see the spindly legs and squat bulk of a water tank, painted a bright scarlet. This water tank was not far from the railway station, but half a mile down the track, and only a few hundred yards from the place where the Hardy boys were seated, rose the bulk of another water station.

But this tower—one of the old style built before the modern tanks came into use—was not freshly painted. It had been allowed to fall into a state of disrepair. Some of the rungs were missing from the ladder that led up the side, and the tower itself had a forlorn and weather-beaten aspect, as though it had been deserted. This, indeed, was the case. The new tower tank closer to the station had been erected to replace it, and although the old structure had not been torn down, it was not now used.

Frank took a huge bite out of his sandwich and began to munch it thoughtfully. The sight of the two water stations had given him an idea, but at first it seemed to him to be too absurd for consideration. He was wondering whether he should mention it to his brother.

Then he noticed that Joe, too, was gazing thoughtfully down the railway tracks. Joe raised a sandwich to his lips absently, essayed a bite and missed the sandwich altogether. Still he continued gazing at the two water towers.

Finally Joe turned and looked at his brother.

In the eyes of both was the light of a great discovery. They knew that they were both thinking of the same thing.

"Two water towers," said Frank slowly.

"An old one and a new one."

"And Jackley said—"

"He hid the stuff in the old tower."

"He was a railwayman."

"Why not?" shouted Joe, springing to his feet. "Why couldn't it have been the old water tower? He used to work around here."

"He didn't say the old tower of Tower Mansion, after all. He just said 'the old tower!'"

"Frank, I believe we've stumbled on the clue!"

"It would be the natural thing for him to come to his old haunts after the robbery. And if he found he couldn't get away with the stuff he would hide it somewhere he knew. The old water tower! Why didn't we think of it before, Joe? Why, that *must* be the place!"

CHAPTER XXII
THE SEARCH

Lunch, motorcycles—everything else was forgotten!

With a wild yell of delight, Frank began to scurry down the embankment that flanked the right of way. At his heels ran Joe.

They raced down the grassy slope until they came to the wire fence. They scrambled over it, heedless of tearing their clothes. They dashed up on to the cinder path beside the rails.

"What if we're wrong, Frank?" panted Joe.

"We can't be wrong. I just know that's what Jackley meant. The old tower. It was the old *water* tower he meant all along. He didn't have time to explain."

The Hardy boys were tingling with excitement.

It seemed that they could never reach the water tower. They dashed along the cinder path with all the speed at their command, but the tower still seemed a long distance away.

"If only we *have* stumbled on the secret after all, Joe!"

"It'll clear Mr. Robinson—"

"We'll get the reward—"

"Dad'll be proud of us."

These thoughts gave them new strength and their hopes were high as they neared the tower.

The structure reared gloomily from beside the tracks. At close quarters it was even more decrepit, even more in a state of disrepair than they had imagined. The old tower had been abandoned for some time in favor of the new tank nearer the station. It sagged perilously. The ladder that led to the top lacked so many rungs that at first the boys feared they would be unable to ascend.

"If Jackley got up this ladder, we can do the same," said Frank, as he stopped, panting, at the bottom. "Let's go."

He began to scramble up the flimsy ladder.

Hardly had he ascended four rungs than there came an alarming crack!

"Look out!"

Frank clung to the rung above, just as a rung snapped beneath his weight. He hung in midair for a moment, then drew up his feet and placed them on the next rung. This proved firmer, and he was able to go on.

"Don't break 'em all," called Joe. "I want to be in on this."

Frank continued up the ladder. Occasionally, when he came to a place where a rung had broken off, he was obliged to haul himself upward by main force, but finally he neared the top. The ladder ran up along the side of the tank to the very top of the great, vat-like receptacle, and there it led to a trapdoor.

The Hardy boys did not look down. They were high above the ground now, and the old water tower was swaying alarmingly. They began to realize their peril, for the tower was old and liable to topple over with them. But the thought did not serve to restrain them, and at last Frank scrambled over the last rung and found himself on the upper surface of the tower. He turned around and helped Joe over.

Far below them lay the countryside, the green fields laid out in neat patterns, the roads in the distance like white ribbons, and the railway tracks glistening in the sunlight. The wind seemed much stronger on top of the tower, and it whistled about their ears. The flimsy structure swayed to and fro with every movement they made.

The trapdoor was closed. Frank went over to it and tugged at it, but the timber was heavy and Joe was obliged to help him. Between the two, however, they managed to raise it, revealing a dark gap that led into the recesses of the abandoned water tower.

The upper part of the tank was a space about four feet in depth and separated from the lower, or main portion by a thick floor. Frank lowered himself through the opening, and he was quickly followed by his brother. They crouched down below the roof of the tank and peered about them in the obscurity.

"It must be in here. There's no other place he could have hidden the stuff," said Frank.

"Let's hunt for it, then. I wish we had brought our flashlights."

Frank, however, had matches. Cautiously, he lit one. Then, crawling on hands and knees, he advanced into the darkness of the tower.

In the faint glow of the match they saw that the place was half-filled with rubbish. There was a quantity of old lumber, miscellaneous bits of iron, battered tin pails, crowbars, and other things piled up pellmell in all parts of the tower.

But there was no sign of hidden loot.

"It must be here somewhere!" declared Joe doggedly. "He wouldn't leave it out in the open. Probably it's in behind all this junk."

Frank held the match. They had to be careful, for the place was as dry as tinder and any negligence might have made the whole place a mass of flame from which there would have been no escape. In the glow, then, Joe searched frantically, casting the old pails and the old bits of board and lumber aside with reckless abandon.

One entire side of the tower top was searched without result. Then, on the far side, they spied a number of boards piled up in a peculiar manner. They did not look as though they had been flung there carelessly or accidentally, but rather as though they had been placed to hide something.

Like a terrier after a bone, Joe made for it. Frantically, he tore away the boards.

There, in a neat little hiding place formed by the wood, lay a bag. It was an ordinary gunny sack, but when Joe dragged it forth he knew at once that their search had ended.

"We've found it!" he exulted.

"The Tower treasure!"

"This must be it."

Joe dragged the gunny sack out into the light beneath the trapdoor. They did not even wait to go out on top of the water tower.

"Hurry!" exclaimed Frank, as with trembling fingers Joe began to open the sack.

It was tied with a piece of twine, and Joe tugged at the stubborn knots. At last, however, the twine fell away, and the bag sagged open.

Joe plunged his hand into the recesses of the sack and he first withdrew an old-fashioned bracelet of precious stones.

"Jewelry!"

"How about the bonds?"

Again Joe groped into the sack. His fingers encountered a bulky packet. He withdrew it and the packet proved to be comprised of long, imposing-looking documents, held together by a rubber band. On the surface of the outer document, when they held it up to the light, they read the information that it was a negotiable bond for $5000 issued by the City of Bayport.

"That settles it," said Frank. "We've found the treasure."

The boys looked at one another in triumph.

"Jackley wasn't lying after all. He *did* hide the stuff in the old tower. And Mr. Robinson wasn't in league with him and didn't find it after it was hidden," ruminated Joe. "We can clear up the whole affair now."

"Let's start, then!" Frank exclaimed. "No use sitting here all day patting ourselves on the back. It's up to us to get right back to Bayport and turn this treasure over to the Applegates."

Hastily, he scrambled up through the trap, and Joe passed the bag of treasure up to him. Frank put the sack carefully to one side, then helped his brother up to the top of the tower. After that he tied the treasure sack to his belt, in order that he might have the full use of his two hands in descending the precarious ladder.

They were so excited by their momentous discovery, by the knowledge that all the days of fruitless search had now ended, that they descended the ladder at break-neck speed. The last two rungs of the ladder snapped under Frank's feet and the boys were obliged to undertake a drop of six feet in order to reach the ground, but they hardly noticed it. Scarcely had they picked themselves up than they were off on a run for their motorcycles, parked far back on the hillside.

"We've shown 'em, eh?" gasped Joe.

"I'll say we have! Oh boy, won't this surprise everybody?"

"*Now* I'd like to see dad tell us we're not cut out to be detectives!"

"Wait till Adelia Applegate sees all her jewelry back again. She'll change her opinion of us."

"Wait till Hurd Applegate sees his bonds back. And wait till Chief Collig and Detective Smuff hear about it!"

So the Hardy boys gloated over their prospective return, but beneath it all they were thinking of what this discovery meant to the Robinsons.

They reached the embankment, scrambled over the fence, and made their way up the slope until at last they regained their motorcycles. Although they had only partly finished their lunch, they were too excited to eat any more, so they stowed the remainder away in the basket, lashed the bag of treasure securely to Frank's carrier, and turned the motorcycles around.

"What a lucky chance for us that we decided to go down this road!" declared Frank. "If we had done as we intended and circled around by Chet's place we would never have found the stuff!"

"And it's ten chances to one that neither of us would have thought of that water tower until his dying day."

The rest of their speculations were drowned by the roar of the motorcycles as the Hardy boys set out on their return to Bayport with the Tower treasure.

HISTORICAL EMPORIUM

Est. 2003

Buy at... HISTORICAL EMPORIUM

Whose **REPUTATION** is *celebrated* world-wide as the pre-eminent clothing source for the **ADVENTUROUS** and *Fashionable*.

We are...

REVERED
by our customers

REVILED
by our competitors

RESPECTED
by all who know us

NO LOCAL DEALER CAN COMPETE WITH OUR QUALITY, VARIETY AND INCOMPARIBLE CUSTOMER SERVICE!

ACCEPT NO SUBSTITUTE!
If you require **clothing and supplies** as stylish and **stout-hearted** as you, contact us immediately to be outfitted.

800-997-4311

HistoricalEmporium.com

CHAPTER XXIII
ADELIA APPLEGATE'S COMPLIMENT

The curtain rolled down on the mystery of the Tower treasure that afternoon in the library of the Applegate home.

The Hardy boys had gone directly to their father with the story of the recovery of the loot, and Fenton Hardy had lost no time in acquainting Hurd Applegate with the facts. Between them, they arranged a little surprise for Chief Collig and Detective Smuff, as well as for Henry Robinson. On the invitation of Hurd Applegate, the chief brought Mr. Robinson to Tower Mansion, "to be faced with additional evidence," as Fenton Hardy suavely put it.

Chief Collig and Detective Smuff entered the library with their prisoner between them. They had confidently anticipated that Mr. Applegate had discovered some new facts that would further serve to tighten the web about the unfortunate caretaker, and when they came into the room there was nothing at first to eradicate this impression.

Hurd Applegate and Adelia Applegate sat by the huge library table, and with them were Mr. Hardy and his sons. Chief Collig did not at first notice the gunny sack lying on the table.

"Well, Mr. Applegate," said the chief, fanning himself, as usual, with his hat. "I brought along Mr. Robinson, just as you asked."

"Good. As I mentioned to you, there has been some new evidence in this case."

"I knew something would turn up," grunted Smuff.

"Not that any new evidence is needed, of course," declared the chief. "We got this fellow dead to rights, as it is. He ain't got a chance in the world. But still, it's just as good to make a real strong case of it."

"I'm afraid you don't understand me," went on Hurd Applegate. "This new evidence will *clear* Mr. Robinson. And when he is cleared, I want him back in my employ again."

"Huh?" gasped Chief Collig.

"What's that you say?" exclaimed Smuff.

"The stolen stuff has been found."

"No!"

"Here it is," put in Fenton Hardy, getting up and dumping the gunny sack upside down on the table. There was a tinkle and clatter as jewels came rolling out on the table, and then there was a rustle of paper as the packets of bonds followed.

"Where was it found?" asked the chief. "This doesn't clear him. He probably hid it some place."

"The stuff was found just where Jackley said he hid it. In the old tower."

"But the old tower was searched high and low."

"There is more than one 'old tower'," went on Mr. Hardy. "Only we didn't happen to think of that at the time. It was found in the old water tower, down at the Junction, where Jackley used to work."

Chief Collig was speechless with surprise. He gazed at Smuff, whose jaw had dropped in astonishment.

"Who found it?" asked Smuff at last.

"These two lads," said Mr. Applegate, indicating the Hardy boys. "They found it this morning."

"Them kids?" scoffed Chief Collig. "I don't believe it."

"Well, there's the stuff to prove it," snapped Fenton Hardy.

"I've got my jewelry back, thanks to them," declared Adelia Applegate shrilly. "They were smarter than the whole pack of you. If it wasn't for them, the stuff would never have been found. And I was the one who didn't want to let them search the old tower and who spoke crossly to them. Why, they're *real* detectives, both of them."

In all the talk and excitement that followed the clearing up of the Tower mystery, the Hardy boys received no compliment that they treasured so much as that remark of Adelia Applegate's.

"Well," said Chief Collig, scratching his head, "I'll be bumped!"

He looked at Smuff.

"I'll be bumped, too," declared Smuff.

"This beats all," said the chief.

"It does," agreed his faithful satellite.

"Shut up!" snapped the chief. "Who asked you to say anything?"

"Nobody."

"Well, then, keep quiet. A fine detective you are! Why didn't you think of that? The old tower! Of course he meant the old water tower. What else could he have meant? But *you* wouldn't think of it. Not in a hundred years—you wouldn't think of it. What kind of a detective are you, anyway? Here was a case that was as simple as A B C and you couldn't think of it. You let yourself be beat by a couple of boys!"

Smuff looked properly ashamed of himself, although it was plain that he was struggling with the temptation to ask the chief why *he* had not thought of the water tower, too. But he stifled the impulse and thereby doubtless saved the chief the trouble of dismissing him for impudence and insubordination.

"Yes," said Hurd Applegate, "the Hardy boys recovered the treasure. And I think you will admit that Mr. Robinson is cleared. Personally, I am satisfied that he knew nothing whatever of the theft and I want to apologize to him for any unjust suspicions I may have had. Mr. Robinson, will you let me shake your hand?"

Trembling, Henry Robinson stepped forward. His face had been illuminated by a glow of incredulous hope from the moment he learned of the discovery of the loot.

"Am I really cleared?" he asked. "I knew things looked bad against me all along. I hardly dared hope—"

"I guess you'll be let off now all right," said Chief Collig grudgingly.

"There will be formalities, of course," said Fenton Hardy. "But I'm pretty sure the prosecution won't continue. The discovery of this loot proves Red Jackley's story was correct from start to finish."

"But how about that nine hundred dollars?" demanded Smuff suspiciously.

Mr. Robinson straightened up.

"I'm sorry," he said, "but even yet I can't explain that. I can in a few days, perhaps; but I've promised to keep silent about that money. It's a private matter entirely."

"I don't think we need bother about that," objected Hurd Applegate. "I've checked over the treasure and it's all there. All the bonds and all the jewelry. There is nothing missing. As for the nine hundred dollars, why, that is Mr. Robinson's own affair."

Reluctantly, Smuff subsided into silence.

"Will you come back into my employ, Mr. Robinson?" asked Hurd Applegate. "Of course, I feel very keenly, because you were unjustly accused, and I want to make it up to you. If you will consent to come back to Tower Mansion as caretaker again I will increase your salary, and I'll also insist that you accept back pay for the time you were away."

"Why," stammered Mr. Robinson, "this is good of you, Mr. Applegate. Of course I'll come back, I'll be glad to. It'll mean a lot to my wife and daughters—and to Perry. He'll be able to go back to school again."

"Good!" exclaimed Joe Hardy impulsively, slapping his knee. Then, finding that he had attracted attention to himself, he sank back into his chair, embarrassed.

"And as for the Hardy boys," proceeded Hurd Applegate, "seeing they discovered the treasure—"

"Real detectives," shrilled Adelia. "Real detectives, both of them! Smart lads!"

"Yes, they showed some real detective work, and I hope they grow up to follow in their father's footsteps. But, as I was saying, they discovered the treasure, so of course they will get the reward."

"A thousand bucks!" exclaimed Detective Smuff, in awe.

"Dollars, Mr. Smuff—dollars!" corrected Adelia Applegate severely. "No slang please, not in Tower Mansion."

"One thousand iron men!" declared Smuff, unheeding. "One thousand round, fat, juicy smackers for a couple of kids! And a real detective like me—!"

The thought was too much for him. He sank his head in his hands and groaned aloud.

Frank and Joe did not dare look at each other. They were finding it difficult enough to restrain their laughter without that.

"Yes, a thousand dollars," went on Hurd Applegate. "I'll write the checks now. Five hundred for each."

With that he took out his fountain pen, reached in a drawer of the table for a check book, and soon the silence was broken by the scratching of pen on paper. Hurd Applegate wrote out two checks, each for five hundred dollars and these he handed to the boys. Frank and Joe accepted them with thanks, folded them up and put them in their pockets.

"And that, I think," concluded Mr. Applegate, "finishes the mystery of the Tower robbery."

"Thanks to the Hardy boys!" chimed in his sister. "Real detectives, both of them. I must ask them up for supper some night."

CHAPTER XXIV

THE LAST OF THE TOWER CASE

The discovery of the Tower Mansion treasure was a Bayport sensation for almost a week—and a week is a long time for any sensation to last, even in Bayport.

People said that they knew all along that Mr. Robinson was innocent of the theft, and went as far out of their way to be nice to him as they had gone out of their way to be unkind to him and ignore him when he was accused of crime.

People too, were loud in their praises of the Hardy boys, and everybody predicted a bright future for them and said they knew all along that the lads were bound to solve the mystery if they kept at it long enough. All of this the boys took with a grain of salt, as the saying is, for they knew that the public is fickle and as quick to condemn failure as it is to praise success.

Frank and Joe did not let the adulation turn their heads.

"When we couldn't find the treasure everybody said we were just nuisances—little boys trying to play detective," laughed Frank. "Now that we have found it, all that is forgotten. The main thing is that we've proved to dad that we know how to keep our eyes and ears open."

"And we've got a thousand dollars between us."

"A mighty nice start for a bank account."

"I'll say it is! I wish another mystery would come along."

"We can't expect to get a reward for every case we work on—and we can't expect to solve 'em all, either," Frank pointed out.

"We can't expect to get many cases to try our hand at. We're not professionals just yet."

"No, but we will be, some day."

This conversation took place as the Hardy boys were on their way up to Tower Mansion about a week later. Adelia Applegate, who had taken a great fancy to the lads, in violent contrast to her dislike of them on the day they had gone to make a search of the old tower, had invited them up to the Tower Mansion for supper.

She had also asked them to invite a number of their chums. So Slim Robinson, Chet Morton, Biff Hooper, Jerry Gilroy, Phil Cohen and Tony Prito had all been invited by the brothers to attend.

When the Hardy boys reached the Mansion they found that the others had already arrived.

"We're waiting for you," shrilled Miss Applegate, who was decked out in an ancient yellow gown with remarkable trimmings of black and red. "Everybody's hungry."

She soon led the way to the dining room, where a long table had been prepared for the boys. They gasped when they saw that array, and Miss Applegate beamed.

"I know you don't want an old woman like me watching you while you eat," she cried. "So go right ahead—and put your elbows on the table if you wish."

There was a scramble for places, as a servant came in with the soup, but Frank Hardy sprang to his feet.

"Three cheers for Miss Applegate!"

They were given with vociferous enthusiasm. Miss Applegate blushed with pleasure, and as she left the room the Hardy boys and their chums were sitting down to a banquet the like of which they had never seen before. For more than half an hour they indulged in roast chicken, crisp and brown, huge helpings of fluffy mashed potatoes, pickles, vegetables and salads, pies and puddings to suit every taste, and when the last boy sank back in his chair with a happy sigh there was still food to spare.

"I never thought I'd see the day when I'd quit eating while there was still some chicken on the table," murmured Chet Morton, "but this is the day."

"We have the Hardy boys to thank for this spread," said Jerry. "Let's give 'em three cheers."

The boys roared out their "hip, hip, hurrah!" three times, while Joe and Frank looked acutely uncomfortable. They looked still more uncomfortable when Slim Robinson got up, pushing back his chair.

"I'd like to say something, fellows, if you don't mind."

"Three cheers for Slim!" yelled some one.

So the boys gave Slim three cheers, and he gulped and blushed crimson.

"Speech!"

The cry was taken up.

"Speech! Speech!"

"I'm not going to make any speech," he said. "I only want to say something."

"Go ahead!"

"I'm not going to hand out any compliments to the Hardy boys."

Joe and Frank looked greatly relieved. They had been afraid of being embarrassed by Slim's gratitude.

"Everybody knows what they've done and everybody knows what it means to me and to my family."

"You bet!"

"Sure!"

"But I just wanted to clear up one point on behalf of my father."

"Three cheers for Henry Robinson! He's all right."

The three cheers for Mr. Robinson were perhaps a little weaker than the others, but that was only because some of the boys were beginning to show slight signs of hoarseness by that time.

"It's about the nine hundred dollars that he got just about the time of the robbery. He couldn't explain it at the time and it looked bad against him."

"It doesn't matter where he got it," shouted Biff Hooper. "I'll bet he got it honestly anyway, and if any one else says different, just let him come outside."

No one else said differently.

"Yes, he got it honestly, of course," said Slim. "The money was paid him by a man who owed it to him. But dad couldn't say anything about it because he promised not to. This man owed two other men besides my father, and those debts should have been paid first. He was afraid the others would sue him if they heard he had paid dad, so he made my father promise to say nothing. And when my dad makes a promise he keeps it."

The boys looked at one another. To tell the truth, few of them had thought of the affair of the nine hundred dollars, but now that it was recalled to them they realized that here was the final angle of the Tower Mansion mystery cleared up at last. They cheered Slim to the echo, they pounded on the table with their knives, and when Hurd Applegate came in to see what the racket was about they gave him three cheers and made him sit at the head of the table.

And that ended the affair of Tower Mansion, but it did not end the career of the Hardy boys as amateur detectives. They were soon to be called on to help solve another mystery, and the story of their adventures in this case will be told in the next volume of this series, entitled "The Hardy Boys: The House on the Cliff."

"Speech! Speech!" the boys were shouting to Hurd Applegate.

The old stamp collector got up, smiling.

"It's been a long time since there's been a crowd of boys in Tower Mansion," he said. "I've been in danger of forgetting that I was ever young once myself. So I want you to come back—often. I want you to know that Tower Mansion is always open to the Hardy boys and their chums."

The Hardy boys looked at one another, as the crowd about the table broke into a yell of delight.

"He's a pretty good old scout after all, isn't he?" said Frank.

"You bet he is," replied his brother.

The End

READING BREAK!!!

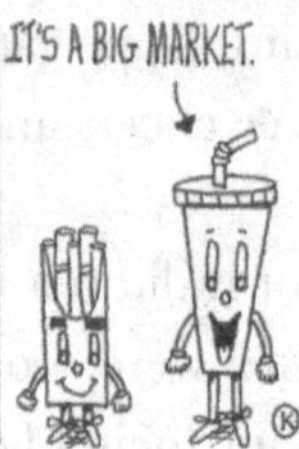

SUDOKU

3		2	7				8	
	6							
	5		2		6			4
		8					9	2
1			5			4	3	
	3				2		1	7
					3			
6					1			8
			4					5

quick

2 out of 3 with someone near.

Want your short story published in Adventures to Go?
Email your entire story, with "Submission" in Subject to:
OffBeatReads@pm.me

A pair of cows were talking in the field. One says, "Have you heard about the mad cow disease that's going around?"
"Yeah," the other cow says. "Makes me glad I'm a penguin."

Excerpt:

Something, a shadow perhaps, caught the corner of his left eye and he turned but didn't see anything. Seconds later, he heard a branch break, and someone also dressed in a camouflage jacket appeared with a gun in his right hand. He didn't recognize him behind his dark goggles but saw he was wearing a crimson armband, so he knew he had to be killed.

Slowly he rose out of his crouch and trailed behind him, curling a finger around the trigger of his gun. He moved tentatively, as if crossing a pond of ice, not wanting to make any sound that would reveal his presence. Soon his heart began to make so much racket he was worried the guy would hear it, so he forced himself to take long, deliberate breaths as he followed him through the thick woods. He didn't have long, he suspected, before the guy realized he was behind him.

From Cruel Earth, by Thomas Healy

OUR AMERICAN COUSIN

A DRAMA IN 3 ACTS

BY TOM TAYLOR

TRANSCRIBER'S NOTE:

Abraham Lincoln was watching this play when
he was assassinated.
(Act III, halfway through Scene 2.)

ORIGINAL CAST OF CHARACTERS:

Lord Dundreary	Mr. E. A. Sothern
Asa Trenchard	” Jos. Jefferson
Sir Edward Trenchard	” E. Varrey
Capt. De Boots	” Clinton
Harry Vernon	” M. Levick
Abel Murcott	” C.W. Couldock
Mr. Coyle	” J.G. Burnett
Mr. Buddicombe	” McDouall
Mr. Binny	” Peters
John Wickens	” Brown
Mrs. Mountchessington	Miss Mary Wells
Florence Trenchard	” Laura Keene
Mary	” Sara Stevens
Augusta	” E. Germon
Georgina	Mrs. Sothern
Sharpe	Miss Flynn
Skillet	Mrs. M. Levick

Act I

SCENE 1

Drawing room in 3. Trenchard Manor, C. D., backed by interior, discovering table with luncheon spread. Large French window, R. 3 E., through which a fine English park is seen. Open archway, L. 3 E.

Set balcony behind. Table, R., books and papers on it. Work basket containing wools and embroidery frame. A fashionable arm chair and sofa, L. 2 E., small table near C. D. Stage handsomely set, costly furniture, carpet down, chairs, etc.

Buddicombe discovered on sofa reading newspaper. Skillet and Sharpe busily arranging furniture as curtain rises.

Sharpe: I don't know how you may feel as a visitor, Mr. Buddicombe, but I think this is a most uncomfortable family.

Bud: Very uncomfortable. I have no curtain to my bed.

Skil: And no wine at the second table.

Sharpe: And meaner servants I never seed.

Bud: I'm afraid Sir Edward is in a queer strait.

Skil: Yes, for only this morning, Mr. Binny, Mrs. Skillet says he—

Enter Binny, L. 3 E.

Binny: Mind your hown business instead hof your betters. I'm disgusted with you lower servants. When the wine merchant presents his bills, you men, hear me, say he's been pressing for the last six months, do you?

Skil: Nor I, that the last year's milliner's bills have not been paid.

Sharpe: Nor I, that Miss Florence has not had no new dresses from London all winter.

Bud: And I can solemnly swear that his lordship's hair has been faithfully bound in this bosom.

Binny: That'll do, that'll do; but to remember to check hidle curiosity is the first duty of men hin livery. Ha, 'ere hare the letters.

Enter John Wickens, L. 3 E., with green baize bag. Binny takes bag, takes out letters and reads addresses.

Binny: Hah! bill, of course, Miss Augusta, Mrs. Mountchessington, Lord Dundreary, Capt. De Boots, Miss Georgina Mountchessington, Lieut. Vernon, ah! that's from the admiralty. What's this? Miss Florence Trenchard, via Brattleboro', Vermont.

Bud: Where's that, Mr. Binny.

John: Why that be hin the United States of North Hamerica, and a main good place for poor folks.

Binny: John Wickens, you forget yourself.

John: Beg pardon, Mr. Binny.

Binny: John Wickens, leave the room.

John: But I know where Vermont be tho'.

Binny: John Wickens, get hout. [Exit John, L. 3 E.]

Bud: Dreadful low fellow, that.

Binny: Halways himpudent.

Bud: [Looking at letter in Binny's hand.] Why, that is Sir Edward's hand, Mr. Binny, he must have been sporting.

Binny: Yes, shooting the wild helephants and buffalos what abound there.

Bud: The nasty beasts. [Looking off, R. 2 E.] Hello, there comes Miss Florence tearing across the lane like a three year old colt.

Sharp & Skil: Oh, Gemini. [Run off, R. 2 E. Bud. runs off, L. 2 E.]

 Enter Florence, R. 2 E.

Flo: [As if after running.] Oh! I'm fairly out of breath. Good morning, Binny, the letter bag I saw coming, Wickens coming with it. I thought I could catch him before I reached the house. [Sits R.] So off I started, I forgot the pond, it was in or over. I got over, but my hat got in. I wish you'd fish it out for me, you won't find the pond very deep.

Binny: Me fish for an at? Does she take me for an hangler?

Flo: Give me the letters. [Takes them.] Ah, blessed budget that descends upon Trenchard Manor, like rain on a duck pond. Tell papa and all, that the letters have come, you will find them on the terrace.

Binny: Yes, Miss. [Going, L. 3 E.]

Flo: And then go fish out my hat out of the pond, it's not very deep Binny [Aside.] Me fish for 'ats? I wonder if she takes me for an hangler? [Exit disgusted, R. 3 E.]

Flo: [Reading directions.] Lieut. Vernon. [This is a large letter with a large white envelope, red seal.] In her Majesty's service. Admiralty, R. N. Ah, that's an answer to Harry's application for a ship. Papa promised to use his influence for him. I hope he has succeeded, but then he will have to leave us, and who knows if he ever comes back. What a foolish girl I am, when I know that his rise in the service will depend upon it. I do hope he'll get it, and, if he must leave us, I'll bid him good bye as a lass who loves a sailor should.

Enter Sir Edward, Mrs. M., Augusta,
Capt. De Boots, Vernon, L. 3 E.

Flo: Papa, dear, here are letters for you, one for you, Mrs. Mountchessington, one for you, Capt. De Boots, and one for you, Harry. [Hiding letter behind her.]

Ver: Ah, one for me, Florence?

Flo: Now what will you give me for one?

Ver: Ah, then you have one?

Flo: Yes, there, Harry. [Gives it.]

Ver: Ah, for a ship. [Opens and reads.]

Flo: Ah! Mon ami, you are to leave us. Good news, or bad?

Ver: No ship yet, this promises another year of land lubbery. [Goes up.]

Flo: I'm so sorry. [Aside.] I'm so glad he's not going away. But where's Dundreary. Has anybody seen Dundreary?

Enter Dundreary.

Dun: Good morning, Miss Florence.

Flo: [Comes down, L.] Good morning, my Lord Dundreary. Who do you think has been here? What does the postman bring?

Dun: Well, sometimes he brings a bag with a lock on it, sometimes newspapers, and some-times letters, I suppothe.

Flo: There. [Gives letter. Dundreary opens letter and Florence goes up R. Dun. knocks knees against chair, turns round knocks shins, and at last is seated extreme, R.]

Dun: Thank you. [Reads letter.]

De B: [Reading paper.] By Jove, old Soloman has made a crop of it.

Dun: A—what of it?

De B: I beg pardon, an event I am deeply in-terested in, that's all. I beg pardon.

Aug: Ah! Florence, dear, there's a letter of yours got among mine. [Gives it.]

Flo: Why papa, it's from dear brother Ned.

Sir E: From my boy! Where is he? How is he? Read it.

Flo: He writes from Brattleboro' Vt. [Read-ing written letter.] "Quite well, just come in from a shooting excursion, with a party of Crows, splendid fellows, six feet high."

Dun: Birds six feet high, what tremendous an-imals they must be.

Flo: Oh, I see what my brother means; a tribe of indians called Crows, not birds.

Dun: Oh, I thought you meant those creatures with wigs on them.

Flo: Wigs!

Dun: I mean those things that move, breathe and walk, they look like animals with those things. [Moving his arms like wings.]

Flo: Wings.

Dun: Birds with wings, that's the idea.

Flo: [Reading written letter.] "Bye-the-bye, I have lately come quite hap-hazard upon the other branch of our family, which emigrated to America at the Restoration. They are now thriving in this State, and discovering our relationship, they received me most hospitably. I have cleared up the mysterious death of old Mark Trenchard."

Sir E: Of my uncle!

Flo: [Reading written letter.] "It appears that when he quarreled with his daughter on her marriage with poor Meredith, he came here in search of this stray shoot of the family tree, found them and died in their house, leaving Asa, one of the sons, heir to his personal property in England, which ought to belong to poor Mary Meredith. Asa is about to sail for the old country, to take possession. I gave him directions to find you out, and he should arrive almost as soon as this letter. Receive him kindly for the sake of the kindness he has shown to me, and let him see some of our shooting." Your affectionate brother, NED.

Sir E: An American branch of the family.

Mrs M: Oh, how interesting!

Aug: [Enthusiastically.] How delightfully romantic! I can imagine the wild young hunter. An Apollo of the prairie.

Flo: An Apollo of the prairie; yes, with a strong nasal twang, and a decided taste for tobacco and cobblers.

Sir E: Florence, you forget that he is a Trenchard, and no true Trenchard would have a liking for cobblers or low people of that kind.

Flo: I hate him, whatever he is, coming here to rob poor cousin Mary of her grandmother's guineas.

Sir E: Florence, how often must I request you not to speak of Mary Meredith as your cousin?

Flo: Why, she is my cousin, is she not? Besides she presides over her milk pail like a duchess playing dairymaid. [Sir E. goes up.] Ah! Papa won't hear me speak of my poor cousin, and then I'm so fond of syllabubs. Dundreary, do you know what syllabubs are?

Dun: Oh, yeth, I know what syllabubs is—yeth—yeth.

Flo: Why, I don't believe you do know what they are.

Dun: Not know what syllabubs are? That's a good idea. Why they are—syllabubs are—they are only babies, idiotic children; that's a good idea, that's good. [Bumps head against Florence.]

Flo: No, it's not a bit like the idea. What you mean are called cherubims.

Dun: What, those things that look like oranges, with wings on them?

Flo: Not a bit like it. Well, after luncheon you must go with me and I'll introduce you to my cousin Mary and syllabubs.

Dun: I never saw Mr. Syllabubs, I am sure.

Flo: Well, now, don't forget.

Dun: I never can forget—when I can recollect.

Flo: Then recollect that you have an appointment with me after luncheon.

Dun: Yeth, yeth.

Flo: Well, what have you after luncheon?

Dun: Well, sometimes I have a glass of brandy with an egg in it, sometimes a run 'round the duck-pond, sometimes a game of checkers—that's for exercise, and perhaps a game of billiards.

Flo: No, no; you have with me after luncheon, an ap—an ap—

Dun: An ap— an ap—

Flo: An ap—an appoint—appointment.

Dun: An ointment, that's the idea. [Knocks against De Boots as they go up stage.]

Mrs M: [Aside.] That artful girl has designs upon Lord Dundreary. Augusta, dear, go and see how your poor, dear sister is this morning.

Aug: Yes, mamma. [Exit, L. 1 E.]

Mrs M: She is a great sufferer, my dear.

Dun: Yeth, but a lonely one.

Flo: What sort of a night had she?

Mrs M: Oh, a very refreshing one, thanks to the draught you were kind enough to prescribe for her, Lord Dundreary.

Flo: What! Has Lord Dundreary been prescribing for Georgina?

Dun: Yeth. You see I gave her a draught that cured the effect of the draught, and that draught was a draft that didn't pay the doctor's bill. Didn't that draught—

Flo: Good gracious! what a number of draughts. You have almost a game of draughts.

Dun: Ha! ha! ha!

Flo: What's the matter?

Dun: That wath a joke, that wath.

Flo: Where's the joke? [Dundreary screams and turns to Mrs. M.]

Mrs M: No.

Dun: She don't see it. Don't you see—a game of drafts—pieces of wound wood on square pieces of leather. That's the idea. Now, I want to put your brains to the test. I want to ask you a whime.

Flo: A whime, what's that?

Dun: A whime is a widdle, you know.

Flo: A widdle!

Dun: Yeth; one of those things, like—why is so and so or somebody like somebody else.

Flo: Oh, I see, you mean a conundrum.

Dun: Yeth, a drum, that's the idea. What is it gives a cold in the head, cures a cold, pays the doctor's bill and makes the homeguard look for substitutes? [Florence repeats it.] Yeth, do you give it up?

Flo: Yes.

Dun: Well, I'll tell you—a draught. Now I've got a better one that that: When is a dog's tail not a dog's tail? [Florence repeats. During this Florence, Mrs. M. and Dundreary are down stage.]

Flo: Yes, and willingly.

Dun: When it's a cart. [They look at him enquiringly.]

Flo: Why, what in earth has a dog's tail to do with a cart?

Dun: When it moves about, you know. A horse makes a cart move, so does a dog make his tail move.

Flo: Oh, I see what you mean—when it's a wagon. [Wags the letter in her hand.]

Dun: Well, a wagon and a cart are the same thing, ain't they! That's the idea—it's the same thing.

Flo: They are not the same. In the case of your conundrum there's a very great difference.

Dun: Now I've got another. Why does a dog waggle his tail?

Flo: Upon my word, I never inquired.

Dun: Because the tail can't waggle the dog. Ha! Ha!

Flo: Ha! ha! Is that your own, Dundreary?

Dun: Now I've got one, and this one is original.

Flo: No, no, don't spoil the last one.

Dun: Yeth; but this is extremely interesting.

Mrs M: Do you think so, Lord Dundreary?

Dun: Yeth. Miss Georgina likes me to tell her my jokes. Bye-the-bye, talking of that lonely sufferer, isn't she an interesting invalid? They do say that's what's the matter with me. I'm an interesting invalid.

Flo: Oh, that accounts for what I have heard so many young ladies say—Florence, dear, don't you think Lord Dundreary's extremely interesting? I never knew what they meant before.

Dun: Yeth, the doctor recommends me to drink donkey's milk.

Flo: [Hiding laugh.] Oh, what a clever man he must be. He knows we enerally thrive best on our native food. [Goes up.]

Dun: [Looking first at Florence and then at Mrs M.] I'm so weak, and that is so strong. Yes, I'm naturally very weak, and I want strengthening. Yes, I guess I'll try it.

> *Enter Augusta. Bus. with Dundreary, who finally exits and brings on Georgina, L. 1 E.*

Dun: Look at this lonely sufferer. [Bringing on Georgina, seats her on sofa, L.] There, repothe yourself.

Geo: [Fanning herself] Thank you, my lord. Everybody is kind to me, and I am so delicate.

Aug: [At table.] Capt. De Boots, do help to unravel these wools for me, you have such an eye for color.

Flo: An eye for color! Yes, especially green.

Dun: [Screams.] Ha! ha! ha!

All: What's the matter?

Dun: Why, that wath a joke, that wath.

Flo: Where was the joke?

Dun: Especially, ha! ha!

Sir E: Florence, dear, I must leave you to represent me to my guests. These letters will give me a great deal of business to-day.

Flo: Well, papa, remember I am your little clerk and person of all work.

Sir E: No, no; this is private business—money matters, my love, which women know nothing about. [Aside.] Luckily for them, I expect Mr. Coyle to-day.

Flo: Dear papa, how I wish you would get another agent.

Sir E: Nonsense, Florence, impossible. He knows my affairs. His father was agent for the late Baronet. He's one of the family, almost.

Flo: Papa, I have implicit faith in my own judgement of faces. Depend upon it, that man is not to be trusted.

Sir E: Florence, you are ridiculous. I could not get on a week without him. [Aside.] Curse him, I wish I could! Coyle is a most intelligent agent, and a most faithful servant of the family.

Enter Binny, L. 3 E.

Binny: Mr. Coyle and hagent with papers.

Sir E: Show him into the library. I will be with him presently. [Exit Binny.]

Flo: Remember the archery meeting, papa. It is at three.

Sir E: Yes, yes, I'll remember. [Aside.] Pretty time for such levity when ruin stares me in the face. Florence, I leave you as my representative. [Aside.] Now to prepare myself to meet my Shylock. [Exit, R. 1 E.]

Flo: Why will papa not trust me? [Vernon comes down, R.] Oh, Harry! I wish he would find out what a lot of pluck and common sense there is in this feather head of mine.

Dun: Miss Florence, will you be kind enough to tell Miss Georgina all about that American relative of yours.

Flo: Oh, about my American cousin; certainly. [Aside to Harry.] Let's have some fun. Well, he's about 17 feet high!

Dun: Good gracious! 17 feet high!

Flo: They are all 17 feet high in America, ain't they, Mr. Vernon?

Ver: Yes, that's about the average height.

Flo: And they have long black hair that reaches down to their heels; they have dark copper-colored skin, and they fight with—What do they fight with, Mr. Vernon?

Ver: Tomahawks and scalping knives.

Flo: Yes; and you'd better take care, Miss Georgina, or he'll take his tomahawk and scalping knife and scalp you immediately. [Georgina screams and faints.]

Dun: Here, somebody get something and throw

over her; a pail of water; no, not that, she's pale enough already. [Fans her with handkerchief.] Georgina, don't be afraid. Dundreary's by your side, he will protect you.

Flo: Don't be frightened, Georgina. He will never harm you while Dundreary is about. Why, he could get three scalps here. [Pulls Dundreary's whiskers. Georgina screams.]

Dun: Don't scream, I won't lose my whiskers. I know what I'll do for my own safety. I will take this handkerchief and tie the roof of my head on. [Ties it on.]

Flo: [Pretending to cry.] Good bye, Dundreary. I'll never see you again in all your glory.

Dun: Don't cry, Miss Florence, I'm ready for Mr. Tommy Hawk.

   Enter Binny.

Binny: If you please, Miss, 'ere's a gent what says he's hexpected.

Flo: What's his name? Where's his card?

Binny: He didn't tell me his name, Miss, and when I haxed him for his card 'e said 'e had a whole pack in his valise, and if I 'ad a mine 'e'd play me a game of seven hup. He says he has come to stay, and he certainly looks as if he didn't mean to go.

Flo: That's him. Show him in, Mr. Binny. [Exit Binny, L. 3 E.] That's my American cousin, I know.

Aug: [Romantically.] Your American cousin. Oh, how delightfully romantic, isn't it, Capt. De Boots? [Comes down.] I can imagine the wild young hunter, with the free step and majestic mien of the hunter of the forest.

Asa: [Outside, L. 3 E.] Consarn your picture, didn't I tell you I was expected? You are as obstinate as Deacon Stumps' forelock, that wouldn't lie down and couldn't stand up. Would't pint forward and couldn't go backward.

Enter Asa, L. 3 E., carrying a valise.

Asa: Where's the Squire?

Flo: Do you mean Sir Edward Trenchard, sir?

Asa: Yes.

Flo: He is not present, but I am his daughter.

Asa: Well, I guess that'll fit about as well if you tell this darned old shoat to take me to my room.

Flo: What does he mean by shoat?

Binny: [Taking valise.] He means me, mum; but what he wants—

Asa: Hurry up, old hoss!

Binny: He calls me a 'oss, Miss, I suppose I shall be a hox next, or perhaps an 'ogg.

Asa: Wal, darn me if you ain't the consarnedest old shoat I ever did see since I was baptized Asa Trenchard.

Flo: Ah! then it is our American cousin. Glad to see you—my brother told us to expect you.

Asa: Wal, yes, I guess you do b'long to my family. I'm Asa Trenchard, born in Vermont, suckled on the banks of Muddy Creek, about the tallest gunner, the slickest dancer, and generally the loudest critter in the state. You're my cousin, be you? Wal, I ain't got no objections to kiss you, as one cousin ought to kiss another.

Ver: Sir, how dare you?

Asa: Are you one of the family? Cause if you ain't, you've got no right to interfere, and if you be, you needn't be alarmed, I ain't going to kiss you. Here's your young man's letter. [Gives letter and attempts to kiss her.]

Flo: In the old country, Mr. Trenchard, cousins content themselves with hands, but our hearts are with them. You are welcome, there is mine. [Gives her hand, which he shakes heartily.]

Asa: That'll do about as well. I won't kiss you if you don't want me to; but if you did, I wouldn't stop on account of that sailor man. [Business of Vernon threatening Asa.] Oh! now you needn't get your back up. What an all-fired chap you are. Now if you'll have me shown to my room, I should like to fix up a bit and put on a clean buzzom. [All start.] Why, what on earth is the matter with you all? I only spoke because you're so all-fired go-to-meeting like.

Flo: Show Mr. Trenchard to the red room, Mr. Binny, that is if you are done with it, Mr. Dundreary.

Dun: Yeth, Miss Florence. The room and I have got through with each other, yeth.

    [Asa and Dundreary see each other for the first time. Business of recognition, ad. lib.]

Asa: Concentrated essence of baboons, what on earth is that?

Dun: He's mad. Yes, Miss Florence, I've done with that room. The rooks crowed so that they racked my brain.

Asa: You don't mean to say that you've got any brains.

Dun: No, sir, such a thing never entered my head. The wed indians want to scalp me. [Holding hands to his head.]

Flo: The red room, then, Mr. Binny.

Asa: [To Binny.] Hold on! [Examines him.] Wal, darn me, but you keep your help in all-fired good order here. [Feels of him.] This old shoat is fat enough to kill. [Hits Binny in stomach. Binny runs off, L. 2 E.] Mind how you go up stairs, old hoss, or you'll bust your biler. [Exit, L. 3 E.]

Dun: Now he thinks Binny's an engine and has got a boiler.

Flo: Oh, what fun!

Mrs M: Old Mark Trenchard died very rich, did he not, Florence?

Flo: Very rich, I believe.

Aug: He's not at all romantic, is he, mamma?

Mrs M: [Aside to her] My dear, I have no doubt he has solid good qualities, and I don't want you to laugh at him like Florence Trenchard.

Aug: No, mamma, I won't.

Flo: But what are we to do with him?

Dun: Ha! Ha! ha!

All: What is the matter?

Dun: I've got an idea.

Flo: Oh! let's hear Dundreary's idea.

Dun: It's so seldom I get an idea that when I do get one it startles me. Let us get a pickle bottle.

Flo: Pickle bottle! [All come down.]

Dun: Yeth; one of those things with glass sides.

   Enter Asa, L. 2 E.

Flo: Oh! you mean a glass case.

Dun: Yeth, a glass case, that's the idea, and let us put this Mr. Thomas Hawk in it, and have him on exhibition. That's the idea.

Asa: [Down L. of Florence, overhearing.] Oh! that's your idea, is it? Wal, stranger, I don't know what they're going to do with me, but wherever they do put me, I hope it will be out of the reach of a jackass. I'm a real hoss, I am, and I get kinder riley with those critters.

Dun: Now he thinks he's a horse. I've heard of a great jackass, and I dreampt of a jackass, but I don't believe there is any such insect.

Flo: Well, cousin, I hope you made yourself comfortable.

Asa: Well, no, I can't say as I did. You see there was so many all-fired fixins in my room I couldn't find anything I wanted.

Flo: What was it you couldn't find in your room?

Asa: There as no soft soap.

De B: Soft soap!

Aug: Soft soap!

Ver: Soft soap!

Mrs M: Soft soap!

Flo: Soft soap!

Geo: [On sofa.] Soft soap!

Dun: Thoft thoap?

Asa: Yes, soft soap. I reckon you know what that is. However, I struck a pump in the kitchen, slicked my hair down a little, gave my boots a lick of grease, and now I feel quite handsome; but I'm everlastingly dry.

Flo: You'll find ale, wine and luncheon on the side-table.

Asa: Wal, I don't know as I've got any appetite. You see comin' along on the cars I worried down half a dozen ham sandwiches, eight or ten boiled eggs, two or three pumpkin pies and a string of cold sausages—and—Wal, I guess I can hold on till dinner-time.

Dun: Did that illustrious exile eat all that? I wonder where he put it?

Asa: I'm as dry as a sap-tree in August.

Binny: [Throwing open, E. D.] Luncheon!

Asa: [Goes hastily up to table.] Wal, I don't want to speak out too plain, but this is an awful mean set out for a big house like this.

Flo: Why, what's wrong, sir?

Asa: Why, there's no mush!

Dun: No mush?

Asa: Nary slapjack.

Dun: Why, does he want Mary to slap Jack?

Asa: No pork and beans!

Dun: Pork's been here, but he's left.

Asa: And where on airth's the clam chowder?

Dun: Where _is_ clam chowder? He's never here when he's wanted.

Asa: [Drinks and spits.] Here's your health, old hoss. Do you call that a drink? See here, cousin, you seem to be the liveliest critter here, so just hurry up the fixins, and I'll show this benighted aristocratic society what real liquor is. So hurry up the fixins.

All: Fixins?

Flo: What do you mean by fixins?

Asa: Why, brandy, rum, gin and whiskey. We'll make them all useful.

Flo: Oh, I'll hurry up the fixins. What fun! [Exit, R.]

Dun: Oh! I thought he meant the gas fixins.

Asa: Say, you, you Mr. Puffy, you run out and get me a bunch of mint and a bundle of straws; hurry up, old hoss. [Exit Binny, L. 3 E., indignantly.] Say, Mr. Sailor man, just help me down with this table. Oh! don't you get riley, you and I ran against each other when I came in, but we'll be friends yet. [Vernon helps him with table to C.]

Enter Florence, followed by servants in livery; they carry a case of decanters and water, on which are seven or eight glasses, two or three tin mixers and a bowl of sugar. Binny enters with a bunch of mint and a few straws.

Flo: Here, cousin, are the fixins.

Asa: That's yer sort. Now then, I'll give you all a drink that'll make you squeal. [To Binny] Here, Puffy, just shake that up, faster. I'll give that sick gal a drink that'll make her squirm like an eel on a mud bank.

Dun: [Screams.] What a horrible idea. [Runs about stage.]

Flo: Oh, don't mind him! That's only an American joke.

Dun: A joke! Do you call that a joke? To make a sick girl squirm like a mud bank on an eel's skin?

Asa: Yes, I'll give you a drink that'll make your whiskers return under your chin, which is their natural location. Now, ladies and gentlemen, what'll you have, Whiskey Skin, Brandy Smash, Sherry Cobbler, Mint Julep or Jersey Lightning?

Aug: Oh, I want a Mint Julep.

De B: Give me a Gin Cocktail.

Flo: I'll take a Sherry Cobbler.

Ver: Brandy Smash for me.

Mrs M: Give me a Whiskey Skin.

Geo: I'll take a Lemonade.

Dun: Give me a Jersey Lightning.

Asa: Give him a Jersey Lightning. [As Dundreary drinks] Warranted to kill at forty rods. [Dundreary falls back on Mrs. M. and Georgina.]

Closed In.

SCENE 2

Library in Trenchard Manor. Oriel Window, L. C., with curtains. Two chairs and table brought on at change.

Enter Binny and Coyle, L. 1 E.

Binny: Sir Hedward will see you directly, Mr. Coyle.

Coyle: Very well. House full of company, I see, Mr. Binny.

Binny: Cram full, Mr. Coyle. As one of the first families in the country we must keep up our position.

Coyle: [Rubbing his hands.] Certainly, certainly, that is as long as we can, Mr. Binny. Tell Murcott, my clerk, to bring my papers in here. You'll find him in the servant's hall, and see that you keep your strong ale out of his way. People who serve me must have their senses about them.

Binny: [Aside.] I should say so, or 'e'd 'ave hevery tooth hout in their 'eds, the wiper. [Exit, L. 1 E.]

Coyle: And now to show this pompous baronet the precipice on which he stands.

Enter Murcott, with green bag and papers.

Coyle: Are you sober, sirrah?

Murcott: Yes, Mr. Coyle.

Coyle: Then see you keep so.

Mur: I'll do my best, sir. But, oh! do tell them to keep liquor out of my way. I can't keep from it now, try as I will, and I try hard enough, God help me!

Coyle: Pshaw! Get out those mortgages and the letters from my London agent. [Murcott takes papers from bag and places then on table. Coyle looks off, R. 1 E.] So; here comes Sir Edward. Go, but be within call. I may want you to witness a signature.

Mur: I will sir. [Aside.] I must have brandy, or my hand will not be steady enough to write. [Exit, L. 1 E.]

Enter Sir Edward, R. 1 E. Coyle bows.

Sir E: Good morning, Coyle, good morning. [With affected ease.] There is a chair, Coyle. [They sit.] So you see those infernal tradespeople are pretty troublesome.

Coyle: My agent's letter this morning announces that Walter and Brass have got judgement and execution on their amount for repairing your town house last season. [Refers to papers.] Boquet and Barker announce their intention of taking this same course with the wine account. Handmarth is preparing for a settlement of his heavy demand for the stables. Then there is Temper for pictures and other things and Miss Florence Trenchard's account with Madame Pompon, and—

Sir E: Confound it, why harass me with details, these infernal particulars? Have you made out the total?

Coyle: Four thousand, eight hundred and thirty pounds, nine shillings and sixpence.

Sir E: Well, of course we must find means of settling this extortion.

Coyle: Yes, Sir Edward, if possible.

Sir E: If possible?

Coyle: I, as your agent, must stoop to detail, you must allow me to repeat, if possible.

Sir E: Why, you don't say there will be any difficulty in raising the money?

Coyle: What means would you suggest, Sir Edward.

Sir E: That, sir, is your business.

Coyle: A foretaste in the interest on the Fanhille & Ellenthrope mortgages, you are aware both are in the arrears, the mortgagees in fact, write here to announce their intentions to foreclose. [Shows papers.]

Sir E: Curse your impudence, pay them off.

Coyle: How, Sir Edward?

Sir E: Confound it, sir, which of us is the agent? Am I to find you brains for your own business?

Coyle: No, Sir Edward, I can furnish the brains, but what I ask of you is to furnish the money.

Sir E: There must be money somewhere, I came into possession of one of the finest properties in Hampshire only twenty-six years ago, and now you mean to tell me I cannot raise 4,000 pounds?

Coyle: The fact is distressing, Sir Edward, but so it is.

Sir E: There's the Ravensdale property unencumbered.

Coyle: There, Sir Edward, you are under a mistake. The Ravensdale property is deeply encumbered, to nearly its full value.

Sir E: [Springing up.] Good heavens.

Coyle: I have found among my father's papers a mortgage of that very property to him.

Sir E: To your father! My father's agent?

Coyle: Yes, bearing date the year after the great contested election for the county, on which the late Sir Edward patriotically spent sixty thousand pounds for the honor of not being returned to Parliament.

Sir E: A mortgage on the Ravensdale estate. But it must have been paid off, Mr. Coyle, [anxiously,] have you looked for the release or the receipt?

Coyle: Neither exists. My father's sudden death explains sufficiently. I was left in ignorance of the transaction, but the seals on the deed and the stamps are intact, here it is, sir. [Shows it.]

Sir E: Sir, do you know that if this be true I am something like a beggar, and your father something like a thief.

Coyle: I see the first plainly, Sir Edward, but not the second.

Sir E: Do you forget sir, that your father was a charity boy, fed, clothed by my father?

Coyle: Well, Sir Edward?

Sir E: And do you mean to tell me, sir, that your father repaid that kindness by robbing his benefactor?

Coyle: Certainly not, but by advancing money to that benefactor when he wanted it, and by taking the security of one of his benefactor's estates, as any prudent man would under the circumstances.

Sir E: Why, then, sir, the benefactor's property is yours.

Coyle: Pardon me, the legal estate you have your equity of redemption. You have only to pay the money and the estate is yours as before.

Sir E: How dare you, sir, when you have just shown me that I cannot raise five hundred pounds in the world. Oh! Florence, why did I not listen to you when you warned me against this man?

Coyle: [Aside.] Oh! she warned you, did she? [Aloud.] I see one means, at least, of keeping the Ravensdale estate in the family.

Sir E: What is it?

Coyle: By marrying your daughter to the mortgagee.

Sir E: To you?

Coyle: I am prepared to settle the estate on Miss Trenchard the day she becomes Mrs. Richard Coyle.

Sir E: [Springing up.] You insolent scoundrel, how dare you insult me in my own house, sir. Leave it, sir, or I will have you kicked out by my servants.

Coyle: I never take an angry man at his word,

Sir Edward. Give a few moments reflection to my offer, you can have me kicked out afterwards.

Sir E: [Pacing stage.] A beggar, Sir Edward Trenchard a beggar, see my children reduced to labor for their bread, to misery perhaps; but the alternative, Florence detests him, still the match would save her, at least, from ruin. He might take the family name, I might retrench, retire, to the continent for a few years. Florence's health might serve as a pretence. Repugnant as the alternative is, yet it deserves consideration.

Coyle: [Who has watched.] Now, Sir Edward, shall I ring for the servants to kick me out?

Sir E: Nay Mr. Coyle, you must pardon my outburst, you know I am hasty, and——

Flo: [Without.] Papa, dear! [Enters gaily, starts on seeing Coyle.] Papa, pardon my breaking in on business, but our American cousin has come, such an original—and we are only waiting for you to escort us to the field.

Sir E: I will come directly, my love. Mr. Coyle, my dear, you did not see him.

Flo: [Disdainfully.] Oh! yes, I saw him, papa.

Sir E: Nay, Florence, your hand to Mr. Coyle. [Aside.] I insist.

Flo: Papa. [Frightened at his look, gives her hand. Coyle attempts to kiss it, she snatches it away and crosses to L.]

Sir E: [Crosses to L.] Come, Florence. Mr. Coyle, we will join you in the park. Come, my love, take my arm. [Hurries her off, L. 1 E.]

Coyle: Shallow, selfish fool. She warned you of me did she? And you did not heed her; you shall both pay dearly. She, for her suspicions, and you that you did not share them. [Walks up and down.] How lucky the seals were not cut from that mortgage, when the release was given. 'Tis like the silly security of the Trenchard's. This mortgage makes Ravensdale mine, while the release that restores it to its owner lies in the recess of the bureau, whose secret my father revealed to me on his death bed. [Enter Murcott, L. 1 E.] Write to the mortgagee of the Fanhill and Ellenthrope estates, to foreclose before the week is out, and tell Walters and Brass to put in execution to-day. We'll prick this wind-bag of a Baronet. Abel, we have both a bone to pick with him and his daughter. [Murcott starts.] Why, what's the matter?

Mur: Nothing, the dizziness I've had lately.

Coyle: Brandy in the evening, brandy in the morning, brandy all night. What a fool you are, Murcott.

Mur: Who knows that as well as I do?

Coyle: If you would but keep the money out of your mouth, there's the making of a man in you yet.

Mur: No, no, it's gone too far, it's gone too far, thanks to the man who owns this house, you know all about it. How he found me a thriving, sober lad, flogging the village children through their spelling book. How he took a fancy to me as he called it, and employed me here to teach his son and Miss Florence. [His voice falters.] Then remember how I forgot who and what I was, and was cuffed out of the house like a dog. How I lost my school, my good name, but still hung about

the place, they all looked askance at me, you
don't know how that kills the heart of a man,
then I took to drink and sank down, down,
till I came to this.

Coyle: You owe Sir Edward revenge, do you
not? You shall have a rare revenge on him,
that mortgage you found last week puts the
remainder of the property in my reach, and I
close my hand on it unless he will consent to
my terms.

Mur: You can drive a hard bargain. I know.

Coyle: And a rare price I ask for his for-
bearance, Abel—his daughter's hand.

Mur: Florence?

Coyle: Yes, Florence marries Richard Coyle.
Richard Coyle steps into Sir Edward's es-
tates. There, you dog, will not that be a
rare revenge. So follow me with those papers.
[Crosses to L.] And now to lay the mine that
will topple over the pride of the Trenchards.
[Exit L. 1 E.]

Mur: He marry Florence! Florence Trenchard!
My Florence. Mine! Florence _his wife_. No,
no, better a thousand times she had been
mine, low as I am, when I dreampt that dream,
but it shan't be, it shan't be. [Trembling-
ly putting papers in bag.] If I can help her,
sot though I am. Yes, I can help her, if the
shock don't break me down. Oh! my poor mud-
dled brain, surely there was a release with
it when I found it. I must see Florence to
warn her and expose Coyle's villainy. Oh! how
my poor head throbs when I try to. I shall
die if I don't have a drop of brandy, yes
brandy. [Exit, L. 1 E.]

SCENE 3

*Chamber in 3. at Trenchard Manor. Large
shower bath near R. 3 E. Toilet table
with draw, L. 2 E. Small bottle in draw
with red sealing wax on cork. Asa dis-
covered seated, R. with foot on table,
smoking a cigar. Valise on floor in front
of him. Binny discovered standing by his
side.*

Asa: Wal, I guess I begin to feel kinder com-
fortable here in this place, if it wan't for
this tarnal fat critter. He don't seem to
have any work to do, but swells out his big
bosom like an old turkey-cock in laying time.
I do wonder what he's here for? Do they think
I mean to absquatulate with the spoons? [Bin-
ny attempts to take valise—Asa puts his foot
on it.] Let that sweat. That's my plunder.

Binny: Will you have the kindness to give me
your keys, hif you please, sir?

Asa: What do you want with my keys?

Bin: To put your things away in the wardrobe,
sir.

Asa: Wal, I calculate if my two shirts, three
bosoms, four collars, and two pair of socks
were to get into that everlasting big bunk,
they'd think themselves so all-fired small
I should never be able to crawl into them
again.

Bin: Will you take a baath before you dress?

Asa: Take a baath?

Bin: A baath.

Asa: I suppose you mean a bath. Wal, man, I calkalate I ain't going to expose myself to the shakes by getting into cold water in this cruel cold climate of yours, so make tracks.

Bin: Make what?

Asa: Vamose!

Bin: Make vamose!

Asa: Absquatulate.

Bin: Ab— what sir?

Asa: Skedaddle.

Bin: Skedaddle?

Asa: Oh! get out.

Bin: Oh! [Going.] If you are going to dress you'll want some hassistance.

Asa: Assistance! what to get out of my unmentionables and into them again? Wal, 'spose I do, what then?

Bin: Just ring the bell, hi'll hattend you.

Asa: All right, come along. [Binny going.] Hold on, say, I may want to yawn presently and I shall want somebody to shut my mouth. [Binny hurries off, L. 1 E.] Wal, now I am alone, I can look about me and indulge the enquiring spirit of an American citizen. What an everlasting lot of things and fixins there is to be sure. [Opens table draw.] Here's a place will hold my plunder beautifully. [Sees bottle.] Hallo, what's this? [Comes down.] Something good to drink. [Smells bottle.] It smells awful bad. [Reads label.] Golden Fluid, one application turns the hair a beautiful brown, several applications will turn the hair a lustrous black. Well, if they keep on it may turn a pea green. I reckon this has been left here by some fellow who is ashamed of the natural color of his top knot. [Knock.] Come in.

Enter Binny, L. 1 E.

Bin: Mr. Buddicombe, sir, my lord's hown man.

Asa: Roll him in. [Binny beckons, enter Buddicombe.] Turkey cock number two, what is it?

Bud: My Lord Dundreary's compliments and _have_ you seen a small _bottle_ in the toilet table drawer?

Asa: Suppose I had, what then?

Bud: My lord wants it particly.

Asa: Was it a small bottle?

Bud: A small bottle.

Bin: Bottle small.

Asa: Blue label?

Bin: Label blue.

Asa: Red sealing wax on the top?

Bud: Red sealing wax.

Bin: Wax red.

Asa: Nice little bottle?

Bin: Little bottle nice.

Asa: Wal, I ain't seen it. [Aside.] If my lord sets a valley on it, guess it must be worth something.

Bud: Sorry to trouble you, sir.

Bin: [Aside to Bud.] What his hit?

Bud: My lord's hair dye, the last bottle, and he turns red tomorrow. [Exit in haste.]

Bin: Orrable, what an hawful situation, to be sure.

Asa: [Aside.] So I've got my ring on that lord's nose, and if I don't make him dance to my tune it's a pity.

Bin: Miss Florence begged me to say she had borrowed a costume for you, for the harchery meeting, sir.

Asa: Hain't you dropped something?

Bin: Where?

Asa: What do you mean by the harchery meeting?

Bin: Where they shoot with bows and harrows.

Asa: There goes another of them, oh! you need'nt look for them, you can't find 'em when you want 'em. Now you just take my compliments to Miss Trenchard when I goes out shooting with injurious weapons I always wears my own genuine shooting costume. That's the natural buff tipped off with a little red paint.

Bin: Good gracious, he'd look like Hadam and Heve, in the garden of Eden. [Exit Binny.]

Asa: Wal, there's a queer lot of fixings. [Sees shower bath.] What on airth is that? Looks like a 'skeeter net, only it 'ain't long enough for a feller to lay down in unless he was to coil himself up like a woodchuck in a knot hole. I'd just like to know what the all-fired thing is meant for. [Calls.] Say Puffy, Puffy, Oh! he told me if I wanted him to ring the bell. [Looks round

room.] Where on airth is the bell? [Slips
partly inside shower bath, pulls rope, water
comes down.] Murder! help! fire! Water! I'm
drown.

*Enter Skillet, Sharpe, R. 1 E. Bin-
ny, Buddicombe, L. 1 E., seeing Asa,
all laugh, and keep it up till curtain
falls.*

CURTAIN.

Act II

SCENE 1

Oriel Chamber in one.

*Enter Mrs. Mountchessington and Augusta,
L. 1 E., dressed for Archery Meeting.*

Mrs M: No, my dear Augusta, you must be very careful. I don't by any means want you to give up De Boots, his expectations are excellent, but, pray be attentive to this American savage, as I rather think he will prove the better match of the two, if what I hear of Mark Trenchard's property be correct.

Aug: [Disdainfully.] Yes, ma.

Mrs M: And look more cheerful, my love.

Aug: I am so tired, ma, of admiring things I hate.

Mrs. M: Yes, my poor love, yet we must all make sacrifices to society. Look at your poor sister, with the appetite.

Aug: What am I to be enthusiastic about with that American, Ma?

Mrs M: Oh! I hardly know yet, my dear. We must study him. I think if you read up Sam Slick a little, it might be useful, and just dip into Bancroft's History of the United States, or some of Russell's Letters; you should know something of George Washington, of whom the Americans are justly proud.

Aug: Here he comes, ma. What a ridiculous figure he looks in that dress, ha! ha!

Mrs M: Hush, my dear!

Enter Asa, in Archery Dress.

Aug: Oh, Mr. Trenchard, why did you not bring me one of those lovely Indian's dresses of your boundless prairie?

Mrs M: Yes, one of those dresses in which you hunt the buffalo.

Aug: [Extravagantly.] Yes, in which you hunt the buffalo.

Asa: [Imitating.] In which I hunt the buffalo. [Aside.] Buffaloes down in Vermont. [Aloud.] Wal, you see, them dresses are principally the nateral skin, tipped off with paint, and the indians object to parting with them.

Both: Ahem! ahem!

Asa: The first buffalo I see about here I shall hunt up for you.

Mrs M: Oh, you Americans are so clever, and so acute.

Aug: Yes, so 'cute.

Asa: Yes, we're 'cute, we are; know soft solder when we see it.

Aug: [Aside.] Ma, I do believe he's laughing at us.

Mrs M: Oh, no, my dear, you are mistaken. Oh! I perceive they are appearing for the archery practice. I suppose we shall see you on the ground, Mr. Trenchard.

Asa: Yes, I'll be there like a thousand of brick.

Aug: A thousand of brick!

Mrs M: Hush, my dear! that is doubtless some elegant American expression. Au revoir, Mr. Trenchard.

Asa: Which?

Mrs M: Au revoir. [Exit with Augusta, R.]

Asa: No, thank you, don't take any before dinner. No use their talking Dutch to me. Wal, I never see an old gal stand fire like that, she's a real old bison bull. I feel all-fired tuckered out riding in those keers. I'd like to have a snooze if I could find a place to lay down in. [Sees curtain on window, L. E.] Oh, this might do! [Pulls curtain, then starts back.] No you don't! One shower bath a day is enough for me. [Cautiously opens them.] No, I guess this is all right, I shall be just as snug in here as in a pew at meeting, or a private box at the Theatre. Hello! somebody's coming. [Goes into recess.]

Enter Dundreary and Buddicombe, L. 1 E.

Bud: My lord—

Dun: [Business.]

Bud: My lord!

Dun: [Business.]

Bud: Your lordship!! [Louder.]

Dun: There, now you've spoiled it.

Bud: Spoiled what, my lord?

Dun: Spoiled what, my lord; why, a most magnificent sneeze!

Bud: I am very sorry, my lord.

Dun: Now that I can speak alone with you, tell me about that hair dye. Have you found it?

Bud: Not a trace of it, my lord.

Dun: If you don't find it, I'll discharge you.

Bud: Very well, my lord. [Bows and exits, L. 1 E.]

Dun: Very well, my lord! He's gone and lost my hair dye, and my hair turns red to-morrow, and when I ask him to find it for me or I'll discharge him, he says, "Very well, my lord." He's positively idiotic, he is— Ah! here comes Miss Georgina, that gorgeous creature— that lovely sufferer. [Exit, L. 1 E.]

Asa: [Looking out.] What's the price of hair dye? Hallo! he's coming again with that sick girl.

Re-enter Dundreary and Georgina, L. 1 E.

Dun: Will you try and strengthen your limbs with a gentle walk in the garden?

Georgina: No, thank you, my lord. I'm so delicate. Oh, my lord, it is so painful to walk languidly through life, to be unable, at times, to bear the perfumes of one's favorite flowers. Even those violets you sent me yesterday I was compelled to have removed from my room, the perfume was too strong for me. I'm _so_ delicate.

Dun: Yes, Miss Georgina; but they're very strengthening flowers, you know.

Geo: Yes, my lord, you are always right.

Dun: Do you know I'm getting to be very robust?

Geo: Would I could share that fault with you; but I am so delicate.

Dun: If you were robust I should not love you as I do. It would deprive you of that charm which enchains me to your lovely side, which—which—

Geo: Oh, my lord, my lord! I'm going to faint.

Dun: And I'm going to sneeze, you faint while I sneeze.

Geo: [Taking his arm.] Oh! my lord.

Dun: Do you know what a sneeze is?

Geo: No, my lord.

Dun: She never sneezed. I'll tell you what a sneeze is. Imagine a very large spider.

Geo: [Screams.] Where, my lord?

Dun: No, no, I don't mean a real spider, only an imaginary one, a large spider getting up your nose, and all of a sudden, much to his disgust, he discovers he has put his foot in it and can't get it out again.

Geo: That must be very distressing.

Dun: For the spider, yes, and not very pleasant for the nose.

Geo: Oh! my lord, do take me to mamma.

Dun: No, you lovely sufferer, let's walk a little more.

Geo: I can't my lord, I'm _so_ delicate.

Dun: Well, then, exercise, imitate that little hop of mine. [Hops.] It isn't a run, it's a—

Geo: What is it?

Dun: No, it isn't a what is it. Well, let me suppose I get you an oyster. [Georgina shakes her head.] Oh! then suppose I get you an oyster.

Geo: No, my lord, I'm too delicate.

Dun: How would you like the left wing of a canary bird?

Geo: No, my lord, it's too strong for me.

Dun: Let me ask you a widdle—why does a duck go under water? for divers reasons. Now I'll give you another—why does a duck come out of the water? for sundry reasons. No! No! see, you live on suction, you're like that bird with a long bill, they call doctor, no, that's not it, I thought it was a doctor, because it has a long bill—I mean a snipe—yes, you're a lovely snipe. [Exeunt, R.]

Asa: [Looking after them.] There goes a load of wooden nutmegs. Hello, here comes somebody else.

Enter Florence, R., with paper.

Flo: [Reads.] "One who still remembers what he ought long since to have forgotten, wishes to speak with Miss Trenchard." Florence scratched out, "on matters of life and death, near the orel, in the west gallery," Written upon a dirty sheet of paper, in a hardly legible hand. What does this mean; it opens like one of Mrs. Radcliffe's romances. Well, here I am, and now for my correspondent.

Enter Murcott, L.

Mur: Oh! for one minute's clear head, Miss Florence.

Flo: I presume you are the writer of this?

Mur: Yes, I am.

Flo: You address me as an old acquaintance, but I do not recognize you.

Mur: So much the better. So much the better.

Flo: I hate mystery, sir; but you see I have come to rendezvous. I must know to whom I am speaking.

Mur: As frank as ever. I am Abel Murcott.

Flo: Starting back! You?

Mur: Do not be ashamed, I have not the strength to injure you, if I had the evil. In this shabby, broken down drunkard you need not fear the madman, who years ago forgot in his frantic passion the gulf that lay between your station and his own. I am harmless except to my self.

Flo: Speak on, sir; I hear you.

Mur: I need not tell you by what steps I came to this, you don't know, maybe you never knew, what a maddening thing a passion is when it turns against itself. After being expelled from my tutorship in this house, I lost my employment, self respect, hope. I sought to drown recollection and draw courage from drink. It only embittered remembrances, and destroyed the little courage I had left. That I have bread to eat, I owe to Mr. Coyle; he employed me as his clerk. You know he has been with your father this morning. I have come to tell you my errand; are you as brave as you used to be when I knew—

Flo: I fear nothing.

Mur: I come to tell you of your father's ruin, his utter ruin.

Flo: My father's ruin? What? What?

Mur: His estates are mortgaged, his creditors clamorous. The Bailiffs will be in Trenchard Manor to-day, disguised as your own servants. This much Mr. Coyle has conceded to your father's respect for appearances.

Flo: Then beggary stares him in the face. Poor father, what a sad blow for him. Is that all, sir?

Mur: No; the worst remains.

Flo: Go on, sir.

Mur: Coyle knows your father's weakness and as a means of escape from ruin to the verge of which he has brought him, he has this day proposed for your hand.

Flo: Mine!

Mur: On consideration of settling on you the Ravensdale Estate.

Flo: And my father, how did he listen to such insolence?

Mur: You know as well as I do how he would hear such a proposal, at first a torrent of rage, then the strong ebb of selfishness set in, and he consented to listen to the terms, to view them as something to be considered, to consider them.

Flo: Good Heavens, can this be true? No, I will not believe it of my father, and from such lips.

Mur: You have full right to think this and to say it, but mark your father and Coyle to-day. You will then see if I speak truth or not.

Flo: Forgive my distrust, Mr. Murcott.

Mur: I am past taking offence or feeling scorn, I have carried more than can be heaped upon me, but I did not come only to give you warning of your danger.

Flo: Can you avert it?

Asa: (Coming down between them). Wal, stranger that's just the question I was going to ask.

Flo: You here, sir, and listening.

Asa: Wal, it wasn't purpose, I went in there to take a snooze, I heard you talking and I thought it wouldn't be polite of me not to listen to what you had to say. I'm a rough sort of a customer, and don't know much about the ways of great folks. But I've got a cool head, a stout arm, and a willing heart, and I think I can help you, just as one cousin ought to help another.

Flo: Well, I do think you are honest.

Mur: Shall I go on?

Flo: Yes, we will trust him, go on.

Mur: I found the Ravensdale mortgage while rumaging in an old deed box of Coyle's father's, there was a folded paper inside the deed. I took both to Coyle unopened, like a besotted fool that I was. My belief is strong that the paper was the release of the mort-gage that the money had been paid off, and the release executed without the seals having been cut from the original mortgage. I have known such things happen.

Asa: Have ye, now? Well, if a Yankee lawyer had done such a thing he would have Judge Lynch after him in no time.

Mur: You can but find that release, we may unmask this diabolical fiend and save you.

Flo: But, surely, a villain of Coyle's stability would have destroyed the paper, the very key-stone of his fraud.

Mur: I fear so.

Asa: Do you, now, wal, you're wrong, you're both wrong. I guess you ain't either on you done much cyphering human nature. The key stone of their fraud is just the point your mighty cute rascals always leave unsecured. Come along with me, stranger, and we'll just work up this sum a little, two heads are better than one. Yours is a little muddled, but mine's pretty clear, and if I don't circumvent that old sarpint, Coyle—

Flo: Well?

Asa: Say I am a skunk, that's all, and that's the meanest kind of an animal. [Exit L. 1st E.]

Flo: I owe you much, Mr. Murcott, more than I can ever repay.

Mur: No, no, no, if you did but know the hope of seeing you has roused all the manhood that drink and misery has left me. God bless you, Miss Florence.

Flo: No, you don't call me Florence as you did when I was the truant pupil and you the indulgent tutor. [Offers her hand.]

Mur: No, no; for heaven's sake do not call back that time or I shall go mad! mad! mad. [Rushes off, L. 1 E., followed by Florence.]

SCENE 2

Park in 4. Rural cottage, L. 1 E., adjoining which, and projecting on stage an inside view of a dairy with sloping roof, painting backing to look like milk pans. The whole scene should have a picturesque appearance. Garden fence run across back, ornamental gate or archway, R. 3 E. Pigeon house on pole near dairy, L. C. Spinning wheel inside cottage door, one or two rustic benches, R. and L.

Enter John, R. 3 E., with two milk pails on a yoke, puts them down near dairy, then looks off, R. 3 E.

John: There they go, that's a bull's eye, I warrant. Dang me though, if I wouldn't rather see Miss Mary than this cock robin sports yonder, here she comes. Good morning, Miss Mary. [Enter Mary from cottage L.]

Mary: Oh, Wickens, you are there. How kind of you to help me with the milk pails to-day, when all the lads and lasses have given themselves a holiday to see the shooting.

John: Ah, Miss Mary, you ought to be among then, with a green hat and feather, if all had their rights.

Mary: [Laughing.] Nay, ladies without a farthing in the world, ought to put aside their ladyships and make themselves: besides I'm proud of my dairy here, just help me with this troublesome fellow, steady, don't shake it, the cream is foaming so beautifully. There. [John carries pan into cottage and returns down, R.]

John: Now, Miss Mary, what can I do for you?

Mary: Let me see; well, really, I do believe, Wickens, I've nothing to do but amuse myself.

John: Dang it, Miss, that's a pity, cos I can't help you at that, you see.

Mary: Oh! Yes, bring me out dear old Welsh nurse's spinning wheel [Exit John into cottage, L. 2 E.] by the side of which I have stood so often, a round eyed baby wondering at its whirring wheel. [Reenter John with wheel, places it near cottage, L. 2 E.] There, that will do famously. I can catch the full scent of the jessamines.

John: [R. C.] Anything more, Miss Mary?

Mary: No, thank you, Wickens!

John: [Going.] Good morning, Miss Mary.

Mary: Good morning, Wickens.

John: [Returning.] Is there anything I can get for you, Miss Mary?

Mary: [Spinning.] Nothing, thank you.

John: Dang me if I wouldn't like to stop all day, and watch her pretty figure and run errands for her. [Exit R. 3 E., crosses behind fence.]

Mary: Poor Wickens is not the only one who

thinks I am a very ill-used young body. Now I don't think so. Grandfather was rich, but he must have had a bad heart, or he never could have cast off poor mamma; had he adopted me, I should never have been so happy as I am now, uncle is kind to me in his pompous, patronizing way, and dear Florence loves me like a sister, and so I am happy. I am my own mistress here, and not anybody's humble servant, I sometimes find myself singing as the birds do, because I can't help it [Song, "Maid with the milking pail," can be introduced here.]

Enter Florence and Asa through gate, R. 3 E.

Flo: Come along, cousin, come along. I want to introduce you to my little cousin. [Kisses Mary.] I've brought you a visitor, Miss Mary Meredith, Mr. Asa Trenchard, our American cousin. [They shake hands.] That will do for the present. This young gentleman has carried off the prize by three successive shots in the bull's eye.

Mary: I congratulate you, sir, and am happy to see you.

Asa: [Shakes hands again.] Thank you, Miss.

Flo: That will do for a beginning.

Asa: [Aside.] And so that is Mark Trenchard's grandchild.

Mary: Why have you left the archery, Florence?

Flo: Because, after Mr. Asa's display, I felt in no humor for shooting, and I have some very grave business with my cousin here.

Mary: You? Grave business? Why I thought you never had any graver business than being very pretty, very amiable, and very ready to be amused.

Asa: Wal, Miss, I guess the first comes natural round these diggins. [Bows.]

Mary: You are very polite. This is my domain, sir, and I shall be happy to show you, that is, if you understand anything about a dairy.

Flo: Yes, by the way, do you understand anything about dairies in America?

Asa: Wal, I guess I do know something about cow juice. [They turn to smother laugh.] Why, if it ain't all as bright and clean as a fresh washed shirt just off the clover, and is this all your doin's, Miss?

Mary: Yes, sir, I milk the cows, set up the milk, superintend the churning and make the cheese.

Asa: Wal, darn me if you ain't the first raal right down useful gal I've seen on this side the pond.

Flo: What's that, sir? Do you want to make me jealous?

Asa: Oh, no, you needn't get your back up, you are the right sort too, but you must own you're small potatoes, and few in a hill compared to a gal like that.

Flo: I'm what?

Asa: Small potatoes.

Flo: Will you be kind enough to translate that for me, for I don't understand American yet.

Asa: Yes, I'll put it in French for you, "petite pommes des terres."

Flo: Ah, it's very clear now; but, cousin, do tell me what you mean by calling me small potatoes.

Asa: Wal, you can sing and paint, and play on the pianner, and in your own particular circle you are some pumpkins.

Flo: Some pumpkins, first I am small potatoes, and now I'm some pumpkins.

Asa: But she, she can milk cows, set up the butter, make cheese, and, darn me, if them ain't what I call raal downright feminine accomplishments.

Flo: I do believe you are right cousin, so Mary do allow me to congratulate you upon not being small potatoes.

Mary: Well, I must look to my dairy or all my last week's milk will be spoiled. Good bye, Florence, dear. Good bye, Mr. Trenchard. Good morning, sir. [Exit into Cottage.]

Asa: [Following her to door.] Good morning, Miss. I'll call again.

Flo: Well, cousin, what do you think of her?

Asa: Ain't she a regular snorter?

Flo: A what?

Asa: Wal, perhaps I should make myself more intelligable, if I said, a squeeler, and to think I'm keepin' that everlasting angel of a gal out of her fortune all along of this bit of paper here.

Flo: What is that? [Takes paper from pocket.]

Asa: Old Mark Trenchard's will.

Flo: Don't show it to me, I don't want to

look at it, the fortune should have come to Mary, she is the only relation in the direct line.

Asa: Say, cousin, you've not told her that darned property was left to me, have you?

Flo: Do you think I had the heart to tell her of her misfortune?

Asa: Wal, darn me, if you didn't show your good sense at any rate. [Goes up to dairy.]

Flo: Well, what are you doing, showing _your_ good sense?

Asa: Oh, you go long.

Flo: Say, cousin, I guess I've got you on a string now, as I heard you say this morning.

Asa: Wal, what if you have, didn't I see you casting sheep's eyes at that sailor man this morning? Ah, I reckon I've got you on a string now. Say, has he got that ship yet?

Flo: No, he hasn't, though I've used all my powers of persuasion with that Lord Dundreary, and his father has so much influence with the admiralty.

Asa: Wal, din't he drop like a smoked possum?

Flo: There you go, more American. No, he said he was very sorry, but he couldn't.

Asa: [Taking bottle out.] Oh, he did, did he? Wal, I guess he'll do his best all the same.

Flo: I shall be missed at the archery grounds. Will you take me back?

Asa: Like a streak of lightning. [Offers arm and takes her to dairy.]

Flo: That's not the way.

Asa: No, of course not. [Takes her round stage back to dairy.]

Flo: Well, but where are you going now?

Asa: I was just going round. I say, cousin, don't you think you could find your way back alone.

Flo: Why, what do _you_ want to do?

Asa: Wal, I just wanted to see how they make cheese is this darned country. [Exits into dairy.]

Flo: [Laughing.] And they call that man a savage; well, I only wish we had a few more such savages in England.

Dun: [Without, R. 2 E.] This way, lovely sufferer.

Flo: Ah, here's Dundreary.

[Dundreary enters with Georgina, places her in rustic chair, R.]

Dun: There, repothe yourself.

Geo: Thank you, my lord; you are so kind to me, and I am so delicate.

Flo: Yes, you look delicate, dear; how is she this morning any better?

Dun: When she recovers, she'll be better.

Flo: I'm afraid you don't take good care of her, you are so rough.

Dun: No, I'm not wruff, either. [Sings.] I'm gentle and I'm kind, I'm — I forget the rest

Flo: Well, good morning, dear—do take care of her—good day, Dundreary. [Exit through gate.]

Dun: Now, let me administer to your wants. How would you like a roast chestnut?

Geo: No, my lord, I'm too delicate.

Dun: Well, then, a peanut; there is a great deal of nourishment in peanuts.

Geo: No, thank you.

Dun: Then what can I do for you?

Geo: If you please, ask the dairy maid to let me have a seat in the dairy. I am afraid of the draft, here.

Dun: Oh! you want to get out of the draft, do you? Well, you're not the only one that wants to escape the draft. Is that the dairy on top of that stick? [Points to pigeon house.]

Geo: No, my lord, that's the pigeon house.

Dun: What do they keep in pigeon houses? Oh! pigeons, to be sure; they couldn't keep donkeys up there, could they? That's the dairy, I suppothe?

Geo: Yes, my lord.

Dun: What do they keep in dairies?

Geo: Eggs, milk, butter and cheese.

Dun: What's the name of that animal with a head on it? No, I don't mean that, all animals have heads. I mean those animals with something growing out of their heads.

Geo: A cow?

Dun: A cow growing out of his head?

Geo: No, no, horns.

Dun: A cow! well, that accounts for the milk

and butter; but I don't see the eggs; cows don't give eggs; then there's the cheese—do you like cheese?

Geo: No, my lord.

Dun: Does your brother like cheese?

Geo: I have no brother. I'm so delicate.

Dun: She's so delicate, she hasn't got a brother. Well, if you had a brother do you think he'd like cheese?

Geo: I don't know; do please take me to the dairy.

Dun: Well, I will see if I can get you a broiled sardine. [Exit into dairy.]

Geo: [Jumps up.] Oh! I'm so glad he's gone. I am so dreadful hungry. I should like a plate of corn beef and cabbage, eggs and bacon, or a slice of cold ham and pickles.

Dun: [Outside] Thank you, thank you.

Geo: [Running back to seat.] Here he comes. Oh! I am so delicate.

Enter Dundreary.

Dun: I beg you pardon, Miss Georgina, but I find upon enquiry that cows don't give sardines. But I've arranged it with the dairy maid so that you can have a seat by the window that overlooks the cow house and the pig sty, and all the pretty things.

Geo: I'm afraid I'm very troublesome.

Dun: Yes, you're very troublesome, you are. No, I mean you're a lovely sufferer, that's the idea. [They go up to cottage door.]

Enter Asa, running against Dundreary.

Dun: There's that damned rhinoceros again. [Exit into cottage, with Georgina.]

Asa: There goes that benighted aristocrat and that little toad of a sick gal. [Looks off.] There he's a settling her in a chair and covering her all over with shawls. Ah! it's a caution, how these women do fix our flint for us. Here he comes. [Takes out bottle.] How are you, hair dye. [Goes behind dairy.]

Enter Dundreary.

Dun: That lovely Georgina puts me in mind of that beautiful piece of poetry. Let me see how it goes. The rose is red, the violet's blue. [Asa tips his hat over his eyes.]

Dun: [Repeats.]

Asa: [Repeats business.]

Dun: [Comes down, takes off hat, looking in it.] There must be something alive in that hat. [Goes up, and commences again.] The rose is red, the violet's blue, sugar is sweet, and so is somebody, and so is somebody else.

Asa: puts yoke on Dundreary's shoulders gently. Dundreary comes down with pails.

Dun: I wonder what the devil that is? [Lowers one, then the other, they trip him up.] Oh, I see, somebody has been fishing and caught a pail. [Goes hopping up stage, stumbling over against spinning wheel. Looks at yarn on stick.] Why, what a little old man. [Sees Asa.] Say, Mr. Exile, what the devil is this?

Asa: That is a steam engine, and will bust in about a minute.

Dun: Well, I haven't a minute to spare, so

I'll not wait till it busts. [Crosses to R., knocks against private box, R. H., apologizes.]

Asa: Say, whiskers, I want to ask a favor of you.

Dun: [Attempts to sneeze.] Now I've got it.

Asa: Wal, but say. [Dundreary's sneezing bus.]

Asa: [Takes his hand.] How are you. [Squeezes it.]

Dun: There, you've spoiled it.

Asa: Spoiled what?

Dun: Spoiled what! why a magnificent sneeze.

Asa: Oh! was that what you was trying to get through you?

Dun: Get through me: he's mad.

Asa: Wal, now, the naked truth is—[Leans arm on Dundreary's shoulder. Bus. by Dundreary.] Oh, come now, don't be putting on airs. Say, do you know Lieut. Vernon?

Dun: Slightly.

Asa: Wal, what do you think of him, on an average?

Dun: Think of a man on an average?

Asa: Wal, I think he's a real hoss, and he wants a ship.

Dun: Well if he's a real hoss, he must want a carriage.

Asa: Darn me, if that ain't good.

Dun: That's good.

Asa: Yes, that is good.

Dun: Very good.

Asa: Very good, indeed, _for you_.

Dun: Now I've got it. [Tries to sneeze.]

Asa: Wal, now, I say. [Dundreary trying to sneeze.]

Asa: What, are you at that again? Dundreary business. Asa bites his finger. Dundreary goes up, stumbles against chair and comes down again.

Dun: I've got the influenza.

Asa: Got the what?

Dun: He says I've got a wart. I've got the influenza.

Asa: That's it exactly. I want your influence, sir, to get that ship.

Dun: That's good.

Asa: Yes, that's good, ain't it.

Dun: Very good.

Asa: Yes, darn me, if that ain't good.

Dun: For you. Ha! ha! One on that Yankee.

Asa: Well done, Britisher. Wal, now, about that ship?

Dun: I want all my influence, sir, for my own w—w—welations. [Stammering.]

Asa: Oh! you want it for your own w—w—welations. [Mimicing.]

Dun: I say, sir. [Asa pretends deafness. This bus. is ad. lib.]

Asa: Eh?

Dun: He's hard of hearing, and thinks he's in a balloon. Mister.

Asa: Eh?

Dun: He thinks he can hear with his nose. I say—

Asa: Eh?

Dundreary turns Asa's nose around with his thumb. Asa puts his two hands up to Dundreary's.

Dun: Now he thinks he's a musical instrument. I say—

Asa: What?

Dun: You stutter. I'll give you a k—k—k—

Asa: No you won't give me a kick.

Dun: I'll give you a c—c—card to a doctor and he'll c—c—c—

Asa: No he won't kick me, either.

Dun: He's idiotic. I don't mean that, he'll cure you.

Asa: Same one that cured you?

Dun: The same.

Asa: Wal, if you're cured I want to stay sick. He must be a mighty smart man.

Dun: A very clever man, he is.

Asa: Wal, darn me, if there ain't a physiological change taking place. Your whiskers at this moment—

Dun: My whiskers!

Asa: Yes, about the ends they're as black as a niggers in billing time, and near the roots they're all speckled and streaked.

Dun: [Horror struck.] My whiskers speckled and streaked?

Asa: [Showing bottle.] Now, this is a wonderful invention.

Dun: My hair dye. My dear sir.

Asa: [Squeezing his hand.] How are you?

Dun: Dear Mr. Trenchard.

Puts arm on shoulder. Asa repeats Dundreary business, putting on eyeglass, hopping round the stage and stroking whiskers.

Dun: He's mad, he's deaf, he squints, stammers and he's a hopper.

Asa: Now, look here, you get the Lieut. a ship and I'll give you the bottle. It's a fine swap.

Dun: What the devil is a swap?

Asa: Well, you give me the ship, and I'll give you the bottle to boot.

Dun: What do I want of your boots? I haven't got a ship about me.

Asa: You'd better make haste or your whiskers will be changed again. They'll be a pea green in about a minute.

Dun: [Crosses to L.] Pea green! [Exits hastily into house.]

Asa: I guess I've got a ring in his nose now. I wonder how that sick gal is getting along?

Wal, darn me, if the dying swallow ain't pitching into ham and eggs and home-made bread, wal, she's a walking into the fodder like a farmer arter a day's work rail splitting. I'll just give her a start. How de do, Miss, allow me to congratulate you on the return of your appetite. [Georgina scream.] Guess I've got a ring in her pretty nose now. [Looks off, R.] Hello! here comes the lickers and shooters, it's about time I took my medicine, I reckon.

> *Enter, from R. 2. E., Sir E., Mrs. M. Florence, Vernon, Augusta, De Boots, Wickens, Coyle, Sharpe, Binny, Skillet, Buddicombe, two servants in livery, carrying tray and glasses, a wine basket containing four bottles to represent champagne, knife to cut strings, some powerful acid in one bottle for Asa—pop sure.*

Sir E: Now to distribute the prizes, and drink to the health of the winner of the golden arrow.

Flo: And there must stand the hero of the day. Come, kneel down.

Asa: Must I kneel down?

Flo: I am going to crown you Capt. of the Archers of Trenchard Manor.

Asa: [Aside to Florence.] I've got the ship.

Flo: No; have you?

Sir E: Come, ladies and gentlemen, take from me. [Takes glasses, Starts on seeing me in livery.] Who are these strange faces?

Coyle: [In his ear.] Bailiffs, Sir Edward.

Sir E: Bailiffs! Florence I am lost.

[Florence supports her father. At the same moment Dundreary enters with letter and money. Georgina appears at dairy door as Dundreary comes down, L. Asa cuts string of bottle, cork hits Dundreary. General commotion as drop descends.]

Act III

SCENE 1

Dairy set as before in Act 2d, Scene 2.

[Asa discovered on bench, R. C., whittling stick. Mary busy with milk pans in dairy.]

Asa: Miss Mary, I wish you'd leave off those everlasting dairy fixings, and come and take a hand of chat along with me.

Mary: What, and leave my work? Why, when you first came here, you thought I could not be too industrious.

Asa: Well, I think so yet, Miss Mary, but I've got a heap to say to you, and I never can talk while you're moving about so spry among them pans, pails and cheeses. First you raise one hand and then the other, and well, it takes the gumption right out of me.

Mary: [Brings sewing down.] Well, then, I'll sit here—[sits on bench with Asa, vis-a-vis.] Well now, will that do?

Asa: Well, no, Miss Mary, that won't do, neither; them eyes of yourn takes my breath away.

Mary: What will I do, then?

Asa: Well, I don't know, Miss Mary, but, darn me, if you could do anything that wasn't so

213

tarnal neat and handsome, that a fellow would want to keep on doing nothing else all the time.

Mary: Well, then, I'll go away. [Rises.]

Asa: [Stopping her.] No, don't do that, Miss Mary, for then I'll be left in total darkness. [She sits.] Somehow I feel kinder lost, if I haven't got you to talk to. Now that I've got the latitude and longitude of all them big folks, found out the length of every lady's foot, and the soft spot on everybody's head, they can't teach me nothing; but here, [Whittling.] here I come to school.

Mary: Then throw away that stick, and put away your knife, like a good boy. [Throws away stick up stage.] I must cure you of that dreadful trick of whittling.

Asa: Oh, if you only knew how it helps me to keep my eyes off you, Miss Mary.

Mary: But you needn't keep your eyes off me.

Asa: I'm afraid I must, my eyes are awful tale-tellers, and they might be saying something you wouldn't like to hear, and that might make you mad, and then you'd shut up school, and send me home feeling about as small as a tadpole with his tail bobbed off.

Mary: Don't be alarmed, I don't think I will listen to any tales that your eyes may tell unless they're tales I like and ought to hear.

Asa: If I thought they'd tell any other, Miss Mary, I pluck them right out and throw them in the first turnip patch I came to.

Mary: And now tell me more about your home in America. Do you know I've listened to your stories until I'm half a backwoodsman's wife already?

Asa: [Aside.] Wouldn't I like to make her a whole one.

Mary: Yes, I can shut my eyes and almost fancy I see your home in the backwoods. There are your two sisters running about in their sunbonnets.

Asa: Debby and Nab? Yes!

Mary: Then I can see the smoke curling from the chimney, then men and boys working in the fields.

Asa: Yes.

Mary: The girls milking the cows, and everybody so busy.

Asa: Yes.

Mary: And then at night, home come your four big brothers from the hunt laden with game, tired and foot sore, and covered with snow.

Asa: That's so.

Mary: Then how we lasses bustle about to prepare supper. The fire blazes on the hearth, while your good old mother cooks the slapjacks.

Asa: [Getting very excited.] Yes.

Mary: And then after supper the lads and lasses go to a corn husking. The demijohn of old peach brandy is brought out and everything is so nice.

Asa: I shall faint in about five minutes, Miss Mary you're a darned sight too good for this country. You ought to make tracks.

Mary: Make what?

Asa: Make tracks, pack up, and emigrate to the roaring old state of Vermont, and live 'long with mother. She'd make you so comfortable, and there would be sister Debby and Nab, and well, I reckon I'd be there, too.

Mary: Oh! I'm afraid if I were there your mother would find the poor English girl a sad incumbrance.

Asa: Oh, she ain't proud, not a mite, besides they've all seen Britishers afore.

Mary: I suppose you allude to my cousin, Edward Trenchard?

Asa: Well, he wan't the only one, there was the old Squire, Mark Trenchard.

Mary: [Starting Aside.] My grandfather!

Asa: Oh! he was a fine old hoss, as game as a bison bull, and as gray as a coon in the fall; you see he was kinder mad with his folks here, so he came over to America to look after the original branch of the family, that's our branch. We're older than the Trenchard's on this side of the water. Yes we've got the start of the heap.

Mary: Tell me, Mr. Trenchard, did he never receive any letters from his daughter?

Asa: Oh yes, lots of them, but the old cuss never read them, though. He chucked them in the fire as soon as he made out who they come from.

Mary: [Aside.] My poor mother.

Asa: You see, as nigh as we could reckon it up, she had gone and got married again his will, and that made him mad, and well, he was

a queer kind of a rusty fusty old coon, and
it appeared that he got older, and rustier,
and fustier and coonier every fall, you see
it always took him in the fall, it was too
much for him. He got took down with the ague,
he was so bad the doctors gave him up, and
mother she went for a minister, and while she
was gone the old man called me in his room,
`come in, Asa, boy,' says he, and his voice
rang loud and clear as a bell, `come in,'
says he. Well I comed in; `sit down,' says
he; well I sot down. You see I was always a
favorite with the old man. `Asa, my boy,'
says he, takin' a great piece of paper, `when
I die, this sheet of paper makes you heir to
all my property in England'. Well, you can
calculate I pricked up my ears about that
time, bime-by the minister came, and I left
the room, and I do believe he had a three
day's fight with the devil, for that old man's
soul, but he got the upper hand of satan at
last, and when the minister had gone the old
man called me into his room again. The old
Squire was sitting up in his bed, his face as
pale as the sheet that covered him, his silk-
en hair flowing in silvery locks from under
his red cap, and the tears rolling from his
large blue eyes down his furrowed cheek, like
two mill streams. Will you excuse my light-
ing a cigar? For the story is a long, awful
moveing, and I don't think I could get on
without a smoke. [Strikes match.] Wal, says
he to me, and his voice was not as loud as it
was afore—it was like the whisper of the wind
in a pine forest, low and awful. `Asa, boy,'
said he, 'I feel that I've sinned in harden-
ing my heart against my own flesh and blood,
but I will not wrong the last that is left of
them; give me the light,' says he. Wal I gave
him the candle that stood by his bedside,
and he took the sheet of paper I was tell-

ing you of, just as I might take this. [Takes will from pocket.] And he twisted it up as I might this, [Lights will,] and he lights it just this way, and he watched it burn slowly and slowly away. Then, says he, `Asa, boy that act disinherits you, but it leaves all my property to one who has a better right to it. My own daughter's darling child, Mary Meredith,' and then he smiled, sank back upon his pillow, drew a long sigh as if he felt relieved, and that was the last of poor old Mark Trenchard.

Mary: Poor Grandfather. [Buries her face and sobs.]

Asa: [After bus.] Wal, I guess I'd better leave her alone. [Sees half burned will.] There lies four hundred thousand dollars, if there's a cent. Asa, boy, you're a hoss. [Starts off, R. 1 C.]

Mary: To me, all to me. Oh Mr. Trenchard, how we have all wronged poor grandfather. What, gone? He felt after such tidings, he felt I should be left alone—who would suspect there was such delicacy under that rough husk, but I can hardly believe the startling news—his heiress—I, the penniless orphan of an hour ago, no longer penniless, but, alas, an orphan still, [Enter Florence.] with none to share my wealth, none to love me.

Flo: [Throwing arms around Mary's neck.] What treason is this, Mary, no one to love you, eh, what's the matter? You've been weeping, and I met that American Savage coming from here; he has not been rude to you?

Mary: On no, he's the gentlest of human beings, but he has just told me news that has moved me strangely.

Flo: What is it, love?

Mary: That all grandfather's property is mine, mine, Florence, do you understand?

Flo: What! he has popped, has he? I thought he would.

Mary: Who do you mean?

Flo: Who? Asa Trenchard, to be sure.

Mary: Asa Trenchard, why, what put that in your head?

Flo: Why how can Mark Trenchard's property be yours, unless you marry the legatee.

Mary: The legatee? Who?

Flo: Why, you know Mark Trenchard left everything to Asa.

Mary: No, no, you have been misinformed.

Flo: Nonsence, he showed it to me, not an hour ago on a half sheet of rough paper just like this. [Sees will.] Like this. [Picks it up.] Why this is part of it, I believe.

Mary: That's the paper he lighted his cigar with.

Flo: Then he lighted his cigar with 80,000 pounds. Here is old Mark Trenchard's signature.

Mary: Yes, I recognize the hand.

Flo: And here are the words "Asa Trenchard, in consideration of sole heir"—etc.—etc.—etc.

Mary: Oh Florence, what does this mean?

Flo: It means that he is a true hero, and he loves you, you little rogue. [Embraces her.]

Mary: Generous man. [Hides face in Florence's bosom.]

Flo: Oh, won't I convict him, now. I'll find him at once.

Runs off, R. 3 E., Mary after her calling Florence!!! Florence!!! as scene closes.

Change

SCENE 2

Chamber as before.

Enter Mrs. Montchessington, and Augusta, L. 1 E.

Mrs M: Yes, my child, while Mr. De Boots and Mr. Trenchard are both here, you must ask yourself seriously, as to the state of your affections, remember, your happiness for life will depend upon the choice you make.

Aug: What would you advise, mamma? You know I am always advised by you.

Mrs M: Dear, obedient child. De Boots has excellent expectations, but then they are only expectations after all. This American is rich, and on the whole I think a well regulated affection ought to incline to Asa Trenchard.

Aug: Very well, mamma.

Mrs M: At the same time, you must be cautious, or in grasping at Asa Trenchard's solid good qualities, you may miss them, and De Boots expectations into the bargain.

Aug: Oh, I will take care not to give up my hold on poor De Boots 'till I am quite sure of the American.

Mrs M: That's my own girl. [Enter Asa L.] Ah, Mr. Trenchard, we were just talking of your archery powers.

Asa: Wal, I guess shooting with bows and arrows is just about like most things in life, all you've got to do is keep the sun out of your eyes, look straight—pull strong—calculate the distance, and you're sure to hit the mark in most things as well as shooting.

Aug: But not in England, Mr. Trenchard. There are disinterested hearts that only ask an opportunity of showing how they despise that gold, which others set such store by.

Asa: Wal, I suppose there are, Miss Gusty.

Aug: All I crave is affection.

Asa: [Crosses to C.] Do you, now? I wish I could make sure of that, for I've been cruelly disappointed in that particular.

Mrs M: Yes, but we are old friends, Mr. Trenchard, and you needn't be afraid of us.

Asa: Oh, I ain't afraid of you—both on you together.

Mrs M: People sometimes look a great way off, for that which is near at hand. [Glancing at Augusta and Asa alternatively.]

Asa: You don't mean, Miss Gusta. [Augusta casts sheeps eyes at him.] Now, don't look at me in that way. I can't stand it, if you do, I'll bust.

Mrs M: Oh, if you only knew how refreshing this ingenuousness of yours is to an old woman of the world like me.

Asa: Be you an old woman of the world?

Mrs M: Yes, sir.

Aug: Oh yes.

Asa: Well I don't doubt it in the least. [Aside.] This gal and the old woman are trying to get me on a string. [Aloud.] Wal, then, if a rough spun fellow like me was to come forward as a suitor for your daughter's hand, you wouldn't treat me as some folks do, when they find out I wasn't heir to the fortune.

Mrs M: Not heir to the fortune, Mr. Trenchard?

Asa: Oh, no.

Aug: What, no fortune?

Asa: Nary red, it all comes to their barkin up the wrong tree about the old man's property.

Mrs M: Which he left to you.

Asa: Oh, no.

Aug: Not to you?

Asa: No, which he meant to leave to me, but he thought better on it, and left it to his granddaughter Miss Mary Meredith.

Mrs M: Miss Mary Meredith! Oh, I'm delighted.

Aug: Delighted?

Asa: Yes, you both look tickled to death. Now, some gals, and mothers would go away from a fellow when they found that out, but you don't valley fortune, Miss Gusty?

Mrs M: [Aside, crosses to Aug.] My love, you

had better go.

Asa: You crave affection, _you_ do. Now I've no fortune, but I'm filling over with affections which I'm ready to pour out all over you like apple sass, over roast pork.

Mrs M: Mr. Trenchard, you will please recollect you are addressing my daughter, and in my presence.

Asa: Yes, I'm offering her my heart and hand just as she wants them with nothing in 'em.

Mrs M: Augusta, dear, to your room.

Aug: Yes, ma, the nasty beast. [Exit R.]

Mrs M: I am aware, Mr. Trenchard, you are not used to the manners of good society, and that, alone, will excuse the impertinence of which you have been guilty.

Asa: Don't know the manners of good society, eh? Well, I guess I know enough to turn you inside out, old gal—you sockdologizing old man-trap. Wal, now, when I think what I've thrown away in hard cash to-day I'm apt to call myself some awful hard names, 400,000 dollars is a big pile for a man to light his cigar with. If that gal had only given me herself in exchange, it wouldn't have been a bad bargain. But I dare no more ask that gal to be my wife, than I dare ask Queen Victoria to dance a Cape Cod reel.

Enter Florence, L. 1 E.

Flo: What do you mean by doing all these dreadful things?

Asa: Which things.

Flo: Come here sir. [He does so.]

Asa: What's the matter?

Flo: Do you know this piece of paper? [Showing burnt paper.]

Asa: Well I think I have seen it before. [Aside.] Its old Mark Trenchard's will that I left half burned up like a landhead, that I am.

Flo: And you're determined to give up this fortune to Mary Meredith?

Asa: Well, I couldn't help it if I tried.

Flo: Oh, don't say that.

Asa: I didn't mean to do it when I first came here—hadn't the least idea in the world of it, but when I saw that everlasting angel of a gal movin around among them doing fixins like a sunbeam in a shady place; and when I pictured her without a dollar in the world—I—well my old Adam riz right up, and I said, "Asa do it"—and I did it.

Flo: Well, I don't know who your old Adam may be, but whoever it is, he's a very honest man to consult you to do so good an action. But how dare you do such an outrageous thing? you impudent—you unceremonious, oh! you unselfish man! you! you, you! [Smothers him with kisses, and runs off, R. 1 E.]

Asa: Well, if that ain't worth four hundred thousand dollars, I don't know what is, it was sweeter than sweet cider right out of the bung hole. Let me see how things stand round here. Thanks to old whiskers I've got that ship for the sailor man, and that makes him and Miss Florence all hunk. Then there's that darned old Coyle. Well I guess me and old Murcott can fix his flint for him. Then there's—[Looks off, L.] Christopher Columbus, here comes Mary.

Enter Mary, L. 1 E.

Mary: Mr. Trenchard, what can I say to you but offer you my lifelong gratitude.

Asa: Don't now, Miss, don't—

Mary: If I knew what else to offer. Heaven knows there is nothing that is mine to give that I would keep back.

Asa: Give me yourself. [Bus.] I know what a rude, ill-mannered block I am; but there's a heart inside me worth something, if it's only for the sake of your dear little image, that's planted right plump in the middle of it.

Mary: Asa Trenchard, there is my hand, and my heart is in it.

Asa: [Seizes here hand, then drops it suddenly.] Miss Mary, I made what folks call a big sacrifice for you, this morning. Oh! I know it, I ain't so modest, but that I know it. Now what's this you're doing? Is this sacrifice you are making out of gratitude for me? Cause if it is, I wouldn't have it, though not to have it would nigh break my heart, tough as it is.

Mary: No, no, I give myself freely to you—as freely as you, this morning, gave my grandfather's property to me.

Asa: Say it again, last of hope and blessed promise. [Clasps her in his arms.] Mary, there's something tells me that you'll not repent it. I'm rough, Mary, awful rough, but you needn't fear that I'll ever be rough to you. I've camped out in the woods, Mary, often and often, and seen the bears at play with their cubs in the moonlight, the glistening teeth, that would tear the hunter, was harmless to them; the big strong claws that would peel a man's head, as a knife would a pumpkin, was as soft for them as velvet cushions, and that's what I'll be with you, my own little wife; and if ever harm does come to you, it must come over the dead body of Asa Trenchard. Mary I know it Asa; and if I do not prove a true and loving wife to you; may my mother's bright spirit never look down to bless her child.

Asa: Wal, if I don't get out in the air, I'll bust. [Exit hastily R. 1 E. pulling Mary after him.]

Enter Binny, L. 1 E. Drunk.

Binny: [Calling.] Mr. H'Asa, Mr. H'Asa! Oh he's gone; well, I suppose he'll come back to keep his happointment. Mr. Coyle's quite impatient. It isn't hoften that han hamerican has the run of the wine cellars of Trenchard Manor, and in such company, too. There's me and Mr. Coyle, which is a good judge of old port wine, and he knows it when he drinks; and his clerk, Mr. Murcott, which I don't hexactly like sitting down with clerks. But Mr. H'Asa wished it and Mr. Coyle hadn't any objections, so in course I put my feelings in my pocket, besides, Murcott is a man of hedication, though unfortunately taken to drink. Well, what of that, it's been many a man's misfortune, though I say it, what shouldn't say it, being a butler. But now to join my distinguished party. [Exit, R. 1 E.]

SCENE 3

Wine cellar in 3.

*Coyle, Murcott and Binny discovered.
Table L., with two cups and bottles.
Coyle L. of table, seated. Binny back
of table. Murcott sitting on barrel, R.
Door in flat with staircase discovered,
dark. Stage half dark. Candles on table,
lighted.*

Coyle: A capital glass of wine, Mr. Binny, and a capital place to drink it.

Asa: [Without.] Bring a light here, can't you. I've broken my natural allowance of shins already.

Enters D. in F., down stairs.

Asa: [To Murcott.] Is he tight yet?

Mur: Histered, but not quite gone yet.

Coyle: Oh, Mr. Trenchard, glad to see you, to welcome you to the vaults of your ancestors.

Asa: Oh! these are the vaults of my ancestors, are they? Wal, you seem to be punishing their spirits pretty well.

Binny: Wines, Mr. Asa? The spirits are in the houter cellar.

Coyle: Oh, Mr. Asa, there is no place like a wine cellar for a hearty bout. Here you might bawl yourself hoarse beneath these ribs of stone, and nobody hear you. [He shouts and sings very loud.]

Asa: Oh, wouldn't they hear you? [Aside.]

That's worth knowing.

Binny: [Very drunk—rising.] That's right, Mr. Coyle, make as much noise as you like, you are in the cellars of Trenchard Manor, Mr. Coyle. Mr. Coyle, bless you, Mr. Coyle. Mr. Coyle, why his hit Mr. Coyle, I am sitting at the present time, in this present distinguished company? I will tell you, Mr. Coyle, hit his because Hi always hacts and conducts myself has becomes a gentleman, hand Hi knows what's due to manners. [Falls in chair.]

Asa: Steady, old hoss, steady.

Binny: Hi'm steady. Hi always was steady. [Staggers across to L.H.] Hi'm going to fetch clean glasses. [Exit, L. 3 R.]

Asa: Now, Mr. Coyle, suppose you give us a song.

Coyle: [Very drunk.] I can't sing, Mr. Trenchard, but I sometimes join in the chorus.

Asa: Wal, give us a chorus.

Coyle: Will you assist in the vocalization thereof?

Asa: [Mimicing.] Will do the best of my endeavors thereunto.

Coyle: [Sings.] "We won't go home till morning." Repeat. Repeat [Falls off chair, senseless.]

Asa: [Finishing the strain.] "I don't think you'll go home at all." Now, then, quick, Murcott, before the butler comes back, get his keys. [Murcott gets keys from Coyle's pocket and throws them to Asa.] Is this all?

Mur: No; the key of his private bureau is on his watch chain, and I can't get it off.

Asa: Take watch and all.

Mur: No; he will accuse us of robbing him.

Asa: Never mind, I'll take the responsibility. [Coyle moves.]

Mur: He is getting up.

Asa: Well, darn me, knock him down again.

Mur: I can't.

Asa: Can't you? Well, I can.

[Pulls Murcott away. Knocks Coyle down; is going towards D. in F., meets Binny with tray and glasses; kicks it, knocks Binny down and exits up staircase, followed by Murcott, carrying candle. Dark state. Binny rises; Coyle ditto. Blindly encounter each other and pummel soundly till change.

Quick Change

SCENE 4

Chamber in 1, same as Scene 2.

Enter Dundreary and Vernon, L. 1 E. Dundreary stops, C., and is seized with an inclination to sneeze. Motions with his hand to Vernon.

Ver: My lord! [Business Dundreary sneezing.] Your lordship! [Dundreary same bus. Louder.] My lord!

Dun: There you go; now you've spoiled it.

Ver: Spoiled what, my lord?

Dun: Spoiled what? why a most magnificent sneeze.

Ver: I'm very sorry to interrupt your lordship's sneeze, but I merely wanted to express my gratitude to you for getting me a ship.

Dun: Sir, I don't want your gratitude, I only want to sneeze.

Ver: Very well, my lord, then I will leave you, and this gives you an opportunity for sneezing. [Crosses to R.] But in return for what you have done for me, should you ever want a service a sailor can offer you, just hail Harry Vernon, and you'll find he'll weigh anchor and be alongside. [Hitches up breeches and exits, R. 1 E.]

Dun: Find him alongside? What does he mean by a long side? and he always wants to weigh anchor. What funny fellows the sailors are. Why the devil won't they keep a memorandum of the weight of their anchor? What's the matter with the sailor's side? [Imitates Vernon.] Oh I see, he's got the stomach ache. [Exit, R. 1 E.]

Change Scene

SCENE 5

Library in Trenchard Manor in 3 or 4.

Enter Buddicombe, R. 1 E., following Lord Dundreary.

Bud: A letter, my lord.

Dun: [Takes letter.] You may go. [Exit Buddicombe, R. 1 E. Opens letter.] "My dear Frederick." He calls me Frederick because my name is Robert. "I wrote you on my arrival." Why, I never heard from him. "But I am afraid you didn't get the letter, because I put no name on the envelope." That's the reason why I didn't get it, but who did get it? It must have been some fellow without any name. "My dear brother, the other day a rap came to my door, and some fellows came in and proposed a quiet game of porker." A quiet game of porker, why, they wanted to kill him with a poker. "I consented and got stuck—" Sam's dead, I've got a dead lunatic for a brother "for the drinks." He got on the other side of the paper, why couldn't he get stuck all on one side. "P. S.—If you don't get this letter let me know, for I shall feel anxious." He's a mad lunatic. [Exit, R. 1 E.]

Change Scene

SCENE 6

Coyle's Office in 2. High desk and stool, R. Modern box center against flat. Cabinet, L.

Asa: discovered looking over papers on box. Murcott looking in desk.

Asa: Have you found it?

Mur: No, Mr. Trenchard. I've searched all the drawers but can find no trace of it.

Asa: What's this?

Mur: That's a cabinet where his father kept old deeds, the key he always carries about him.

Asa: Oh, he does, does he? Well I reckon I

saw a key as I came in that will open it.
[Exit, R. 1 E.]

Mur: Key, oh, my poor muddled brain, what can he mean!

Asa: [Re-enters with axe.] Here's a key that will open any lock that Hobb ever invented.

Mur: Key? what key?

Asa: What key, why, Yankee. [Shows axe, begins to break open Cabinet.]

   Enter Coyle, R. 2 E.

Coyle: Villains! would you rob me?

Mur: Stand off, Mr. Coyle, we are desperate. [Now seizes him.]

Asa: Here it is a sure as there are snakes in Virginia. Let the old cuss go, Murcott.

Coyle: Burglars! oh, you shall dearly pay for this.

Asa: Yes, I'll pay—but I guess you'll find the change.

Coyle: The law—the law shall aid me.

Asa: Wal, perhaps it would be as well not to call in the law just yet. It might look a little further than might be convenient.

Mur: It's no use to blunder, Mr. Coyle, you are harmless to us now, for we have that, that will crush you.

Coyle: Well, what are your conditions? money, how much?

Asa: Wal, we warn't thinking of coming down on your dollars. But you have an appointment with Sir Edward at two, haven't you?

Coyle: Well?

Asa: Well, I want you to keep that appointment.

Coyle: Keep it?

Asa: Yes, and that's all I do want you to keep of his, and instead of saying you have come to foreclose the mortgage, I want you to say, you have found the release which proves the mortgage to have been paid off.

Coyle: I accept. Is that all?

Asa: Not quite. Then I want you to pay off the execution debts.

Coyle: What, I pay Sir Edward's debts?

Asa: Yes, with Sir Edward's money that stuck to your fingers naturally while passing through your hands.

Coyle: [To Murcott.] Traitor!

Mur: He knows all, Mr. Coyle.

Coyle: Is there anything more!

Asa: yes, I want you to apologize to Miss Florence Trenchard, for having the darned impudence to propose for her hand.

Coyle: What more?

Asa: Then you resign your stewardship in favor of your clerk, Abel Murcott.

Coyle: What, that drunkard vagabond?

Asa: Well, he was, but he's going to take the pledge at the first pump he comes to.

Mur: Yes, I _will_ conquer the demon drink, or die in the struggle with him.

Coyle: Well, anything more?

Asa: Yes, I think the next thing will be to get washed. You're not a handsome man at best, and now you're awful. [Coyle makes a dash at Murcott. Asa catches him and turns him round to R.] Mr. Coyle, in your present state of mind, you had better go first.

Coyle: [Bitterly.] Oh, sir, it is your turn now.

Asa: Yes, it is my turn, but you can have the first wash. Come along Murcott. [Exeunt, R. 1 E]

Change Scene

SCENE 7

Library in Trenchard Manor in 3 or 4.

Sir Edward discovered seated R. of table.

Sir E: The clock is on the stroke of two, and Coyle is waiting my decision. In giving her to him, I know I shall be embittering her life to save my fortune, but appearances—no, no, I will not sacrifice her young life so full of promise, for a few short years of questionable state for myself, better leave her to the mercy of chance [Enter Florence, R. U. E.] than sell her to this scoundrel; and to myself, I will not survive the downfall of my house, but end it thus. [Raises pistol to his head. Florence seizes his arm and screams.]

Flo: Father, dear father, what despair is this? [Sir Edward buries his face in his hands.] If it is fear of poverty, do not think of me, I will marry this man if I drop dead in my bridal robes.

Enter Binny, R. 1 E.

Binny: Mr. Coyle, sir who has come by happointment.

Sir E: I will not see him.

Flo: Yes, yes, show him up, Mr. Binny. [Exit Binny, R. 1 E.]

Sir E: Florence, I will not consent to this sacrifice.

Enter Asa, Coyle and Murcott, R. 1 E.

Sir E: How is this Mr. Coyle, you are not alone?

Asa: No, you see, squire, Mr. Coyle wishes me and his clerk to witness the cutting off the seals from the mortgage, which he has been lucky enough to find the release of.

Sir E: Heavens, is it so?

Coyle: Yes, Sir Edward, there is the release executed by my father, which had become detached.

Asa: [To him.] Accidentally.

Sir E: Saved, saved at last from want!

Coyle: Meanwhile I have paid the execution debts out of a fine which has just fallen in.

Asa: Accidentally. It's astonishing how things have fallen in and out to-day.

Sir E: But your demand here? [Points to Florence.]

Coyle: I make none, Sir Edward. I regret that I should have conceived so mad a thought; it is enough to unfit me for longer holding position as your agent, which I beg humbly to resign—

Asa: [Aside to him.] Recommending as your successor—

Coyle: Recommending as my successor Abel Murcott, whose knowledge of your affairs, gained in my office, will render him as useful as I have been.

Asa: Yes, just about.

Sir E: Your request is granted, Mr. Coyle.

Asa: And now, my dear Mr. Coyle, you may a-b-s-q-u-a-t-u-l-a-t-e.

Coyle: I go, Sir Edward, with equal good wishes for all assembled here. [Darts a look at Murcott and exits, R. 1 E.]

Asa: That's a good man, Sir Edward.

Sir E: Yes.

Asa: Oh, he's a very good man.

Sir E: Yes, he is a good man.

Asa: But he can't keep a hotel.

Sir E: Mr. Murcott, your offence was heavy.

Flo: And so has been his reparation. Forgive him, papa. Mr. Murcott, you saved me; may Heaven bless you.

Mur: Yes, I saved her, thank Heaven. I had strength enough for that. [Exits L. 1. E.]

Flo: You'll keep your promise and make Mr. Murcott your clerk, papa?

Sir E: Yes, I can refuse nothing; I am so happy; I am so happy, I can refuse none anything to-day.

Asa: Can't you, Sir Edward! Now, that's awful lucky, for there's two gals want your consent mighty bad.

Sir E: Indeed; for what?

Asa: To get hitched.

Sir E: Hitched?

Asa: Yes to get spliced.

Sir E: Spliced?

Asa: Yes, to get married.

Sir E: They have it by anticipation. Who are they?

Asa: There's one on 'em. [Points to Florence.]

Sir E: Florence! and the other?

Asa: She's right outside. [Exit, hastily, R. 1. E.]

Sir E: Well, and who is the happy man, Lord Dun—

Flo: Lord Dundreary! No, papa—but Harry Vernon. He's not poor now, though he's got a ship.

Re-enter Asa, with Mary.

Asa: Here's the other one, Sir Edward.

Sir E: Mary? Who is the object of your choice?

Mary: Rough-spun, honest-hearted Asa Trenchard.

Sir E: Ah! Mr. Trenchard you win a heart of gold.

Flo: And so does Mary, papa, believe me. [Crosses to Asa. Mary and Sir Edward go up.]

Flo: What's the matter?

Asa: You make me blush.

Flo: I don't see you blushing.

Asa: I'm blushing all the way down my back.

Flo: Oh, you go long. [Goes up stage.]

Asa: Hello! here's all the folks coming two by two, as if they were pairing for Noah's ark. Here's Mrs. Mountchestnut and the Sailor man. [Enter as Asa calls them off.] Here's De Boots and his gal, and darn me, if here ain't old setidy fetch it, and the sick gal, how are you, buttons? [Dundreary knocks against Asa, who is in C. of stage.]

Dun: There's that damned rhinocerous again. [Crosses to L. with Georgina, and seats her.]

Asa: Here comes turkey cock, number two, and his gal, and darn me, if here ain't Puffy and his gal.

Sir E: Mr. Vernon, take her, she's yours, though Heaven knows what I shall do without her.

Mrs M: [Rising.] Ah, Sir Edward, that is just my case; but you'll never know what it is to be a mother. [Comes down, L. C.] Georgina, Augusta, my dears, come here. [They come down each side of her.] You'll sometimes think of your poor mamma, bless you. [Aside to them.] Oh, you couple of fools.

*[Bumps their foreheads. Dundreary has
business with Georgina, then leads her
to a seat, L.*

De B: [To Dundreary.] Why, Fred, we're all
getting married!

Dun: Yes, it's catching, like the cholera.

Binny: I 'ope, Sir Edward, there's no objec-
tions to my leading Miss Sharpe to the hyme-
nial halter.

Sir E: Certainly not, Mr. Binny.

Bud: [To Dun.] And Skillet and I have made so
bold, My lord—

Dun: Yes, you generally do make bold—but
bless you, my children—bless you.

Asa: Say, you, lord, buttons, I say, whis-
kers.

Dun: Illustrious exile? [Comes down.]

Asa: They're a nice color, ain't they?

Dun: Yes, they're all wight now.

Asa: All wight? no, they're all black.

Dun: When I say wight I mean black.

Asa: Say, shall I tell that sick gal about
that hair dye?

Dun: No, you needn't tell that sick gal about
that hair dye!

Asa: Wal, I won't, if you don't want me to.

Dun: [Aside.] That man is a damned rattle-
snake.

[Goes up, sits in Georgina's lap—turns

to apologize, sits in Augusta's lap—same business with Mrs. M, then goes back to Georgina.]

Asa: Miss Georgina. [She comes down.] How's your appetite? shall I tell that lord about the beefsteak and onions I saw you pitching into?

Geo: Please don't, Mr. Trenchard, I'm so delicate.

Asa: Wal, I won't, if you don't want me to.

Geo: Geo: Oh, thank you.

[Backs up stage and sits in Dundreary's lap, who has taken her seat.]

Asa: Miss Gusty. [Augusta comes down.] Got your boots, hain't you?

Aug: Yes, Mr. Trenchard.

Asa: How do they fit you? Say, shall I tell that fellow you were after me first?

Aug: [Extravagantly.] Not for the world, Mr. Trenchard.

Asa: [Mimicing.] Wal, I won't, if you don't want me to.

Asa: [To Mrs M.] Mrs. Mountchestnut.

Dun: [Coming down.] Sir, I haven't a chestnut to offer you, but if you'd like some of your native food, I'll order you a doughnut?

Asa: I dough not see it.

Dun: [Laughs.] That's good.

Asa: Yes, very good.

Dun: For you.

Asa: Oh, you get out, I mean the old lady.

Dun: Mrs. Mountchessington, this illustrious exile wishes to see you. [Mrs M. comes down.]

Asa: Wal, old woman?

Mrs M: Old woman, sir?

Asa: Got two of them gals off your hands, haven't you?

Mrs M: I'm proud to say, I have.

Asa: Shall I tell them fellows you tried to stick them on me first?

Mrs M: You'll please not mention the subject.

Asa: Wal, I won't, if you don't want me to. [Backs up;—curtseying;—knocks back against Dundreary, who is stooping to pick up a handkerchief. They turn and bunk foreheads.] Say, Mr. Puffy. [Binny comes down.] Shall I tell Sir Edward about your getting drunk in the wine cellar?

Binny: You need not—not if you don't like unto.

Asa: Wal, I won't, if you don't want me to.

Binny: Remember the hold hadage. "A still tongue shows a wise ead."

Asa: X Q's me.

Binny: O, I, C. [Goes up.]

Flo: [Comes down, L.] Well cousin, what have you to say to us? [Mary comes down R. of Asa.]

Asa: Wal, I ain't got no ring, to put in your noses, but I's got one to put on your finger. [To Mary.] And I guess the sailor man has one to put on yours, and I guess you two are as happy as clams at high water.

Flo: I am sure you must be very happy.

Asa: Wal, I am not so sure about my happiness.

Flo: Why, you ungrateful fellow. What do want to complete it?

Asa: [To Audience.] My happiness depends on you.

Flo: And I am sure you will not regret your kindness shown to Our American Cousin. But don't go yet, pray—for Lord Dundreary has a word to say. [Calls Dundreary.]

Dun: [Sneezes.] That's the idea.

CURTAIN

ACTRESS CAROLE LOMBARD
1929

ACTRESS CAROLE LOMBARD
BONUS PICTURE

Read about Miss Lombard and the other women we have
showcased in our 2 Year Anniversary Issue
COMING THIS FALL

Dark Corners
Elmedina Hota

ELMEDINA HOTA IS AN ARTIST
BASED IN SARAJEVO, BOSNIA
AND HERZEGOVINA.
FOR MORE ABOUT HER
BREATHS OF LIFE VISIT
INSTAGRAM & TWITTER:
@HELLMEDINCIC

Paralysed

The moonlight across her room
descends and claims its place,
as she is burdened with an unsettling,
yet oddly pleasant embrace
that slithers into the linen, wrapping around her back,
the terror that consumes her reveals an impending attack

The sound grows - of the restless sea,
whispering to surrender and become forever free,
a strong pull on her legs drags her onto the floor,
she can hear the echo of a crow's caw ashore

Frightened to the bone, unfit to move,
her body betrays her - it feels alarmingly heavy;
the setting which she's trapped in she's desperately
trying to improve,
as she feels the void:
to consume her entirely it might be ready

Bursting in an attempt to scream,
still not a sound that could be heard,
as her eyes catch a glimpse of the abyss,
into the water she's being suddenly lured

As the void below her reflection greets her with a smile,
offering beauty, turning into an inviting kiss;
horrified, with teary eyes, she finally whimpers:
'God, allow this to be but a distressing dream that I can
dismiss!'

The moonlight soothes her eyes
as she travels back to reality,
escaping her demise;
the seagull can be heard — no sight of a crow,
still in bed she lies despite the feeling of a fall,
of this nightmare that, at last, ended she'll have no more.

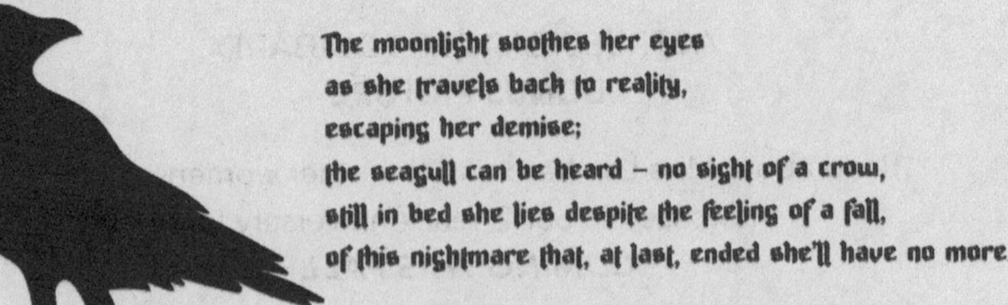

ADVENTURES ON THE GO
Volume 1 Book 1
FEATURING:
OffBeatReads Original:
The Journal of Eye Collector D.R. Melvin
by Robert Kimbrell
Edgar Allan Poe's:
THE SYSTEM OF DOCTOR TARR AND PROFESSOR FETHER
Sci-Fi:
LADY INTO HELL-CAT
by Stanley Mullen
AND MORE!
3 Complete Stories!

ADVENTURES ON THE GO
Take a book on your travels and never be bored.
Volume 1 Book 2
WINTER 2021
FEATURING: THE VAMPYRE
INSIDE:
The Good Guy
Detective Wolfram Gets A Case
Friend Island
WE COULD NOT RESIST THIS
A GHOSTLY CHRISTMAS EVE TALE!
AND MORE!
Exclusive: 3 Questions With Award-Winning Crime Fiction Author Joni M. Fisher
TRUE ACCOUNT: DOES RACHEL HAUNT SPRINGFIELD HIGH?

ADVENTURES ON THE GO
Multi-Genre entertainment to take with you. Wherever.
Volume 1 Book 3
Spring 2022
AGATHA CHRISTIE TRIBUTE EDITION
2 COMPLETE AGATHA CHRISTIE MYSTERIES!
ALSO INSIDE ORIGINAL STORY BY DARRYLE PURCELL
PARADISE LITE
MORE ABOUT AGATHA INSIDE- AND WHY DID SHE DISAPPEAR?
Agatha Christie (ca.1910)

ADVENTURES ON THE GO
Take an adventure with you and never be bored.
Volume 1 Book 4
Summer 2022
COVER: SCREEN QUEEN MARY PICKFORD
STAR OF THE 1918 FILM STELLA MARIS-Based on Book included Inside!
STELLA MARIS!
Martians already own the world in: DON'T LOOK NOW
ORIGINAL STORY GHOSTS AND HEARTBEATS IN THE RAIN by Miranda Maples
TWO OLD LOVERS
A NEW EDITORIAL
EXCLUSIVE INTERVIEW: SAVANNAH J. GOINS
Author, Writing Coach, Dragon-Wrangler

COLLECT EVERY ISSUE

ADVENTURES
FALL 2022
TOLKIEN FANS: POETRY BY THE WRITER YOU DON'T KNOW YOU KNOW
SEVEN KEYS TO BALDPATE
ILLUSIONS OF EVIDENCE
THE DAY TIME STOPPED MOVING
MULTI-GENRE READING ENTERTAINMENT

ADVENTURES To Go
WINTER 2022
OUTWITTING THE HUN -THE NEARLY FORGOTTEN TRUE STORY OF A LIEUTENANT WHO ESCAPED A GERMAN PRISON CAMP
KURT VONNEGUT 2BR02B
THE TUNNEL UNDER THE WORLD
THE MAN OF FLESH AND BLOOD
INTERVIEW WITH AUTHOR MIRANDA MAPLES & MORE
COVER MODEL PAIGE OF WARBIRD PINUP GIRLS
MULTI-GENRE READING ENTERTAINMENT

MULTI-GENRE READING ENTERTAINMENT
ADVENTURES
SPRING 2023
A LOOK BACK AT REAL GLAMOUR WITH ELMEDINA HOTA
THREE NEW ORIGINAL STORIES
DARK CORNERS POETRY
RAY BRADBURY'S A LITTLE JOURNEY
A JURY OF HER PEERS by SUSAN GLASPELL
SOUTHWEST SCENARIOS
AND MORE

PEOPLE AND STORIES THAT SHOULD NOT BE FORGOTTEN
ADVENTURES
SUMMER 2023
INSIDE:
OUR AMERICAN COUSIN
THE STAGEPLAY LINCOLN WAS WATCHING
THE FIRST HARDY BOYS MYSTERY: THE TOWER TREASURE
STORIES O. HENRY KATE CHOPIN AND THREE NEW AUTHORS

TAPPING AT THE DOOR

BY DAVID PAYNE

There was a tapping at the air lock door. In space, we shouldn't have been able to hear anything through the door at all, but yet here we were and there was most definitely a knocking. A tapping.

Rick, he stood next to me and froze at the sound. He was an engineer out of New England, turned astronaut mostly on a bet from his friends who doubted he could do it. We looked at each other, not taking a move forward or away and then the sound went away. We were silent for a minute or more, our bodies refusing to move, until Elsy came down the corridor, calling to me.

"Rin - you got those specs I need?"

"Hmm?" I responded, still quite distracted. "Specs? Yeah. They're uh... right here." I picked up the clipboard and pushed it in her direction, my eyes not really straying far from the door.

"Thanks... What's up?" she asked, touching Rick on the shoulder which made him jolt as if he hadn't heard her coming. He exhaled, blinked his eyes, then turned away from the door.

"Nothing," he said. He turned around to look at me and said it again: "Nothing, right?"

I nodded, not really sure that was the right answer. "Nothing."

"Ok, you two. You want to keep a secret that's fine. Just remember we're on a really small boat up here."

Rick shrugged off the horror in his body, and left me floating near the door. There was something I should have been doing. Something indeed, but I had no memory of what it was, and I couldn't force myself to move on. Rick left. Elsy continued on her way, now that she had her specs, and that left me there. Alone. With the tapping.

But it had stopped. So maybe it was just my imagination. I could remove the doubt by looking through the viewport of the door, I supposed. What would be my options then though? If I saw something, we had a real problem we would have to find a solution to. If I didn't see anything, did that really mean there was nothing there?

I couldn't do nothing though, so that meant checking the viewport.

So, I pushed myself along the handholds to the door and took a peek through. I punched the button to activate the lights within. The small air lock sprang to vibrant white light. Still, even with the light on, I couldn't see much in the room at all. It was a small window, and it was positioned off set, so it didn't give me a good vantage point within.

Still, I looked and looked, angling my head one way and the next, just making sure there was nothing. And there was nothing. I had to accept that, maybe it was just my imagination. And Rick's. He heard it too. I couldn't forget that.

Opening the door without anyone else around seemed like the most foolish I could be, and besides we were supposed to get clearance before opening any of the air lock doors. Not that we would be locked out of the system or anything. Just policy. And one that I thought was a good idea, even without the idea of something being stuck in it. Who knew what it could be? Certainly not me. I didn't even have a baseline for the best case scenario. Nothing just meant I was likely going crazy. Something inert had to have gotten in there somehow. Something alive meant some sort of alien. None of these were good. In fact, all of them were bad. Very very bad.

"Rick?" I tapped the intercom to get his attention and gave him a minute to respond.

"Rick here." the sound was eerie, but only because I was already freaked out.

"Let's gather everyone and talk about this."

"I don't think that's necessary."

"Well I do. I'm calling everyone over."

"Roger."

I clicked off the comm, then back on for a general call to the station.

"Everyone, please report to air lock four," I announced.

There were only six of us on the station, and I dreaded waiting there by myself, but soon Elsy and Rick were there, then the others.

"What's all this about?" Naomi asked.

"Rick and I heard something tapping at the air lock door." I didn't see any reason to sugarcoat it. "It has stopped, obviously, but there was something making a noise on the other side. I want to check it out, but I needed to make sure we all are aware of what that means."

Rick raised his hand. "What does that mean?" He seemed genuinely curious. Elsy took a cautious look out the viewport, but pushed herself away after a moment.

I stammered for a second while I collected myself. "Well, the way I see it, there is either something out there making the noise - whether an object or a being of some sort..."

"An alien?" Rick blurted out, trying to hide a nervous chuckle.

"I'm not saying an alien... but yeah. Maybe. I don't know. Something. Or there is nothing out there and maybe Rick and I heard something that is wrong with the air lock. I'm not an engineer though, and I wouldn't know how to poke through the door's workings if there is something. So yeah. I called you all here to make sure I'm not crazy, okay?"

"I heard the noise too," Rick admitted, though I didn't think that was much of an admission since I had said it already. "But I don't think it is aliens."

"Fine. Not aliens. Wonderful. Then what is it?"

Rick looked through the viewport, doing the same kind of dance I did to look at all the angles. He turned around and shrugged with his whole body.

"I don't know."

"If there is something out there, we can't just let it in though." Elsy pointed out, nervously.

"Too right," I agreed. "But what other option do we have?"

"We could vent out the air lock." Naomi ventured. I had to admit it was the best idea, and I hadn't thought of it.

"Okay. Let's do that then," I agreed, probably a little too eagerly.

"We'll need to clear it with ground control," Elsy said

The discussion went on for far too long. While they were all discussing it though, Naomi just came to the door and punched in the commands to vent the air lock. She was done before anyone had a moment to speak up, except for me, and I just watched and stayed quiet.

"Done."

"I can't believe you just did that!" Rick said, a little bit of envy in his voice.

"All right. Show's over. Back to work?" Naomi said, pulling herself through to the corridor to get back to her tasks.

I lingered at the door for a moment, trying to see if anything had gone out the air lock from the venting. I didn't see anything though.

"Yeah, I guess." I said. The others murmured agreement and moved on from the door. I was the last one there again, but then I grabbed the nearest handhold and sent myself towards the lab. I had more tests to run. That's what I had been doing, remembering it suddenly.

I was almost at the lab door, when I heard the tapping coming from the air lock again.

David Payne is a father, writer, streamer.

With the support of his partner and children, he has been creating stories daily since late 2021. He participates ferociously in Stories on Fire (previously known as 31 Stories, 31 Days), National Novel Writing Month, and Game of Tomes.

On stream, he writes each day both as a form of accountability and to inspire others to the craft. His focus is entirely on getting the words on the page and letting the editing table sort out the details later.

Link:

starstolenwritings.wordpress.com

NEW BOOK! 265-PAGE HARDCOVER NOW
AVAILABLE ON AMAZON WORLD-WIDE!
THE NEW WWII NOSE-ART PICTORIAL BY PHOTOGRAPHER AND AUTHOR CHRISTIAN KIEFFER
Warbird Pinup Girls
THE COLLECTION
Warbird Pinup Girls
CHRISTIAN MICHAEL KIEFFER
THE COLLECTION
2009-2022
WWW.AMAZON.COM/DP/B09XSZPPY1

VINTAGE & Velvet
CLOTHING
Style from the Past for the Woman of Today
www.vintageandvelvetclothing.com

TREASURES

BY SUZANNE ELSON

The hinge on the screen door was too tight, causing it to swing back quickly. It was old, inexpensive and had mesh stapled around the frame that easily could become detached. The young boy had developed a trick of beating the quick door by placing his stick between it and the frame, and masterfully diving underneath without knocking his magical wand out. This little game sometimes captivated him for hours. It seemed anything could, as long as it kept him away from his annoying older brother. On his fifth dive through to the kitchen linoleum the screen door abruptly snapped back, catching his bare legs. He quickly turned around to see how he could have messed up, and saw his big brother towering over him, cigarette in the mouth of a face not old enough to be shaved, remorseless, piercing eyes.

Eddie felt the sharp pain of the cuts on his calves. Colin pressed his hand on the door, preventing Eddie from wiggling out. He bit his lower lip as the tears rolled down his cheek. "Aw. All my friends were right about you Eddie. You're nothing but a sissy girl and a loser kid. That's what Dad always called you too."

"You're lying," Eddie cried. "You don't remember Dad. And he wouldn't call me that. Ma said he really loved me." The older boy glared at the younger one, jealousy trickling across his face. He let go of the frame, spat out his cigarette, and was gone. Eddie slowly stood up, holding his legs, whispering, 'I'm not a loser. Dad did love me. It's not my fault you weren't wanted.'

Angry and hurt, Eddie dried his face and cleaned his scrapes. He did some exploring to pass the afternoon. Eddie dragged an old ladder from the spare room and set it under the loft. He carefully climbed the steps and heaved the heavy attic door over. Once up inside, he relaxed. This is where he always escaped from Colin. Hidden under heavy wool blankets in the corner lay his secret project: an old Hope chest. He ran over, uncovered it and started twisting the lock. The little boy wrestled with it, jamming an old screwdriver through the handle, and after what seems like a lifetime of grunts and moans, the rusty lock fell apart. Eddie sat back in astonishment. This was a long project for him, one that had him dreaming of its contents for hours. Eddie struggled to open the dusty wooden lid. He sighed. There wasn't much there, except old yellowed papers. He gazed through the ones on top, not making much sense of the handwriting, until he noticed an elasticized bundle jammed in the corner. Eddie stretched the old elastic and stared at what he had found— a dozen or so hand drawn cartoon caricatures. To a young boy, this was sheer joy. Eddie ran around the floorboards, making voices and stories for each character. Hours passed before he finally climbed down the ladder, a thick bulge under his shirt. His quiet life away from Colin had taken on a new dimension. For the first time he felt superior—he had found a magical treasure!

The young boy said cross legged on the floor of his play tent amusing himself with the drawings. "Edgar smiled to himself, as he knew he was a tougher and stronger cat than the others," he stated in a deep authoritative voice, falling back in the tent laughing. The floor was covered in the drawings, along with some of his own that he tried to copy. As he was gathering up the old ones to hide, Colin burst into his tent. "Who are you talking to in here, you loser, your imaginary friends? And what are all these stupid drawings doing all over the floor, and on Ma's good paper? Boy are you ever gonna get it." Colin picked up a few drawings and laughed. "You don't honestly think you are any good, do ya?" He ripped them down the middle, watching them fall onto Eddie's legs. Eddie sat in the middle of the ripped up drawings, breathing in the cloudy secondhand smoke, feeling the anger build up inside him, watching his fists clinch, and feeling his face burn. He was sick of him. 'You're the loser Colin. Just wait till I'm a famous artist,' he muttered to himself.

The little boy skateboarded down Main Street, drawings shoved in his back pocket. He was on his way to the variety store, and couldn't help notice the older man sitting alone on the park bench. He was beginning to look familiar to him. The stranger never approached him, and Eddie never felt unsafe, just curious. He lacked a father figure in his life. Eddie purposely skated close, hoping he would speak.

Many years passed with Eddie regularly seeing the elderly man sitting on the bench observing him, never speaking. On his 15th birthday Eddie was walking through the park. The usual occurrence of seeing the old man did not take place. Eddie sat on the roundabout, wondering where he was. He had recently entered a local art contest run by the town newspaper. Eddie knew in his heart that this was how he wanted to spend his life. He was about to rise when the roundabout started moving. The old man appeared in front of him, looking thoughtfully into his eyes. "Don't give up on your dreams, no matter who criticizes you. This is your life, not theirs. Follow your own path," he quietly said and left. Eddie ran after him. "You spoke to me after all these years? Who are you?" he asked excitedly. The old man kept walking, but glanced over. "What's important is you heed what I say."

Eddie stopped. He stood there, and watched him walk away.

Eddie's older brother had become a rebellious young adult, hanging around a fast crowd. He lived at home one week per month, and didn't do much when he was there, except hassle Eddie. Colin was sitting at the kitchen table, cigarette dangling from swollen lips. "Hey cartoon loser." Eddie ignored him and walked into the living room. "Hey Ma, how would you feel if I took off out west for a bit, you know, look up Uncle Mark in Alberta? He mentioned good art schools out there." His mother took off her glasses and looked up at him. She knew he was too good for this little town. "Eddie, you're only 15. I know you have big dreams, but at least wait a few more years, you're not even done high school. Stay and keep me company a little bit longer sweetheart," she replied.

"It's not good for me to be here Ma. I won't live there long, I promise. I'll be back. I know you don't like being alone here with all your memories of Dad," he said. His mother dropped her head. His father was rarely mentioned. All Eddie had gathered over the years was that he had died when he was an infant, and that things weren't good between them.

Over the next few months Eddie tirelessly argued with his mother. He eventually convinced her to allow him to live with her brother. It was 45 minutes from a small college that housed a very good arts program. He was delighted when she finally agreed. They both knew a fresh start with a father figure was what he needed. At the end of school term, Eddie packed his leather bag, stuffing a few articles of clothing on top of the drawings. As he waved good-bye from the bus, he yelled, "Don't cry Ma. I'll be back soon. You'll be real proud of me, you'll see."

The handsomely dressed man grabbed the handle of the screen door and opened it, struggling to pass himself and his suitcase through before the hinge snapped back. Once inside, he dropped his bags and quietly crept into the living room where an older lady was dozing, knitting spilling from her lap. With tears in his eyes, he watched her sleep. It had been 6 years since he had last seen her. Her curly hair was now white and her plump hands rested on her belly, rising slowly with her breathing. He leaned forward and whispered, "Ma, your baby's home, all grown up." The older lady opened her tired eyes and shrieked with excitement. "Eddie, my darling!" she cried, wrapping her arms around his neck. "My baby's home, after all these years. Oh, aren't you handsome!" The tall lean man held his mother for many minutes, rocking and crying with her. "Ma, I am so sorry I stayed away all this time, but I've been having such a beautiful life. Did you get my last letter?" The old lady smiled and reached under her chair. She pulled out a shoebox stuffed with letters. "Yes. I've saved every one and read them at least four times, Colin and I."

"Colin read them?" Eddie asked in surprise.

"Yes. You don't know how proud he is of you. He's also green with envy. He's home you know, I'm sure he'd really like to see you."

Eddie turned and walked towards the bedrooms. He peeked in them, finding them both empty. He noticed the old ladder resting against the wall. Eddie climbed up into the loft. All his childhood memories came flooding back. His brother was sitting in the corner, on the old chest, in a thick cloud of smoke.

"Now I know why you always hung out up here," Colin said without looking up. "It's very safe from the world, isn't it? Quiet, freeing. You always did your own thing, exploring up here, figuring yourself out. Now look at you—a great success, doing what makes you happy. Now I'm the loser brother."

Eddie didn't know what to say. He bit his lip, looking down at his tired brother, thinking of all the things he'd wanted to say over the years. "Colin…what happened to you?"

Colin put out his cigarette and stared up at the ceiling. "When you left I had to deal with a lot—life, the truth. See, through you I hid who I was and what frightened me. I used you as a scapegoat, I guess." Eddie sat down beside him. "What or who were you afraid of? You always seemed so indestructible to me."

Colin kept his head down and quietly answered, "Dad." Eddie looked at him for a while, this fragile man with more skeletons than he had ever knew. "Huh?"

"I lied to you about Dad," Colin began, "and I'm not proud of it. He *is* alive. He left when you were an infant. Ma told you he died because it was easier for her to handle it that way. It was a very dark time for her. I don't know the full story, but I do remember him. I was almost 7 when he left and I remember the horrible fight they had. I also remember how much he adored you. Maybe he saw himself in you, I don't know."

Eddie's face turned red. His eyes stung. He couldn't believe what he was hearing.

"He's in a nursing home in Nairn and isn't doing well. We should go up and visit him soon. I try to go once a week. Sometimes he recognizes me, sometimes he doesn't. Ma's been up once or twice." Colin lit another cigarette and squinted out the attic window.

Eddie climbed down the ladder and stared out the kitchen window. 'My father's alive. My God,' he whispered. 'I can't believe he's been alive all this time! And he really *did* love me.' The quiet gentlemen stood there for a long time, not wanting to leave this memory, this moment, this feeling. He looked out at the old trees on the lawn, watching them dance in the wind.

The brothers walked up the steps and along the hallway of the nursing home. The younger brother was beside himself with excitement and nerves. They turned the corner together and stood outside a closed yellow door. The younger one held onto the handle, squeezing it open. There were two beds. The first one was empty. An old man lay in the second, his back facing them. Eddie walked over and sat down. The old man struggled to turn around. Eddie braced himself, biting his lip, his emotions running high. When the old man finally faced him, Eddie cried out, the noise filling the still room. The old man with the pale watery eyes was the same man he had encountered in the park year after year, the same man that was his inspiration for his trip out west. His father smiled and nodded.

"Your mother forbade me from visiting you, but I was damn sure I wasn't going to miss seeing you growing up," he breathed, "so in my own way I watched you without her ever knowing." He slowly held out his hand.

Eddie let the tears freely fall. "I can't believe that was you all these years. I truly thought you were dead!" He squeezed his father's hand. All that time trying to figure out the quiet stranger were quickly fitting together. "What did you mean when you told me years ago about following my dreams? How did you know what they were?"

The old man smiled at him as he answered. "Your cartoon strip. I've been following it all these years. Thanks for bringing my dreams to life." He closed his eyes and rested his head on his pillow. "That fat cat was my childhood friend, but your mother didn't want me to do anything with it," he continued.

"Those were *your* drawings?" Eddie asked incredulously, standing up. "I had no idea whose they were or why they were in our attic. You don't know how many hours of pleasure they gave me!" he said.

"Oh I know. I used to watch you talk to yourself on the roundabout. You didn't realize I was there as much as I was. I knew what you were doing and what you saw in those old drawings of mine," he struggled.

Eddie sat back down again and smiled through his tears. He hugged his dad and rocked with him, holding onto a lifetime of love and dreams and memories. He held and rocked his father for a very long time, not ever wishing to let go—of his Dad, of the present, or of the past.

Now his life was just going to keep getting better. He finally has a chance to make amends with his brother, to build a relationship that they never really had. Life is full of treasures.

Suzanne has had several poems and short stories published in literary magazines while completing her BA in English Literature. She currently has a 6-picture book contract with Black Harbor Press. The first book is scheduled to be published early summer, 2024. Suzanne recently had a second picture book accepted by Smarty Pants Magazine For Kids. She is very active in the twitter writing community @writerofPB and on kidlit411.

Suzanne has been an ESL teacher in London, Canada for 18 years. She is an avid 4-seasons camper who feels those unplugged adventures are absolutely perfect for writing. She lives with her husband and son. Her other two sons and two grandbabies are never far away!

MOMENT IN TIME

Johnson, Rev. J.A. and family. Glass negatives; between
February 1901 and December 1903.

THANOS

BY MICHAEL FOWLER

Thorne came to Thanos to retrieve a lost love. Two years ago Cara had left Earth and him for a death cultist and this overcrowded mausoleum of a planet.

It wasn't fair to call Hector a cultist, perhaps. He had not founded Thanos, the realm of doom, but only lived in it and loved it. He forced no one to accompany him here; Cara had gone voluntarily, according to her last communications with Thorne. She loved Hector and believed in his vision, and so farewell.

Until a week ago, when a message from her reached him on Earth, "Come for me, Cara." Except for an address, that was all. He surmised that Hector had now died, or abandoned her, and that at long last she had rejected his love of dying and its attendant rituals.

Then too, Cara was approaching age thirty, and no denizen of Thanos expected to live beyond that. After two years there, she might be suffering the natural embalming effects of the place, rendering her weak and helpless. Those effects were, according to the warnings he had read, quite dire: "The seeming fresh air and mild climate reduces the people to a tan-colored, hard crust, like the shells of locusts, by age thirty, due to unknown chemical properties. Natives call this process the *burnishing* or the *embalming*, and the residual husks do not decompose and resist burning."

Rather ghastly, and just like the weirdo Hector to choose such a hellish locale. He hadn't been that healthy to start with and was perhaps already ill when he took Cara away. He had coughed a lot the few times Thorne met him, coming out the door of his makeshift church with Cara in tow, constantly holding the crook of his arm to his face.

A scavenger vessel, for a hefty fee, transported Thorne from the space station Solace IV to an air hub near her town, Point Noe. The hub itself was marked by an enormous hangar filled with castoff vehicles, household appliances, furniture, toys, artworks, books and musical instruments, all to be shipped to more vibrant cradles of civilization elsewhere in the galaxy, perhaps as junk. Thorne didn't doubt that the planet's natural resources, if any, were being siphoned off too. In their place fresh empty coffins and unmarked tombstones waited to be unloaded on moribund Thanos. Vicious dogs were chained around the place to discourage theft.

Thorne had a choice of vehicle to take from the hub, a van or a hovercraft, but the man in charge of rentals warned him that a van might be inconvenienced by stacks of coffins or funeral processions crowding the streets. Thorne wanted the hovercraft anyway, and as he took the keys, the fellow told him to hover back within two hours; otherwise he'd have to wait till tomorrow for the next vessel back to the space station and catch it at a different town nearby. He also warned Thorne to watch out for the government orderlies, robots that roamed the streets in packs and acted like they owned the place. "They're pretty much all show, but they're a pain," he said. "If you try to destroy them, it only eggs them on." Thorne said he'd be careful.

A minute later Thorne, a skilled pilot of small craft with the Department of Forests at home, was in the air above Point Noe, following the vocal advice of his tracker to Cara's street number. What he saw below were streets lined with parked cars but little moving traffic, sidewalks empty but for stacks of household effects, private lawns and church yards lined with coffins, and an apparently endless cemetery engulfing all, baring tombstones like rows of teeth. It was a town ground to a halt by death, its sole preoccupation. He'd seen pictures before and heard descriptions; what amazed him is that anyone would want to stay long or live here.

He set down gently in the empty driveway, already taking note of Cara's modest circumstances. Hector hadn't been well off, nor she, and Thanos wasn't a place to grow rich, except perhaps for undertakers. The location reminded him of a rural neighborhood at home, where most people worked for the same large company or industry, in this case the death industry, and obtained their food from local growers. Her yard was overdue for trimming by several weeks, he guessed, and the single-story clapboard house, the white paint peeling here and there, was the size of a largish condo. The open garage revealed a lot of bare wooden boards and carpentry tools, woodchips and shavings showing recent use.

She came out to greet him looking somewhat harder, he wouldn't say more haggard, than he remembered. Still beautiful with her long straight black hair, she combined fond remembrance and clear independence in her smile. She looked flushed by what in the best scenario was her pleasure in seeing him.

"Something you need to help me with before we go," she said after the briefest of hugs. "I need to get Hector and his casket over to his church. I promised him as he lay dying I would do that. I'd bury him in the back yard, but it's full of caskets already, all his family. They say the deeper you dig anywhere here, the more bodies you find, and it's true. The church people will watch over it if there's no room to inter it there. I think it's a beautiful casket; Hector made it himself in the garage, using planks from our living room floor and the top from the kitchen table."

"I was admiring the tools," Thorne said. "Are we loading it onto a van or something? I don't know if my hovercraft can handle the three of us. Let's have a look."

The tall, wasted Hector lay bent like an archer's bow in a casket considerably too long and too wide for him, dressed in a white cotton robe, his hair in a tight ponytail, his feet bare, his skin a translucent yellow. Alongside the body Cara had laid two framed portraits of them as a couple, a marriage photo and another of them holding hands here in the front yard.

"There's no van. We gave that up. And don't say what you're thinking," she admonished him.

"What do you mean?" But he was certain he knew.

"That I look a lot younger in the pictures, though they're only from two years ago."

"Maybe you don't look younger, but Hector sure does." He felt a small surge of remorse even as he said it.

She let his remark pass. Thorne found it impossible to imagine how this defunct death worshipper had attracted so yea-saying a person as her, and wondered if she were still under his spell. Would she benefit from some sort of deprogramming? He attempted to move the coffin with one hand; it was heavy but not immobile. Still, it was too large for the hovercraft, even if he and Cara could lift it.

Another dilemma he noted was the sudden grouping of six mechanical men on the street corner, already marching in formation toward them and shouting something. The words became clearer as they closed in: "We are order! Stop your looting! Go away now!" they chanted in raucous unison, all six pointing a riveted hand at Thorne.

"If those are the orderlies I've heard about, I'm not supposed to be alarmed, but I am," said Thorne. "Can you advise me on a defensive strategy?"

"They're harmless dolts. A last-ditch effort on the part of the government to control the break-ins and lootings that keep ticking up. Watch."

"You there, orderlies!" she turned toward them and bellowed. They halted at the edge of her driveway and stared back at her like upright vacuum cleaners with eyes. Their raised hands fell to their sides.

"I am a citizen of Thanos!" Cara continued. "You know me! Who will now assist me, raise one hand!"

Three of the vacuum cleaners raised one hand, the other three two hands.

"Who will give his life to aid a citizen of Thanos, now raise two hands!" Cara shouted.

The orderlies who had raised one hand now raised a second, and the ones who had raised two lowered both. They reminded Thorne of the classic TV show *F Troop*.

"Take this coffin, after I seal it, to the First Church of Tulu on Front Street two blocks east of here," Cara said to the attentive six. "Tell

Reverend Endsworthy that it contains the body of Hector Mortes. Then you many disband."

As Thorne and the orderlies watched, she placed a translucent white shroud over Hector's yellowed visage, and then signaled to Thorne to assist her with the lid. This was a broad, heavy piece of wood, its top hand-carved by Hector into complex figures and whorls, as arcane to Thorne as the lid of Queequeg's watertight box was to Ishmael. Like the rest of the coffin, it was painted a light blue. The two maneuvered it into the slots Hector had built to hold it. Cara then hammered it shut with six long nails, her blows strong and precise.

"To the church," Cara instructed the orderlies, and they hefted the heavy box as if they were pallbearers, three on a side, except there were no handles or rails to assure their grip, and they appeared off balance and liable to lose their cargo at any moment. Somehow they managed to head down the sidewalk at a steady pace, looking as self-important as vacuum cleaners can look.

"I guess Hector caught a ride after all," Cara smiled at Thorne. "But I'm not sure I trust those idiots."

"Care to show me the abode?" said Thorne, glad to see them go. "There's time."

They entered the house through the garage, passed through a kitchen where two coffins lay on the floor against the wall, and into a living room where a tarnished, desiccated corpse in a natty leisure suit sat in a recliner before a dark TV. Next to him a plump, brownish shell in a fluffy bathrobe sat in an easy chair, and across the room two bodies rapped in gossamer linen reclined lengthwise on the sofa, almost embracing. In a corner by the sofa a shrunken, formally dressed body sat in a still rocker. The boards for the coffin had been taken from another corner, and a bedspread covered the resultant gape.

"Who are they?" said Thorne.

"Hector's parents and grandparents, also an aunt and uncle. It's the same in all the homes here; all are stuffed with the lovely corpses of entire families."

"Can't they be buried?"

"The cemeteries and everybody's private yard are chockfull of caskets already, just like ours, so almost no more burials can take place. And the bodies don't decompose and won't burn, so most of the deceased have to remain where they died. There's nowhere to put them. Their families clothe them in the finest long-lasting, weatherproof garments and stage them to evoke poignant scenes from their lives. As a reverend-in-training at the church, Hector's an exception."

"Who's in the rocker?"

"That's Hector's grandmother Dinka, dressed as when she died at thirty-two, on her way to church. Grandpa Petro still hangs out in the cellar, if you care to take a peak downstairs. He's the standing figure fastened to plumbing pipes, wearing a sweatsuit and holding a favorite bong. He looks as if he were still twenty-nine and about to inhale, only slimmer. The soulmates on the sofa are Hector's parents. Care to see the other rooms?"

"I'd prefer a breath of air," said Thorne. "What's the situation out back?"

She accompanied him to the back yard, where he discovered a patio table and five occupied chairs covered by a plastic tarp. The occupants of the chairs were concealed except for their shod feet; these the tarp didn't descend low enough to cover. More coffins lay in the yard, and most disturbingly, a body tied to a child's swing beneath a thick tree limb. It looked so doll-like that Thorne thought it might be a child. It was arrayed in what looked like silk pajamas, its arms fastened to the chains of the swing by entwined scarves.

"It's not a child," Cara assured him. "Few children die on Thanos. Instead, everyone kicks at thirty."

"Does it happen overnight?" Thorne's voice betrayed his apprehension.

"Pretty much. You reach thirty or thereabouts, suddenly turn a bit stiff and yellowish, and the next day you're a husk. Fewer people are being born too, as you can probably tell from the lack of activity."

"That's enough. Are you ready?"

Once they were airborne in the hovercraft, she had him do a flyover of the church where Hector was bound. She wanted to check on the progress of the orderlies there.

"Who exactly is Tulu?" said Thorne, recalling the church's namesake.

"One of the chief gods of death. The main teaching of Tulu is that death is a dignified and honorable event for all, not to be preceded by immoral or ignoble acts in life, and not to be forgotten by those yet to pass. As death is permanent, so must remembrance be of those who have left us."

"When I was growing up in Ohio," said Thorne, "there was a rock DJ who called his listeners 'tulus.' He would open his show by saying, 'Hello to my tulu babies and all my ducky friends.' Then he would spin 'Odorless' by the Hairy Ones. He was spouting nonsense syllables of course. There is no conceivable way he was referring to your and Hector's Tulus, if I may call them that."

Cara shot him a glance that indicated it really wasn't the right time for his jokes. He often thought that was a reason, perhaps a main reason, he had lost her to Hector. He was always joking, and Hector was always serious, or so he had appeared on those occasions Thorne encountered him. Tall, thin, dark and brooding was Hector, whereas Thorne was a smartass, serious only about her.

She pointed below and he brought the craft over a large, towered church. Tidy rows of tombs covered an adjacent graveyard, but unlike his home planet, there were no crosses. Instead a multitude of thin white columns of varying heights, tipped by small o's, spread over the grounds. Maybe the o's stood for omega, Thorne thought. Unburied coffins lay everywhere, including the parking lot, and she wagged her finger to indicate that she had pinpointed the party in question below.

"There," she said. "Those six. That's him, I recognize the light blue color of the coffin. There's the reverend meeting them by the side door."

He did a flyover once and then again, and when she seemed satisfied that all was in accordance with her wishes, he veered toward the air hub, leaving the blue coffin far behind. They didn't speak along the way.

Joining a dozen or so other passengers, they buckled themselves into their seats above the wing of a huge recently loaded transporter. From the window beside her, Thorne saw the now familiar hangar of commerce— all the detritus of a dying planet changing hands. After a lengthy wait the massive vessel took off, and she at last relaxed enough to talk.

"I haven't thanked you yet for coming to my rescue. I certainly owe you for that. I completely broke down when Hector passed, and you were my only salvation. Sorry to drag you this far. I'm feeling a bit less helpless now, I admit, and maybe I could have carried on without you."

"I would have come even if you cancelled. I had a week's vacation to use up anyway, and I always wanted to steal you away from here, if possible. I still live where I used to, by the way, and I'm still with the forestry service. I do enjoy the green of our home planet, and the vitality of its plants *and* people. I especially like *old* plants and people; a hundred years or older is good by me."

"Uh huh." She was not much amused. "Still in your place with the spare bedroom for women, hoping to find one who'll take permanent refuge there?" She was getting her rebuttal in.

"That's the one. And you're right, the ladies all eventually run out on me, you included. I wonder why. Do you suppose it's because they consider the spare bedroom a trap? Or do you think it's because I haven't joined an end-of-life cult?" He immediately apologized, saying his words were far harsher than he intended.

"It isn't a cult, and Hector was a religious proselyte, not a cult member. He was born and grew up on Thanos; you know that, don't you?"

Thorne wasn't sure what he knew. "I never understood Hector's goal on Earth. Did he actually expect Tulu to catch fire?"

"Don't try to make his mission sound nonsensical or pointless. Hector was serious, but he soon tired of especially Americans' fear and revulsion toward death, and how in the view of most people he met death was somehow synonymous with defeat. He decided to return home to Thanos and study under a Tulu reverend, and chose Endsworthy at the church. Eventually he was to be a reverend himself. If he had he started his spiritual journey at age eighteen instead of twenty-five, he might have lived to achieve his goal. But the embalmment struck him hard when he got home, and he quickly succumbed to what Tulus call the burnish, the everlasting shell of death."

"I can't get over that you came here in the first place. You had to know what this place was."

"I knew exactly what it was. But Hector had a confidence about him, that it was right for him and for us. He was oddly seductive that way. And he knew the language and had started teaching it to me, so we wouldn't be completely at sea. And I had nothing to hold me where I was."

"Nothing but me." He looked a bit hurt. "I knew I should have been more seductive with you. That's always been my problem with women. I'm never seductive enough."

"It wouldn't have done you any good. I confess I was starry-eyed then. And for two years we did well. You saw our house, that Hector's grandfather owned. He and his wife were already deceased when we arrived, but Hector's parents made us welcome though the home was already crowded with living beings and non-living beings, all relations. Then his parents died too, after our first year, and it became Hector's and my place."

"Your place to die."

"And live in. I worked in a local food and herb store for spending money, and Hector continued his church-sponsored training. It was ideal for us. We even had a small circle of friends. We knew a few couples like us, young in body and mind, or perhaps only beginning to tarnish and stiffen a little, who worked hard to maintain an active lifestyle. Aside from preparing to die, they knew how to cut loose and have fun, too."

"Fun doing what, visiting graveyards?"

"Doing what vital young people anywhere do. The people are happy if you ask them. Being doomed is no hardship to them, and they approach the inevitable end with assurance and gladness. The planet is a glorious cemetery, and they are essential to its well-being. That is the meaning of life on Thanos, by the grace of Tulu."

Thorne was amazed that she called her friends vital, despite the obvious fact that they were all at death's door, and perhaps dead as they spoke.

"But now you're leaving," he said. "Why? There must be another Hector here who would take a lively interest in you."

"Not as many as you might think. Young people here don't take much joy in paring off and reproducing. Certainly Hector's views weren't those of a founding father. When a man carries on through death, he doesn't require progeny. One hesitates even to go to the doctor here, since the purpose of life is to die. I was never able to convince Hector that we should have our child."

"Well, eureka!" He almost slapped his forehead for effect. "I was just thinking you were starting to burnish a bit, as the people on Thanos do, when here it's maternal glow."

"The mother planet has begun to pull a tiny moon into her orbit," she confessed.

She fell silent then, and Thorne followed her gaze out the window. The giant sphere of Thanos seemed to recede and shrink by the moment, its hue the same beige that stained its doomed inhabitants. Good riddance, he thought.

"I would love the child as if it were my own," he said. "You're welcome to come with me."

"I was sure you would say that, and maybe your love would embrace us both. But I'm not about to test you. I'd like to stay with you for a short period, check out that spare room again where your women can hide from you. But then, I warn you, I'll be off."

"To quote Tulu, 'my journey availeth not.'" Thorne was joking glumly, with little idea of what Tulu might have said. She corrected him at once.

"Tulu says, the journey begins when it's over."

"That does sound more Tulu-like. Where will you go?"

"I'll see my family first, I suppose. Do you know in the two years I was on Thanos, my parents didn't visit me once? Only my sisters came for a brief call, and they wore ridiculous paper masks over their faces the whole time, as if to ward off some infection. But I suppose I can't blame them for that."

"You know Thanos is on a travel advisory list. You'll have to undergo a physical when we arrive. So will I."

"I understand. The baby's health is my priority. On Thanos there's a high incidence of health problems in newborns, as if they're born knowing that life is a faulty start and not their real purpose. But I want life for my child."

She suddenly leaned over to him. "Poor Thorne," she said. "He was hoping for a greater reward, wasn't he?"

Thorne gave a slight shrug. He understood now why she had to leave Thanos, and it wasn't to draw closer to him. The miles and miles they progressed toward home seemed to expand the distance between them. She moved in her seat to slip out of her jacket, as if preparing to nap, and he caught sight of her bare arm: as smooth and rigid as an artificial limb.

It was a trick of the light, he told himself, only a trick of the light. When she dozed off, he would look again.

The End

Michael Fowler is a playwright and speculative fiction writer living in Ohio. His farce *The Resurrectionist*, may be read at **Fleas on the Dog** online, and recent stories have appeared in **Not One of Us** and **The Horror Zine**.

Because humankind fails to learn from past lessons, we find that many circumstances from yesteryear are repeating themselves yet again. The commentaries that follow here and in future issues were originally published by *The Mohave Valley Daily News between 1993 & 2013--an*d in many ways they apply to today.
We are grateful to republish these commentaries written by Darryle Purcell in full and unedited. His own brand of humor and style can deliver insight, provoke thought, and even boil blood.

Editor takes a stand on cockroach survival

From June 23, 2000

PEOPLE FOR THE ETHICAL TREATMENT OF ANIMALS (PETA) IS A LARGE ORGA-nization well known for its advocacy for animal rights. We've all either seen, heard about or read about their work against the use of animals in circus acts. These are people who really love animals.

Most of us are animal lovers in our own way. I like dogs and cats.... and I really love a good steak. The only hunting I ever did was in Vietnam — and it was a mutual situation — so I can understand those who want to protect Bambi and Dumbo from what they perceive to be uncaring acts by man.

But a letter I recently received from the PETA people really bugs me. They are no longer just complaining about sadistic circus clowns poking slapsticks into elephants and cosmetic scientists forcing bunnies to wear experimental tacky lipstick and eye shadow. They have launched an assault to protect the persecuted cockroach!

In the letter dated June 9, PETA staff writer Paula Moore states, "Instead of reaching for the Raid, why not show a little kindness to a cockroach?"

She goes on to explain that cockroaches "are really quite fascinating once you get to know them." She states that cockroaches "smell with their mouths and with the long antennae" and describes their cute little versions of eyes and ears.

"They also feel pain," she claims.

Well, maybe Bill Clinton would, but when it comes to cockroaches, I just don't feel their pain. Call me just plain mean, but I really don't care whether these disgusting creatures smell with their mouths or any other filthy chunks of their slimy bodies. And I don't want to "get to know them."

I can picture animal-nut actress Kim Basinger cuddling up to a sad-eyed crippled-up cockroach on a PETA public-service television commercial to explain the horrors that particular bug had to endure at the hands of some uncaring "speciesist." Perhaps Sally Struthers could also launch a "feed the cockroaches" program for PETA. (She should be very careful where she steps while filming.)

Will their next press release advocate a meals-on-wheels program for sewer rats? Will they sue Marine sergeants for calling recruits "maggots" on behalf of the Maggot Anti-Defamation League? How many Hollywood stars will wear Save The Roach ribbons at the next Academy Awards celebration?

Although many of us have considered the PETA people to be extremists, I think we all gave them credit for standing up on their hind legs for their beliefs. But their stand on cockroach preservation has dramatically increased the number of nuts that their image has over the average fruitcake.

A SERVICE OF LOVE

BY O. HENRY

When one loves one's Art no service seems too hard.

That is our premise. This story shall draw a conclusion from it, and show at the same time that the premise is incorrect. That will be a new thing in logic, and a feat in story-telling somewhat older than the great wall of China.

Joe Larrabee came out of the post-oak flats of the Middle West pulsing with a genius for pictorial art. At six he drew a picture of the town pump with a prominent citizen passing it hastily. This effort was framed and hung in the drug store window by the side of the ear of corn with an uneven number of rows. At twenty he left for New York with a flowing necktie and a capital tied up somewhat closer.

Delia Caruthers did things in six octaves so promisingly in a pine-tree village in the South that her relatives chipped in enough in her chip hat for her to go "North" and "finish." They could not see her f—, but that is our story.

Joe and Delia met in an atelier where a number of art and music students had gathered to discuss chiaroscuro, Wagner, music, Rembrandt's works, pictures, Waldteufel, wall paper, Chopin and Oolong.

Joe and Delia became enamoured one of the other, or each of the other, as you please, and in a short time were married—for (see above), when one loves one's Art no service seems too hard.

Mr. and Mrs. Larrabee began housekeeping in a flat. It was a lonesome flat—something like the A sharp way down at the left-hand end of the keyboard. And they were happy; for they had their Art, and they had each other. And my advice to the rich young man would be—sell all thou hast, and give it to the poor—janitor for the privilege of living in a flat with your Art and your Delia.

Flat-dwellers shall indorse my dictum that theirs is the only true happiness. If a home is happy it cannot fit too close—let the dresser collapse and become a billiard table; let the mantel turn to a rowing machine, the escritoire to a spare bedchamber, the washstand to an upright piano; let the four walls come together, if they will, so you and your Delia are between. But if home be the other kind, let it be wide and long—enter you at the Golden Gate, hang your hat on Hatteras, your cape on Cape Horn and go out by the Labrador.

Joe was painting in the class of the great Magister—you know his fame. His fees are high; his lessons are light—his high-lights have brought him renown. Delia was studying under Rosenstock—you know his repute as a disturber of the piano keys.

They were mighty happy as long as their money lasted. So is every— but I will not be cynical. Their aims were very clear and defined. Joe was to become capable very soon of turning out pictures that old gentlemen with thin side-whiskers and thick pocketbooks would sandbag one another in his studio for the privilege of buying. Delia was to become familiar and then contemptuous with Music, so that when she saw the orchestra seats and boxes unsold she could have sore throat and lobster in a private dining-room and refuse to go on the stage.

But the best, in my opinion, was the home life in the little flat—the ardent, voluble chats after the day's study; the cozy dinners and fresh, light breakfasts; the interchange of ambitions—ambitions interwoven each with the other's or else inconsiderable—the mutual help and inspiration; and— overlook my artlessness—stuffed olives and cheese sandwiches at 11 p.m.

But after a while Art flagged. It sometimes does, even if some switchman doesn't flag it. Everything going out and nothing coming in, as the vulgarians say. Money was lacking to pay Mr. Magister and Herr Rosenstock their prices. When one loves one's Art no service seems too hard. So, Delia said she must give music lessons to keep the chafing dish bubbling.

For two or three days she went out canvassing for pupils. One evening she came home elated.

"Joe, dear," she said, gleefully, "I've a pupil. And, oh, the loveliest people! General—General A. B. Pinkney's daughter—on Seventy-first street. Such a splendid house, Joe—you ought to see the front door! Byzantine I think you would call it. And inside! Oh, Joe, I never saw anything like it before.

"My pupil is his daughter Clementina. I dearly love her already. She's a delicate thing—dresses always in white; and the sweetest, simplest manners! Only eighteen years old. I'm to give three lessons a week; and, just think, Joe! $5 a lesson. I don't mind it a bit; for when I get two or three more pupils I can resume my lessons with Herr Rosenstock. Now, smooth out that wrinkle between your brows, dear, and let's have a nice supper."

"That's all right for you, Dele," said Joe, attacking a can of peas with a carving knife and a hatchet, "but how about me? Do you think I'm going to let you hustle for wages while I philander in the regions of high art? Not by the bones of Benvenuto Cellini! I guess I can sell papers or lay cobblestones, and bring in a dollar or two."

Delia came and hung about his neck.

"Joe, dear, you are silly. You must keep on at your studies. It is not as if I had quit my music and gone to work at something else. While I teach I learn. I am always with my music. And we can live as happily as millionaires on $15 a week. You mustn't think of leaving Mr. Magister."

"All right," said Joe, reaching for the blue scalloped vegetable dish. "But I hate for you to be giving lessons. It isn't Art. But you're a trump and a dear to do it."

"When one loves one's Art no service seems too hard," said Delia.

"Magister praised the sky in that sketch I made in the park," said Joe. "And Tinkle gave me permission to hang two of them in his window. I may sell one if the right kind of a moneyed idiot sees them."

"I'm sure you will," said Delia, sweetly. "And now let's be thankful for Gen. Pinkney and this veal roast."

During all of the next week the Larrabees had an early breakfast. Joe was enthusiastic about some morning-effect sketches he was doing in Central Park, and Delia packed him off breakfasted, coddled, praised and kissed at 7 o'clock. Art is an engaging mistress. It was most times 7 o'clock when he returned in the evening.

At the end of the week Delia, sweetly proud but languid, triumphantly tossed three five-dollar bills on the 8×10 (inches) centre table of the 8×10 (feet) flat parlour.

"Sometimes," she said, a little wearily, "Clementina tries me. I'm afraid she doesn't practise enough, and I have to tell her the same things so often. And then she always dresses entirely in white, and that does get monotonous. But Gen. Pinkney is the dearest old man! I wish you could know him, Joe. He comes in sometimes when I am with Clementina at the piano—he is a widower, you know—and stands there pulling his white goatee. 'And how are the semiquavers and the demisemiquavers progressing?' he always asks.

"I wish you could see the wainscoting in that drawing-room, Joe! And those Astrakhan rug portières. And Clementina has such a funny little cough. I hope she is stronger than she looks. Oh, I really am getting attached to her, she is so gentle and high bred. Gen. Pinkney's brother was once Minister to Bolivia."

And then Joe, with the air of a Monte Cristo, drew forth a ten, a five, a two and a one—all legal tender notes—and laid them beside Delia's earnings.

"Sold that watercolour of the obelisk to a man from Peoria," he announced overwhelmingly.

"Don't joke with me," said Delia, "not from Peoria!"

"All the way. I wish you could see him, Dele. Fat man with a woollen muffler and a quill toothpick. He saw the sketch in Tinkle's window and thought it was a windmill at first. He was game, though, and bought it anyhow. He ordered another—an oil sketch of the Lackawanna freight depot—to take back with him. Music lessons! Oh, I guess Art is still in it."

"I'm so glad you've kept on," said Delia, heartily. "You're bound to win, dear. Thirty-three dollars! We never had so much to spend before. We'll have oysters to-night."

"And filet mignon with champignons," said Joe. "Where is the olive fork?"

On the next Saturday evening Joe reached home first. He spread his $18 on the parlour table and washed what seemed to be a great deal of dark paint from his hands.

Half an hour later Delia arrived, her right hand tied up in a shapeless bundle of wraps and bandages.

"How is this?" asked Joe after the usual greetings. Delia laughed, but not very joyously.

"Clementina," she explained, "insisted upon a Welsh rabbit after her lesson. She is such a queer girl. Welsh rabbits at 5 in the afternoon. The General was there. You should have seen him run for the chafing dish, Joe, just as if there wasn't a servant in the house. I know Clementina isn't in good health; she is so nervous. In serving the rabbit she spilled a great lot of it, boiling hot, over my hand and wrist. It hurt awfully, Joe. And the dear girl was so sorry! But Gen. Pinkney!—Joe, that old man nearly went distracted. He rushed downstairs and sent somebody—they said the furnace man or somebody in the basement—out to a drug store for some oil and things to bind it up with. It doesn't hurt so much now."

"What's this?" asked Joe, taking the hand tenderly and pulling at some white strands beneath the bandages.

"It's something soft," said Delia, "that had oil on it. Oh, Joe, did you sell another sketch?" She had seen the money on the table.

"Did I?" said Joe; "just ask the man from Peoria. He got his depot to-day, and he isn't sure but he thinks he wants another parkscape and a view on the Hudson. What time this afternoon did you burn your hand, Dele?"

"Five o'clock, I think," said Dele, plaintively. "The iron—I mean the rabbit came off the fire about that time. You ought to have seen Gen. Pinkney, Joe, when—"

"Sit down here a moment, Dele," said Joe. He drew her to the couch, sat beside her and put his arm across her shoulders.

"What have you been doing for the last two weeks, Dele?" he asked.

She braved it for a moment or two with an eye full of love and stubbornness, and murmured a phrase or two vaguely of Gen. Pinkney; but at length down went her head and out came the truth and tears.

"I couldn't get any pupils," she confessed. "And I couldn't bear to have you give up your lessons; and I got a place ironing shirts in that big Twenty-fourth street laundry. And I think I did very well to make up both General Pinkney and Clementina, don't you, Joe? And when a girl in the laundry set down a hot iron on my hand this afternoon I was all the way home making up that story about the Welsh rabbit. You're not angry, are you, Joe? And if I hadn't got the work you mightn't have sold your sketches to that man from Peoria."

"He wasn't from Peoria," said Joe, slowly.

"Well, it doesn't matter where he was from. How clever you are, Joe—and—kiss me, Joe—and what made you ever suspect that I wasn't giving music lessons to Clementina?"

"I didn't," said Joe, "until to-night. And I wouldn't have then, only I sent up this cotton waste and oil from the engine-room this afternoon for a girl upstairs who had her hand burned with a smoothing-iron. I've been firing the engine in that laundry for the last two weeks."

"And then you didn't—"

"My purchaser from Peoria," said Joe, "and Gen. Pinkney are both creations of the same art—but you wouldn't call it either painting or music."

And then they both laughed, and Joe began:

"When one loves one's Art no service seems—"

But Delia stopped him with her hand on his lips. "No," she said—"just 'When one loves.'"

SODUKO ANSWERS

3	9	2	7	4	5	6	8	1
4	7	6	1	8	9	2	5	3
8	5	1	2	3	6	9	7	4
7	6	8	3	1	4	5	9	2
1	2	9	5	7	8	4	3	6
5	3	4	6	9	2	8	1	7
2	1	5	8	6	3	7	4	9
6	4	7	9	5	1	3	2	8
9	8	3	4	2	7	1	6	5

Thanks for reading!
Next Issue Fall 2023